WITCH BAY

by

P. L. Crompton

Publisher: Crompton Fiction

Copyright: © P. L. Crompton 2014

ISBN: 978-0-9866701-1-4

Cover photograph: Llangrannog
picturenation.co.uk

plcrompton dot wix dot com/CromptonFiction

To Lisa and Colton
and
Elizabeth

WITCH BAY
TRANSLATIONS:

Arswyd	Gracious me
Bach / fach	Little m / f
Bachgen	Boy
Bore da	Good morning
Cariad	Love, darling
Diawl	Damn
Duw Mawr	Great God
Nos da	Goodnight
Merch	Girl
Prynhawn da	Good afternoon

P L Crompton

CHAPTER ONE

Headlights flashed and a horn blared, jarring Beth's attention back to the road. She was in the wrong lane. Knuckles white where she clutched the steering wheel; she swerved back across the white line. The tyres slipped on a strip of earth beneath a banked hedge, then caught as the car brushed against overgrown vegetation. She steered into a gateway, slammed her foot on the brake, and took a calming breath. In an unfamiliar car, a two-lane country road was not the place to drop her guard. The lorry passed and she glimpsed the words Penmawr Trucking printed in luminous white on the side.

She hadn't been concentrating; she had been allowing her thoughts to fill with questions about her aunt's death. The solicitor said they found her in early morning, her cardigan snagged on the Witch; otherwise, the sea would have carried her away. The police thought Aunty Meg had been walking on the beach and caught by the tide.

The answer didn't satisfy Beth. Aunty Meg lived in Derwen all her life, and the locals knew about tide treachery. But what other answer could there be? Murder? Who would murder an elderly spinster who ran a small guesthouse? Why?

The questions killed the last morsel of relief she felt on getting out of London undetected. The change started with disorientation when she got off the train in Carmarthen. Most signs were in Welsh with English subtitles, and the majority of people spoke a language she didn't understand. The salesman where she bought the used car claimed not to speak much English. She would have walked away if she hadn't needed a car for the last leg of her journey. Her heritage was Welsh but as Beth drove deeper into the west the feelings of alienation grew. She hadn't been back for ten years. It was unsettling as the week spent in Paris with only one or two words of French, but this was Britain!

For now, the oak trees that gave the place its name hid Derwen Bay. Derwen—oak, the tree sacred to the Druids. Moonlight turned everything to shades of grey and the sea shone like a sheet of silver ice in the dip between the headlands. She took her foot off the brake and steered onto the road.

The stand of trees fell behind as Beth drove on with caution. She remembered the steepness of the road with the many field run-ins for drivers whose brakes failed. In winter, it would be a nightmare, but she didn't intend to be here when black ice shrouded the slope.

Beth dimmed the lights when she entered the lower village and yellow streetlights eclipsed the moon. She paused beside the sea wall and rolled down her window to listen.

The seagulls were at rest and the sea emerging from its quiet hour. Waves of the retreating tide made no more noise than a dog lapping at a water dish, except around the Witch. The ocean ravaged her skirts, spray rising like a cloud to hide her.

From the cave came a muted rumble as the Atlantic savaged the cliff. The Witch's lair according to legend. Some thought the Witch a love-struck girl turned to stone by Neptune, and she waited for him, her fist raised in anger. Others claimed she came from Atlantis and she pointed out to sea to her drowned home. They said she walked when no one watched.

Years ago, to catch the Witch on the move, Beth spent a night on the beach with her friend, Dil, huddled in sleeping bags. They listened to the revellers leave the Anchor and the last of the cars drive away. Then held their breath as PC

Rogers checked each door along the Front on his last round of the day.

"She moved!" Dil whispered, fingers seeking and clinging to Beth's hand.

Beth concentrated on the Witch and, for a moment, believed she took a step. From the distance of years, logic told her it was impossible. Anchored deep beneath the sand, the rock couldn't move but, as a child, she had no doubt they'd seen the Witch walk.

Beth rolled up the window, eased her foot off the brake, and drove onto Beach Road. She pulled up outside Derwen House and doused the headlights.

Darkened houses flanked Meg's so no one gave the curtains a nosy twitch. Beth switched off the engine and picked up her overnight bag. Before she let herself into the house, she squinted at her watch: one o'clock. She should have booked into a hotel in Carmarthen and continued her journey in the morning because now she didn't have the energy to make up a bed. Beth locked the front door at her back and fumbled her way to the sitting room. With a sigh of exhaustion, she dropped onto the sofa, and dragged Meg's crocheted blanket over her shoulders.

* * *

Someone ran up the stairs and the sounds woke Beth. The house was supposed to be empty.

She eased into sitting position and glanced at her watch: Six o'clock.

Feet thudded across the upstairs landing. A door opened and heavy footsteps moved around in the bedroom overhead.

Beth crept to the door and peeped into the dark hallway. One eye on the stairs, she sidled towards the front door. The key squeaked. She hauled the door open, rushed out, and collided with the man reaching towards the knocker. Beth shrieked.

"*Pwy i chi?*"

Beth pulled away from the arms steadying her, gave a shudder when she saw the helmet and uniform, and cried, "Somebody's in the house! Upstairs."

The police officer repeated the question in English: "Who are you?"

"Bethan Davies." Why was he just standing there? "Somebody broke in; he's upstairs."

He stepped into the house and glanced along the hallway. Tall and broad shouldered, with what seemed to be agonising leisure, he strolled to the foot of the stairs, found and clicked on the light switch. He took out his truncheon and began to climb.

Poised for flight, Beth waited at the newel post while he checked each bedroom on the upper floor.

"There's nobody up here." The officer appeared at the top of the stairs.

"I heard someone!" Beth protested. "He was in the front bedroom. Did you look in the wardrobes and under the beds?"

"No one's there." He made his way to the ground floor. "Do you want me to check down here?"

"Yes!" Beth stood in doorways while he examined every nook and cranny.

"The back door isn't locked," he commented. "Was it locked last night?"

"I arrived late and I didn't check it."

"I think it's safe to say that if anyone were here, he— you did say *he*, didn't you—is gone now."

"There was someone." Weak-kneed, Beth dropped onto a chair beside the kitchen table.

"You said it was a man, did you?"

"I didn't see anyone, but the footsteps sounded heavy."

He was studying her intently. Beth looked away and clasped her hands together to still their trembling.

"It's obvious you've had a fright."

"I didn't imagine it."

He dragged a chair from under the table and sat. "Sometimes, these old places creak and groan. They make noises that sound like someone is in the house."

"Someone was here!" Her words were close to being a shout. For a moment, she was back in London, in the cold interview room facing detectives with hard and accusing eyes. "I didn't dream it. Somebody was upstairs, I tell you."

Unperturbed by her outburst, he removed his helmet and placed it on the table. "I'm Gwyn Thomas, by the way, a friend of your Aunty Megan's."

Without the helmet, he looked younger, more vulnerable. The light brown hair had a wave. His eyes were sky blue flecked with gold.

"I'm sorry about your aunty dying. I came here with the solicitor to see they did everything proper, and I've kept an eye on the place. It took us a while to find you. In London, were you?"

"I moved about the time Meg died. The telegram the solicitor sent never reached me."

"And you didn't have a phone in your new place?"

"I lived with a friend so the telephone wasn't in my name. I learned Meg had died when a friend saw the solicitor's search in *The Times*."

He leaned back. "I don't suppose the place has changed much since you were here before."

Beth recognised the chatty-police-officer approach, but she wouldn't be taken in again. The locals would have told him, as a child she often came to stay with Meg. The gossips would have added other things with a great deal of embellishment.

As if he had read her mind, he said, "You were a child then."

"I haven't been back for ten years."

He nodded. "Going to live here now, are you?"

"I haven't decided yet."

"Don't speak Welsh, do you?"

"Only a few words. I suppose you do."

"You couldn't uphold the law in a land where you don't speak the language. Every police officer in Wales speaks Welsh and English."

"Why were you coming to the house in the middle of the night?" she asked abruptly.

A tinge of colour suffused his face and his gaze slid away from hers. "I got a call about a strange car parked outside."

He was lying, Beth realised, and she spoke with a bite of anger in her voice. "Meg ran a guest house. Strange cars would be normal, wouldn't they?"

"Not when everyone knows the house is empty."

"I'm sorry they disturbed you for no good reason."

He shrugged. "Megan was a special lady. I did what I could to keep things safe for her. I knew she'd left you the house but not when you would arrive."

"Well, now you know who I am, there's no reason for you to be here. Is there?"

At the dismissal, a glimmer of resentment flickered in his eyes. "None at all," he said, rising and putting on his helmet, "but if you hear other noises . . ."

"I'll let you know."

"It's my job to offer assistance to anyone in the village."

No more the friendly bobby, piercing eyes bored into hers. She had no doubt that if it were not for his job he wouldn't bother with her again. Beth followed him to the door and closed it firmly at his back.

CHAPTER TWO

Without hurry, Gwyn walked down the path and onto the road. Megan's niece, then: like her aunty she was. Oh, not in looks, although Megan gave glimpses of the pretty girl she'd been. Some old people were like that. It was the bone structure, he supposed. It endured beneath the wrinkles and age spots.

He'd loved Megan but not as most people thought of love these days. There was nothing sexual in his feelings, no more than in his love for his mother. She was a friend he could rely on, someone to talk to, to go to when things got to him.

It had been an unlikely friendship. Him, the police officer pushing thirty, Megan, the ageing landlady of a guesthouse, and Ishmael, the beachcomber who washed up in the bay donkey's years ago. Ishmael brought them together when he ran to bang on the police station door late one night to tell him about trouble at Derwen House.

Domestic dispute is what Gwyn put in his report. Megan answered the door, her face white as the streaks in her dark hair. Behind her, someone had ripped the phone out of the wall, and the clamour from the kitchen sent a fright wave through the house. A woman with her children, escaping from her husband and stopping at Derwen Bay while she decided what to do; but he'd tracked her. They'd barricaded themselves in the kitchen when Gwyn got there, that man and woman, that husband and wife screaming hate at each other. Another guest had the children huddled in the sitting room. It was odd how shattering china often accompanied words of anger.

Strange, too, how the phrase *this is the police* affected people, but he could never guess their reaction. Some adopted a calm demeanour while others went into a frenzy, their rage directed towards him. One man, six-foot and broad shouldered, but still only a man. The uniform did it. No guns, not even a truncheon in hand, just the uniform; the damned uniform that stood like a wall between him and the public.

Take that girl now. If he'd been a concerned neighbour she'd have welcomed him and offered tea, but she wanted the uniform gone. Frightened she'd been when she opened the door. Somebody upstairs, she said, talking to the uniform, asking the uniform for protection, for a giving of life to save her own. And it wasn't just the recent fright that bothered her, either. There was something else, deeper, and older. Something in her past made her afraid, made her nervous of the uniform once she learned she was in no immediate danger.

Damn, but she was like Megan, and he'd glimpsed the tongue on her. Now he heard Megan's last words. *"Dere draw. 'rwy'n barod i ddweud wrtho ti beth 'rwy'n gwybod."* Come over. I'm ready to tell you what I know.

The words haunted him. He'd tried to get to her but dealing with a three-car accident and the storm worked against him. He took statements, wrote reports, and then helped with the boats tossed together by the rabid waves, dragging them up the sand to tie at the sea wall. Drenched, he'd gone to Megan as soon as he could get away. No one answered; no smiling woman to respond to his knock. He'd tried back and front, shouted above the wind and rain, but no lights came on to show she was home.

I'm ready to tell you. In light of what happened, he often wondered what she wanted to tell him. She was missing for over a day before her body turned up on the beach.

He'd asked for an investigation of her death from Carmarthen. The Sergeant, after listening to the scant details, said there was nothing to look into. The coroner pronounced it an accidental death.

Neither of them knew Megan. She wasn't one to make up stories. If she said something was going on in the Bay he should know about, he believed her. After all, she'd kept it to herself until she was sure there was no mistake.

Prowlers targeted Derwen House. They opened the back door somehow and got in, and now the girl heard something. She believed his lie that someone phoned him about her car, but it wasn't what made him rush to Derwen House so early in the morning.

Had it been a dream? Asleep, a boy again, his mother called him for school. In his dream, somebody prodded him, poked through the quilt and a voice called:

"Gwyn! *Codwch!*" Get up!

Half-awake, he'd thrown back the covers and peered into the empty gloom.

"*Cer i'r ty.*" Go to the house.

Had he dreamed Megan's voice? Wide-awake, he got up and, as if an outside agency propelled him, rushed into his uniform. Something in the air infused him with nervous energy—and with an urgent need to visit Derwen House.

What if he'd ignored the urge? What if the girl had confronted the intruder? He had no doubt someone had been there.

Lost in thought, Gwyn walked up Beach Road and away from the Front. Larger houses gave way to smaller ones and to a huddle of thatched cottages where the road ended. From there Peartree Lane, nothing more than a steep footpath, meandered up the hill and skirted the chapel graveyard. Rooks were busy in the oaks, raucous calls cutting through the morning like knives scraped across a plate.

At the entrance to the campground, Debbie Lewis was trying to untie the scarf her mother seemed equally determined to tie around her neck.

"*Bore da*, Gwyn." Good morning, Catrin called as she knotted the scarf.

"*Bore da*." Gwyn crossed the road. "*Bore da*, Debbie."

"Have you got time for coffee?" Catrin asked.

"I wouldn't say no, if there's one going."

"Go on in the house; Ifor's there. I'll wait with this one until the bus comes otherwise she'll have this scarf off in a flash." Catrin faced Debbie. "You had a sore throat last night so you've got to be careful, my girl."

Gwyn walked towards the sprawling farmhouse. Five years earlier, about the time Gwyn came to Derwen Bay, Catrin sold off much of the farmland and opened a campground. Several caravans sat permanently in the field overlooking the Bay and there were places reserved for touring caravans.

In the kitchen, Ifor was tucking into bacon and eggs. Mouth full, he waved a greeting and pointed to the coffee pot. Gwyn took a mug from the stand on the worktop and poured a coffee he carried to the table.

"Can I get you one, Ifor?"

Ifor swallowed. "No, you're all right. Did you see Catrin?"

Gwyn dropped into a chair opposite Ifor and reached for the sugar and milk. "She's waiting for the bus with Debbie."

"Getting too big for her boots, that girl is."

"Nonsense," Catrin responded to Ifor's comment as she entered the kitchen. "She's a big help around here, and don't you forget it. Guess who's back? Tom Rowland. I just saw him going down the hill."

Uneasiness settled between Gwyn's shoulder blades like a wet towel. For the past two years, several visitors like

Tom stayed longer than the usual two-week holiday. Artists for the most part, they never stepped out of line yet something about them troubled Gwyn.

"Tom was here at Christmas," Ifor said. "Last summer he came for three months and now he's back again. He must like this place."

"We've got two caravans full already this year," Catrin said, pouring a coffee and bringing it to the table.

"Nothing but trouble if you ask me; loud music half the night, they had."

"Only until midnight," Catrin said. "They turned it down after that, but they were up until the early hours."

"Do you want me to have a word with them?" Gwyn asked.

"Yes!" Ifor said.

"Well . . . Perhaps just a word about the music," Catrin said.

"Which caravans have the rowdies?"

"Number eighteen, the one at the far end overlooking the bay. We let the other caravan to a young couple. On their honeymoon, I think."

Gwyn finished his coffee and made his way to the caravans at the far end of the field. Number 18 had a dog tied up outside. A big dog, it stood as he approached and barked a warning.

Gwyn stopped and they eyed each other with caution. He saw Rottweiler in the shape of the head and black-and-tan colouring, but mixed with another breed that gave it height, probably Doberman, but no one had cropped the ears and tail. He took a step closer. "Good dog."

It wagged its tail in greeting, and Gwyn bent to pat it before he knocked on the door. No answer. He knocked again. Still no answer. He tried the door and found it locked. Either they were in a drunken stupor or gone out for the day. He patted the dog again and left.

11

Gwyn took the south road down to the bay. This was his village, this Lower Derwen. The one above wasn't a true village, just a church, an ancient pub with a smoke-blackened bar, and a few houses, but down here—this was the heart of Derwen. Here was the hub that could suck you in. It sucked him in a long time ago. Part of it now, not even a deserved promotion could drag him away. Let others climb the ranks and claw their way to the top; this was where he wanted to be.

"*Bore da,* Gwyn," a voice called. "How are you this morning, boyo?"

"I'm doing fine, Emrys," Gwyn called across the road to where Emrys was setting up the garage forecourt for the day.

"Fancy a cup of tea?"

"Just had coffee up at Catrin's, ta. I'd better see if there's anything in from Carmarthen."

The fax machine was devoid of messages and the light wasn't flashing on the answering machine. The place felt dead. And empty. And cold. With a sigh, Gwyn switched on the electric fire and approached the papers on his desk. A pile of mushrooms rested on the top.

The sun didn't reach this side of the valley until mid-morning. It would be shining on the other side, on Bethan, like a welcoming. But did she feel welcome?

Why did he think she was uneasy about something, frightened about something before she arrived in Derwen? What happened in London to make her nervous of his uniform?

Gwyn had no doubt she'd heard a prowler. Whoever it was hadn't approached the front door or he would have seen Bethan's car and known someone was in the house.

What was he looking for? How much danger was Bethan in if she confronted the prowler? Gwyn didn't like the thought of her alone in the house but there was little he could do about it.

CHAPTER THREE

Someone had been upstairs. It wasn't her imagination and it hadn't been a dream. Beth climbed to the upper floor and found all the doors open. Meg always kept them closed in case of fire. Beth glanced into the main guest bedroom, then locked the door and took the key.

The next bedroom faced the bay. The window gave glimpses of the ocean between branches of the oak at the side of the house. Meg often threatened to chop it down to open up the view.

Surprised to feel a draft, Beth saw the window was ajar, and she crossed the room to close it. On the outside ledge, the imprint of a shoe marred the white paint. She pushed the window wide and leaned out. Green leaves and twigs littered the ground. The intruder must have climbed from the window and leapt into the tree. He had left before they checked the house. She contemplated calling the bobby back to prove she hadn't imagined the intruder, but the less she had to do with the police, the better.

Beth passed the bedroom she'd shared with Meg and checked the two at the back. They faced the hill that was once an oak forest. A few straggly gorse bushes survived erosion and the eruption of cottages, but several trees surrounded the gardens at Plas Mawr, the mansion at the top of the hill.

With all the doors locked, Beth took the keys to the kitchen. Over a cup of tea, she relaxed for the first time since the shock of opening the door to a policeman. In a way, it was worse than waking to hear someone prowling about upstairs.

A hammering on the doorknocker thudded throughout the house interrupting her thoughts. Beth rose and grumbled her way into the hall. The summons repeated as she reached the door to drag it open. "Yes?"

The man on the doorstep stepped back. "Who are you?"

She studied his unshaved and rumpled appearance. "Who are you?"

"I'm looking for Miss Davies."

His accent was London English. A tingle of fear raised goose bumps on her upper arms. He might . . . She brought her thoughts under control. "I'm Miss Davies."

"I mean Miss Megan Davies."

"My aunt—great-aunt that is, was."

"Was?"

"She passed away."

"I'm sorry. Were you close?"

"Look, I don't know who you are but, right now, I'm in no mood to discuss my aunt's death." She started to close the door.

"I'm Tom Rowland. I've been coming here for the past two years. This is still a guest house, isn't it?"

Was it? Beth hadn't decided. "I don't know yet."

An eyebrow rose to meet the tousled hair.

"What I mean is— Damn! Why am I explaining anything to you?"

"Perhaps because I paid a month's board in advance."

Beth stared at him. "A month? How long do you normally stay?"

"The whole summer: three months."

One month, maybe not even that long. She could refund his money and be rid of him right away.

Next door, the nosy parker emerged to sweep the path. Overweight, brown hair permed in a tight poodle cut, her beady eyes focussed on them.

"Good morning, Mrs Williams," Tom called. "How are you today?"

"As well as can be expected, Mr Rowland," she replied.

Beth had never liked the woman, but at least she validated the man. She relaxed. "You'd better come in." She led him through to the kitchen. "You know Mrs Williams?"

"I know all the locals, but I've never seen you before."

"I hadn't seen my aunt for years."

"I remember her mentioning a niece."

"Bethan Davies."

"Megan said you had a dress shop."

"Used to; a land development company made me an offer I couldn't refuse." Somehow, she had to persuade him to accept a refund and leave. She topped up the kettle and plugged it in. "Tea or coffee?"

"Coffee in the morning, tea at night," he answered. "When did you last see your aunt?"

"I was fourteen."

"And you haven't been back since? How many years do that make it?"

"Is that your coy way of asking how old I am, Mr Rowland?" She unplugged the kettle when it began to blow steam.

"You caught me out; and it's Tom, please. If it makes any difference, I'm twenty-nine."

"Why would it make a difference?" She made two mugs of coffee and carried them to the table.

He grinned, his eyes the colour of the sea on a cloudy day. "Some would say I'm old enough to be married and settled down with two or three youngsters."

Beth heeled a chair from under the table and dropped onto it. "There's no milk."

He shrugged and added sugar to his coffee.

"I suppose all this opening up is designed to encourage me to tell you about myself."

"Yes."

"I only arrived last night, and I might not stay."

"What is there in London? Now you've sold your shop, I mean."

How did he know she was from London? She quelled the jolt of fear; Meg probably told him. "I have friends there."

"You must have friends here, too. Did you spend a lot of summers here?"

"A few."

"Derwen Bay isn't big. I doubt I'll be able to find another place to stay."

"There are other seaside places up and down the coast."

"But this is where I want to be."

The petulant edge to his voice and his persistence angered Beth. "It's only the end of May; few places will be booked up. There used to be a pub that took in guests."

"The Anchor; I can try there but they're booked solid most of the time. That's how I came to stop with Megan the first time. The Anchor had double booked and I was late arriving."

"Unlike this morning when you turned up at the crack of dawn."

"Nine o'clock is hardly the crack of dawn," he pointed out.

"If the Anchor is full, you could always try next door with Mrs Williams."

"I'd rather sleep on the beach."

"Now there's a thought for you."

He smiled.

"Why are you smiling?"

"I heard a touch of Welsh lilt in your voice just then."

"With a name like Bethan Davies that isn't surprising now, is it?" she said dryly. "Why do you want to stay in Derwen Bay?"

"I paint. The coastline here is unique."

"After two summers, I should have thought you would have painted everything for miles around."

"The sea is changeable."

"You paint seascapes?"

He nodded.

Beth drained her mug and carried it to the sink. "Well, you will have to find somewhere else. Even if I decide to open the house, I'm not ready for guests."

"But you have a legal obligation to put me up for at least a month."

Beth whirled to face him. "You're not welcome here, Mr Rowland, and the agreement you had was with my aunt, not with me."

"It is a matter for our lawyers to thrash out. In the meantime, I will stay here."

"PC Thomas might say something about that."

He glanced at his watch. "Nine-fifteen; I think Gwyn Thomas will be eating his breakfast about now. Megan's phone is in the hallway."

She glared at him. The solicitor said they'd left the telephone connected in case she tried to ring Meg and they could trace her that way. She could call the police, but she didn't want further dealings with them, even a local bobby. "Look, if I agree to let you lodge here for a week . . ."

"Perhaps I'll be able to find somewhere else for the rest of the summer. Is that what you were about to say?"

Beth nodded.

"I'll get my things." He rose and walked out into the hallway. "The usual arrangement was that I would have breakfast and dinner here. Megan would make sandwiches and a flask for me to take for lunch."

Beth took a set of bedroom keys from the drawer and followed him as far as the front door. Tom disappeared around the side of the house and returned with a rucksack and an easel. She noted the empty driveway she was too tired to negotiate the night before, and asked, "You don't have a car?"

"I hitched here." He headed for the stairs. "I always took a bedroom at the back."

"The view is better from the front."

"The light is better at the back."

She went to change the keys she had and then followed him up. She unlocked a bedroom door and indicated the bare mattress and pillows. "As you can see, I'm not ready for guests."

"It won't take me two minutes to put on sheets." He dropped his things under the window and opened it. "Unless, of course, you want to do it, seeing as you're the landlady."

"Of course," Beth said, stomping to the airing cupboard on the landing and taking out sheets, pillowcases and a quilt. While she made up the bed, he continued to stare out the window. "I can't see there's anything of interest out there you haven't seen before."

"The O'Malleys changed their curtains."

"O'Malleys?" Beth joined him at the window. "I don't remember a family by that name."

"They live up there," he said, pointing to a house half way up the hill, "just below Plas Mawr. The curtains used to be puke green, now they're a puke orange."

"Do you include houses in your paintings?"

"It depends on the scene. People too. If an old sea dog is leaning against the sea wall or an old boat, I'll include him in the painting."

"Do you sell many?"

"Enough."

But not enough to buy a car. "The bed is done, so I'll get the shopping. Do you have any particular likes or dislikes?"

Attention on the view from the window, he answered, "None."

Beth pulled a face at his back. This was going to be the worst month of her life. Well, maybe not the worst, but pretty close.

P L Crompton

CHAPTER FOUR

Beth brought her luggage from the car and took a shower. In the bedroom-cum-office once shared with Meg, she opened a suitcase and took out jeans and a shirt. Before shoving the suitcase under the bed, she removed a brown envelope and extracted a handful of banknotes to put in her pocket. Intent on putting the envelope where she'd hidden her treasures as a child, she pulled back the rug and pried up the loose floorboard in the corner.

She'd taken everything with her that last time, but now a plastic bag occupied the cavity. Beth took it out.

Inside was a bundle of money, not British pounds but French francs. Meg vowed she would never travel abroad but must have changed her mind. Odd she didn't mention it during one of their infrequent phone conversations. Beth counted the notes. If the exchange rate was what it had been three years earlier, she held the equivalent of £10,000. It was more than the average person would take for a holiday. More than thrifty Meg would spend. Perhaps several French guests paid her in cash. Beth replaced the money and stuffed her own envelope on top. She dropped the board into place and spread the rug over it before writing a shopping list and leaving the house.

In the graveyard on the side of the hill, Beth found Meg's grave in the shade of an oak. A shiny black headstone marked it, and a posy of wild flowers wilted lop-sided in a jam jar.

Megan Davies

1914 – 1985

Rest in peace

Beth knelt in grass still wet with dew and rearranged the flowers. Her heart ached with a sense of loss but she couldn't cry. Some said the shock of death held tears at bay until something unexpected set them free.

She remembered Meg as feisty, the way older people sometimes were, but she had many friends and involved herself in all the social events this place had to offer. For years, she ran the drama club, led the chapel choir, and organised the Women's Institute. She said the village came to life in winter after the tourists left.

"So you have come at last, Bethan Louise Davies."

Beth looked up, a hand raised to shield her eyes from the shaft of sunlight lancing between the trees. Reverend Powell-Pritchard. He made her summers in Derwen a misery and, in her mind, the tight-lipped man epitomised most of the villagers. "Yes." She rose, surprised that the man who seemed so big to a child was hardly taller than she was.

"It is a pity they didn't find you in time for the funeral. Megan would have liked you to be there."

"I would have come, had I known."

"Yes." He clasped his hands together at crotch level, white against the black suit. "You hadn't seen much of her these past years. She missed you, Bethan. We did what we could, of course, but we weren't family. Shall we see you in chapel on Sunday?"

Something in the mild reproach stiffened Beth's spine and clenched her jaw. She hissed, "If I don't attend, Mr Powell-Pritchard, I'll be—what is the phrase—sent to Coventry?"

"What do you mean?"

"I know the way it is in Derwen."

The clasped hands tightened as if he expected a blow. "You were always sharp tongued, Bethan."

"Like my aunt, you mean? No, I will not be in chapel on Sunday or any other day." With that, she stomped out of the graveyard.

Beth had not intended to walk farther up the hill but, when she made her dramatic exit from among the gravestones, her feet carried her in that direction. She'd have to pass Powell-Pritchard if she walked back, so it wasn't an option. She could have said a lot more to the man who made her summer holidays hell on earth.

Daunted by the steep stretch ahead, Beth turned off onto the narrow lane to Plas Mawr. She had often walked past the mansion and cut across the fields to take the cliff path down to the village. A dirt track then, now a layer of chipped stone pressed into the surface.

Two whitewashed cottages contrasted a third in need of a coat of paint, its garden a tangle of weeds. Lurid orange curtains covered the windows. The O'Malley place, she decided, remembering Tom Rowland's description. As she prepared to walk by, a lorry loaded with rocks and timber lumbered down the hill. Beth stepped into the cottage gateway and waited for it to pass. The red-haired man at the wheel looked in her direction and studied her from head to toe. He made her feel naked and she raised a defiant chin and stared back. He wasn't someone she had known as a child.

The road ended at Plas Mawr. At the gates, a big black dog with white fangs barked and salivated as it threw itself at the wrought iron. Beth sprinted past.

An overgrown footpath led to the cliffs with only the boundary wall to show her where to walk. At one time, she could see into the garden, but since then someone had added to the top and it was higher than her head. The stone was the same colour as the cliffs and the chunks carried away in the lorry.

Still barking, the dog marked her progress from the other side of the wall. Ahead, where Plas Mawr's garden edged pastureland, there had never been anything more than a barbed-wire fence and a faded sign to warn off trespassers. She slowed her pace and stopped. Should the dog be heading for the wire fence, the safest place was on top of the wall.

Rough-cut stone offered toeholds as Beth leapt up and peered into the garden. To replace the old wire one, someone had built a wooden fence at least six feet high. It continued along the side of the garden and around the back, effectively keeping the dog in.

Rubble littered the garden. Ten years ago, the lawn had been smooth as a bowling green, tended by Old Griff for an absent owner from London. Beth never knew the owner's name but, when he visited with friends, she often spied on the garden parties, envying the women their flowing dresses and wide-brimmed hats. It was probably why she'd entered the fashion industry when she left school and then opened her own boutique.

Beth was about eleven when one woman in particular had drawn her attention because she looked like Miss Brahms on the TV show *Are You Being Served;* but she didn't have the same Cockney accent. When Beth heard her speak, she didn't sound British. Although she didn't know the woman's name, she would never forget the quarrel she'd witnessed when one of the men punched the woman in the face and knocked her to the ground.

Beth saw a man watching her from one of the windows and she dropped back onto the footpath.

A flock of sheep grazed in the field next to the fence, but only one curious lamb glanced in her direction as she made for the cliff. She sank onto the grass a few feet from the edge. Close by, a trail led to the north beach. She often used the walk when she wanted to be alone.

"Be careful. The edge is breaking away over there." A voice came from behind.

Unaware anyone else was on the cliff she looked around. Half hidden by a clump of gorse, a man sat with a canvas resting across his knees. "Thanks for the warning." She rose and wandered towards him. Another English visitor and an artist like Tom.

"I heard someone had fallen over the cliff a while back."

"It isn't the safest of walks." Beth looked over his shoulder at the painting; the south headland. "Oh!" A woman with cropped black hair sat in the foreground. "Is that me?"

"Do you object?"

With her back to the artist, no one in London would recognise her. "I suppose not."

"Thank you. Do you live locally?"

"No. I used to spend my summer holidays here. Are you on holiday?"

"I've been here a couple of months, trying to capture springtime in the bay. The wild flowers hereabouts are fantastic."

"They would be different from those flowering now."

"It rained so much the flowers were beaten down. Are you on your way to the north beach?"

"No. I just needed to get away for a while, feel the sea air on my face without having it mixed with diesel and petrol fumes."

He chuckled. "I know what you mean. The best part of painting seascapes is the air one breathes."

Beth realised he'd stopped painting. "Well, I'd best get back and leave you to your work."

"Watch yourself on the way down; some parts are tricky."

Beth raised a hand in farewell and followed the path. Always slick in parts, she had travelled it often and in safety.

Halfway down, she caught her first glimpse of the entire lower village. Nestled between grassed hills, nothing much seemed to have changed. One or two houses had new coats of paint, and one had grown an addition complete with garage. One close to Meg's sported a greenhouse in a corner of the garden.

She reached the deserted seafront car park where the stench of diesel lingered. The place was almost empty during the week but, at weekends, day-trippers filled it with cars and buses. She paused at the sea wall and looked across the beach. So early in the season, with children still at school, there were few people.

The Witch dominated the shoreline a few yards from where the dark maw of the cave gaped. The tide was out, half-hearted breakers rippling as they withdrew from the sand. Beyond the rock, she glimpsed the second, smaller beach. Easily reached across the sand now, high tide cut it off. The only access then was via the cliff path or by way of a long swim for anyone silly enough to risk being close to the Witch. She winced at the memory.

Meg often took evening walks on the beach. Like all the locals, she knew to the minute when the tide would turn, and it would never have caught her. The police were wrong. She would question the locals who might know something, and she would prove the police wrong.

Beth walked along the Front and saw several faces she remembered, but no one recognised the teen with a ponytail as the woman with the gamine haircut.

The grocer's shop seemed larger, but it smelled the way she remembered: oranges, spices, earthy potatoes, bread baking somewhere behind the back wall, strong disinfectant. A freezer squatted next to a glass-fronted cooler filled with soft drinks. The man restocking it crushed an empty cardboard box against his hip and eyed her.

"*Bore da.*" Daniel Jones. Daniel-the-Shop who'd called the police on her.

"Good morning." She returned the greeting without warmth.

"Can I 'elp you?"

Beth took the list from her pocket. "I need the things on here."

"Staying in the caravan park, are you?" Daniel began to put her order together.

"No."

"Oh?" He paused to glance at her. "In Ty Goch, then?" He mentioned a house let out to summer visitors.

"No."

"Oh." He checked a carton of eggs for breakage. "Where are you staying, then?"

"Derwen House."

The egg carton slid from his hands onto the counter. "You're Megan's niece, from London?"

She ignored the question. "Did any of the eggs break?"

"*Arswyd!*" He opened the carton, set it to one side and chose another. "Bethan, is it? Well, there's grown you have, girl; too big now to take sweeties, eh?"

Beth gave her attention to a rack of magazines. He'd caught her once, but it was enough for Meg to send her home and tell her never to come back. "I'll take the bread, milk, butter and tomatoes with me. Can you deliver the rest?"

"As soon as the delivery boy gets back; gone up to the caravan park, he is. There's people up there early this year, see."

"And I want the Sunday papers, *News of the World* and the *Sunday Mirror*." She waited as he made a note in a book he brought from under the counter. "How much is it?"

He tapped figures into the till, and then called out the total as he ripped out the receipt. "Paying by cheque, are you?"

"Cash." Beth reached into her pocket for the money.

"Staying here long, are you?" he asked as he made change.

"Probably not." Beth pocketed the coins he held out and hoisted the bag he'd packed.

"I was sorry to hear about your aunty. She didn't deserve what happened to her."

Beth stared at him.

"I know you won't want to talk about it, but it must be said. Megan should not have died the way she did. Nobody should."

"What are you talking about, Mr Jones?"

"Your Aunty Megan's murder, of course." A telephone rang at the back of the shop and he rushed to answer it.

Murder . . . He'd given voice to her thoughts. Someone murdered Meg. A knot rose from the pit of Beth's stomach to the base of her throat. In a daze, she walked to the sea wall and rested the bag of groceries on it. How many others thought Meg murdered? Why hadn't the solicitor mentioned it, or the bobby? Did the police investigate? How far did they get with the investigation?

Whatever qualms she had about dealing with the police, she had to find out what the police report said. Beth picked up the groceries bag and marched towards the police station.

The Derwen Bay branch of the Dyfed-Powys Police Force was a house tucked around the corner and away from the seafront. The blue sign above the door announced in Welsh and English that this was where one could find the *Heddlu*—Police. The door was the traditional blue, but the blue lamp to one side had only the sun to brighten it. Beth had her hand on the doorknob when a man called from the garage across the street.

"He isn't there, *cariad*. Gone up to the caravan park to sort out rowdies, he has."

The mechanic had a smudge of oil on his cheek, a spanner in one hand, and the other hand buried in the bowels of a car engine. They were of an age, and something familiar about him plucked at her memory. "Any idea when he'll be back?"

The man shrugged. "Depends if anybody offers him tea; he could be there all day unless he gets a phone call to bring him back."

"Thanks." Beth retraced her steps. She could ring Gwyn Thomas, but she didn't want him coming to the house. She didn't want Tom Rowland involved, either, but until she knew what the police report said, she couldn't rest.

Numb, Beth walked along the Front and up Beach Road. As she turned in at the gate, she realised she had never appreciated how pretty Meg's house was. Built of red brick, ivy clambered over the side shaded by the oak branching over the parking spot. Roses clung around the front door and sitting room window and rambled over an arch leading to the back of the house. In the front garden, someone had cut the grass, but standard rose bushes drooped among the weeds smothering the primroses and daffodils. Here and there, fragrant wallflowers struggled. She had to do something. Meg always kept a garden that was the envy of her neighbours. Beth decided to brave the spidery shed and find the tools necessary to bring the garden into good order. It might help to take her mind off the shock of learning other people thought someone murdered Meg.

Beth put the groceries away and went into the back garden. Weeds choked the herb patch and almost obliterated the little gnome Meg had placed there. Beth pulled the greenery away from the grinning face. They chose the gnome during a trip to Carmarthen and spent an evening painting his pointy cap and clothes in bright reds and blues. She stopped abruptly, shaken by the thought that Meg would never see the silly gnome again.

Without warning, tears blurred the painted face and Beth was sobbing into the scrunched and inadequate tissue she found in her pocket. She ran into the house for a hand towel to mop her face. Crudely embroidered, in one corner of the towel were the initials MD, her work, a Christmas gift to Meg.

Beth raced up to her room, fell onto the bed, and cried herself to sleep.

CHAPTER FIVE

There was still no answer at the caravan with the rowdies. Gwyn stepped onto the road and bent to brush dog hairs from his trousers. A nice dog of undetermined breed, she hadn't jumped at him as other dogs would, but she pressed against him when he knocked on the caravan door.

"Is that a new style of furry uniform you are wearing, Mr Policeman?"

Gwyn looked up and grinned at Ishmael. "What're you doing up here?"

"Gathering mushrooms." Ishmael held up a basket. "Would you like a few for your table?"

"I've nowhere to carry them." Gwyn waited until a lorry passed carrying rubble he knew came from Plas Mawr, and crossed the road to join Ishmael at the stile.

"I will leave a few at the station."

"Thanks." Gwyn perched on the stile and looked down over the bay.

To the south, he could just see the top floor of Hill Farm. In the meadow between the farm and the edge of the cliff, an artist's white tent sat pegged next to a motorbike. At the height of summer, tents would blanket the field right up to the wire fence signalling danger. More rugged than the north cliff, deep granite steppes lay beneath the shallow sprinkling of grass and gorse, not the place for anyone to build a home.

"Megan's niece has arrived," he informed Ishmael.

"I surmised it was she I saw earlier; she has the look of Megan. What is your opinion of her?"

"I'm not sure."

"She is attractive. Few women manage to appear elegant while wearing jeans and a shirt, but she has attained that goal."

"Goal? That's an odd word to use."

"Not necessarily," Ishmael explained. "Megan told us Bethan worked in the fashion industry before she purchased the boutique. Ergo, she would aim at elegance, whatever her mode of dress."

"She said someone was in the house this morning."

"Our inveterate prowler, do you think?"

"I didn't think anyone would be on the prowl at dawn."

"And a resident in the house was unexpected."

Gwyn nodded. "Just like before. Whoever it is gets in without doing damage. It's as if he's got a key."

"He?"

"Bethan said the footsteps sounded heavy enough for it to be a man. What can he be searching for?"

"Some proof of what Megan wanted to disclose to you, perhaps."

"Do you have any idea what she wanted to tell me?"

Ishmael shook his head. "You have asked me many times. Had I an answer in the affirmative, I would divulge the information."

"You're a lot like Megan in that respect, aren't you?"

"Conjecture is often useless."

"In my job, conjecture is sometimes all we have. It worries me that this girl may be in danger."

"Not now, surely, for the artist is back. I recall Megan did not hear the prowler when he was in residence."

"That bothers me. It's a coincidence that he came back the same morning Bethan arrived, isn't it?"

"History is filled with coincidences, Gwyn. You waste your time trying to make sense of them."

"I suppose you're right."

"Something interesting happened last night."

"Oh?"

"Two men who are staying at the caravan site paid Plas Mawr a visit."

"Friends of Plews?"

Ishmael shook his head. "They climbed over the wall and a skirmish ensued. The dog attacked them, too. I didn't wait to learn the outcome because they might have observed me watching from the gates."

"They didn't call me in, so there isn't much I can do." Gwyn climbed from the stile. "If you learn anything more . . ."

"As always." Ishmael hooked the basket over one arm and strode off across the field with a wave of his hand.

Gwyn watched him walk away. *Who are you, Ishmael? From where did you come? Why are you in this place and living as you do?*

He had never uttered the questions aloud. Such enquiries from someone in his job would appear suspect, but they haunted Gwyn. Most thought Ishmael a halfwit, but Ishmael was an educated man and, if genetics had a basis of truth, he came from an aristocratic family. It showed in the long, narrow feet, in the elegance of the calloused hands and in the long, vaguely horsey face; a face seen on photographs of high-society's darlings, but friends didn't pry. It was enough to accept who the friend was, not who he had been.

Gwyn's predecessor had no time for the man named by Eleri-the School after a character in a book the children were reading, but Gwyn sought him out. It had taken time; time when Gwyn asked him no personal questions and imposed no restrictions on the man's wanderings about the village. A bit like training a dog, he mused. You gentled them, showed patience, and the results were far greater than Gwyn expected. The bond of friendship went further. Ishmael was his eyes and ears, the discoverer of lies and truths. No one in Derwen knew

Ishmael's value to the community was far more than painting a wall or mending a fence.

From the road, Gwyn studied the north cliff. The area around Plas Mawr was a hive of activity. Reginald Plews was enlarging the cellar, but he hadn't hired local workmen. Red hair marked Sean O'Malley, one of two brothers who lived in a cottage down the hill from the mansion. The one wearing the blazer and light-coloured slacks would be Reginald who fancied himself Lord of the Manor. Something about the man raised Gwyn's hackles, though he was never anything but polite to Derwen's only law officer. There were two others at work alongside O'Malley. They never came to the village, not even to the pub, so Gwyn had no idea of their names. Perhaps now was the time to find out.

At Plas Mawr, a bullmastiff leapt at the wrought-iron bars and the gate shook under Gwyn's hand. The words he uttered in an attempt to calm the animal were lost under ferocious barking. He couldn't see O'Malley and the only man visible kept his back to Gwyn while he tossed pieces of rock into a wheelbarrow. Gwyn raised a hand in greeting as Reginald Plews hurried across the rubble-strewn garden. The man spoke, but the dog's ruckus drowned out the words until he caught a hand under its collar and clipped it on the nose. The dog resorted to threatening growls.

"What can I do for you, Constable?" Reginald's words came in jerks as he fought to restrain the lunging animal.

"Just passing and I wondered how the work was progressing."

"Very well." The dog yanked Reginald forward in its effort to reach Gwyn.

"You've got a lot of clearing up to do." With a tip of his head, Gwyn indicated the garden.

"We're getting it done bit by bit."

Gwyn nodded. "I've seen the lorries carrying the rubble away. One or two people complained about them going through the upper village late at night."

"Have they?" At first, the look Reginald gave Gwyn showed a lack of concern for the villagers. Then he appeared to take note of the uniform and added, "I'll try to make sure the drivers stick to early evening."

"It's the O'Malley's doing the driving for you, is it?"

"Sometimes. It depends."

"How many other workmen do you have here?"

"Only two now."

"So four in total, as well as yourself."

Reginald nodded. "That's right."

"With that many, it shouldn't be long before the renovations are finished."

Reginald shrugged. "There is still carpentry and painting to do, once the excavating is done."

"And that's after Town Planning approves, right?"

"Of course. Look, Constable, I have a great deal to do so, if you don't mind . . ."

Gwyn nodded. "I'll let you get to it." He turned away.

It was the second time that day he'd been dismissed, first that girl and now Plews. The thought they were both outsiders consoled Gwyn, but the observation that both were wary of the uniform didn't offer any comfort.

* * *

The delicious smell of cooking filled the house when Beth woke. She inhaled in appreciation and then splashed cold water on her face. A glance in the mirror showed a slight redness around her eyes to show she had been crying, and her hair was a tangled mess. She ran a brush through it before descending the stairs in search of the aroma's origin.

Tom looked at home, a tea towel tied at his waist as he stirred something in a pot on the stove. If he saw she'd been crying, he said nothing.

"I hope you don't mind. I raided Megan's store and found a jar of spaghetti sauce."

"And spaghetti, I trust." A flicker of anger twitched Beth's mind. Even from the back, he looked like the cop who had accused her of having stolen goods. "Is this your coy way of telling me I'm being lax in my duties as a landlady?"

"It's my way of saying I'm hungry."

Beth checked her watch; just after five. "What time did Meg make dinner?"

"Around six, but I missed lunch, and you did, too."

Food had been the last thing on her mind. "Shall I make a salad?"

"All done and in the fridge." He indicated a paper bag. "You can slice the tomatoes, though. I hate that job; I always get them mashed."

She retrieved the bowl of salad and added sliced tomatoes. "I see you found the chives."

"Eventually, it's a jungle out there."

"And at the front. I've decided to do what I can after dinner to tidy it."

"I can give you a hand, if you want."

"Doing the gardening on top of the cooking? And you a paying guest! These are a landlady's jobs, and I'm the landlady, as you keep reminding me."

He strained the spaghetti and glanced at her. "You're the one who keeps bringing that up, not me."

"Since our conversations weren't memorable, I cannot dispute what you just said."

He divided the spaghetti onto two plates and put them on the table. "Had a bad day, have we?"

"I can't speak for yours, but I wouldn't say mine was good." Beth put the salad bowl on the table and sat as he brought the tureen of sauce. "From now on, paying guests eat in the dining room."

He shrugged. "If that's the way you want it."

"It's what Meg did."

"When there were other guests, yes."

"And when there weren't, you and she got cosy out here?"

"Or we ate off trays in the sitting room and watched the telly."

"In other words, you made yourself at home."

"Does that bother you?" He took salad from the bowl onto a side plate. "There were times when she was lonely. At the height of the season, most of her friends were too busy to come around, and so was Megan. This place was always packed to bursting with people coming and going but with no time for their landlady."

Beth looked down at her plate. "Is this your way of telling me I neglected her?"

"Without being coy? Yes. Your boutique could have done without you for a few days. You could have spared the occasional weekend."

"You do realise I had a shop open six days a week, and that it's a nine-hour journey here from London, don't you?"

"So you couldn't find time for a lonely old lady. At least you rang her at Christmas."

"How do you know?"

"Because I spent Christmas with her. She was excited to hear from you. She missed you."

Beth pushed away from the table and got to her feet. On top of Powell-Pritchard's words, this was too much. "I don't need you to make me feel guiltier than I already do, especially since someone told me this morning they thought Meg was murdered!" She stomped into the hall and dragged the front door open so hard it bounced against the wall and almost hit her as she rushed outside.

"Bethan! Wait!"

Beth ignored him and ran along the path, snubbing Mrs Williams in the garden next door.

How dare he! How dare he talk to her like that! Meg was her aunt, not his. Just because he'd been coming here for two years didn't give him any rights. When she got back, she would throw his things out of the house, give him his marching orders and lock the doors.

But she'd let Meg down. Ashamed of being caught stealing, she hadn't dared visit Derwen even though Meg asked her to come. She'd made weak excuses. I was easy to say she worked six days a week, and then had the boutique open six days a week, but she'd managed to spend a week in Paris three years earlier. It didn't matter how many excuses she made for not visiting for ten years, the real reason was the petty theft and the way people in Derwen had memories that went back to the year dot.

Beth reached the car park, ran into the public toilets, and locked herself in a cubicle. Muffling her sobs in case anyone should come in, she pulled herself together and blew her nose.

She recognised that the grief she felt as Meg's passing as partly guilt from the way she'd neglected her. A nine-hour journey each way, there hadn't been enough time.

Calmer, she flushed the handful of paper and went to the hand basin to splash her face with cold water. In the chipped mirror, she saw only a tinge of redness. Beth checked to see if Tom was hanging around outside, and left.

A strong wind blew off the sea, tossing the seagulls in squalling circles as they wheeled around the fishing boats making for the beach. A few women with baskets gathered at the edge of the breakers. Beth remembered waiting with Meg so the mackerel and herring they ate would be fresh from the sea. There were days when she shivered and huddled next to her aunt, and other days she played chicken with the wavelets and earned a scolding for getting her sandals wet.

It was too cold to wander on top of the cliffs, but she couldn't go home. Emotionally, she didn't feel strong enough to deal with Tom or to confront the bobby about Meg's murder. When she did, she wanted to be in control.

Where could she go? She wasn't hungry, so the restaurant was out of the question; mid-week and out-of-season, the coffee shop and the Blue Café had already closed. The only alternative was the Anchor.

P L Crompton

CHAPTER SIX

Gwyn's computer skills were the keyboarding equivalent of dancing with two left feet. Exasperated, he rang HQ in Carmarthen and they patched him through to Sergeant Driscoll.

When she answered, the image of her was clear in his mind. Brawny, and on the wrong side of thirty, she once tried to get on the police rugby team. The main objection to her joining was that none of her fellow officers relished having her take him down in a tackle. They had a macho image to uphold. To everyone's surprise, when they brought in the latest computer equipment, Dorothy Driscoll showed an aptitude and earned promotion to head of the department. Rumours said she managed to break into files few could access.

"What do you want, Thomas?"

Her booming voice always made him quake. "Is it possible to check if planning permission was given for enlarging the cellar at Plas Mawr?"

"Where in hell is Plas Mawr? Is it on your patch?"

"Yes. The owner's name is Reginald Plews. He bought the place about five years ago."

"I can check it in the morning. Right now, I'm going off duty."

"The morning will be fine." Gwyn forced his voice to a steadiness he didn't feel. "Also, please check with London Metro if they have anything on a Bethan Davies?"

"She a new girlfriend?"

"She arrived in Derwen Bay last night."

"Any reason you want her checked?"

What reason could he give? That Bethan was frightened of something; that something in her past made her uneasy in his presence.

"Thomas? Are things so quiet in that backwater of yours that you're checking into everyone who visits the hole?"

"If she's to become part of the community, I'd like to find out if Metro knows anything about her when she lived in London."

"So it isn't a priority. I'll get to it when I get to it."

"Thank you."

"Is this through official channels?"

Instantly, Gwyn was alert. Dorothy Driscoll, wasn't above doing work outside official channels. He had never been one of her favourites, none of the officers on the rugby team was, and they said she bore a grudge. Some even said she demanded certain favours—sexual favours—in return for computer checking that wasn't part of an investigation. That made Gwyn shudder more than the realisation that, if his superiors learned he was investigating something outside official channels, he'd be in for it. He cleared his throat. "I'm shocked you should ask such a thing, Sergeant. Naturally, the checks I want done will be reported to my superiors."

"Then you won't mind faxing me the request."

"I'll do it right away." Gwyn hung up.

What made him ask about Bethan? That she wasn't partial to police officers was no reason to suspect she had a record. His years in Derwen, when most of the villagers looked upon him as one of them, had erased from his mind the mistrust many people and visitors felt towards those of his profession. Of course, it was possible it was just to him she wasn't partial. That would be a new experience. Normally women were a bit too partial to him, and it always came as a surprise to Gwyn who considered himself very ordinary looking. Still, there was a first time for everything.

At the computer, he typed out a quick request for information on Reginald Plews' planning permission, the reason easily supplied. When it came to the request for information on Bethan, he left the space blank. He had only his intuition to go on, but it had never let him down.

* * *

Dilys was at the bar, giving change to a man with a tray of pints. Petite and blonde, she glanced up as Beth entered and a puzzled look crossed her face. "Bethan? Is it you?"

Beth grinned. "Have I changed that much?"

"*Duw mawr!*" Dilys ran around to the front of the bar, her arms open wide. "Welcome home!"

Beth laughed and hugged her. "I didn't know if you'd remember me."

"Remember my blood sister?" Dilys held up her thumb to show the scar, twin of the one on Beth's thumb. They became blood sisters after watching a film about American Indians. "This calls for a celebration. What'll you have? It's on the house."

"Bailey's, please."

Dilys went behind the bar to pour a generous liqueur. She picked up a bottle of pineapple juice and an empty glass, and inclined her head. "Come on, let's go into the snug. It's quiet at this time of day and Dat can serve whoever comes in. He'll be pleased to see you, Beth."

"Will he?" Davy, Dil's father, always blamed her for the scrapes his daughter got into.

Dilys led Beth to a small table. "I'm sorry about your aunty."

Beth took a sip of her drink. "I only learned about it a few days ago. The solicitor told me she'd died, but . . ." She couldn't repeat the word Daniel-the-shop used.

"But?" Dilys paused in her pouring of the fruit juice. "Why is there a *but?*"

"Someone told me today that people thought Meg was murdered."

"*Duw mawr!* Who told you a thing like that, then?"

"Daniel Jones."

"Oh, Daniel! You didn't believe him, did you?"

"I assumed she'd died of natural causes. How did she die, Dil?"

"The tide caught her," Dilys said quietly. "They found her caught on the Witch the next morning. Her cardigan snagged on the rock, otherwise she'd have been washed out to sea."

"If they found her in the morning, she must have gone onto the beach at night, but why?"

Dilys gave her attention to the juice she swirled in her glass. "There was a storm that night. Thunder and lightning, and the breakers right up to the wall. Dat was getting sandbags ready to put at the door, in case the sea came over."

"And Meg went out in it? No, nothing would induce her to go onto the beach at night and in a storm. And why would Daniel Jones say someone murdered her?"

"Daniel is always making whales out of tiddlers."

"But he can't be the only one who thinks that way."

"There was talk . . ."

"What talk?" Beth leaned forward.

"Well . . ."

"Tell me, Dil."

"You've got to remember, Beth, people like to make more of things than they really are, especially in a small place like this."

"Had I been here at the time, I would probably have agreed with them. Look at the painting behind you. How could anyone be swept close to the Witch?"

Dilys swung around on her stool to look at the painting. "The tide might have carried her there. By the way, Tom Rowland painted that. He used to stay at your aunt's place."

"He arrived this morning and forced his way in."

"Tom did? You surprise me."

"You know him?"

"He's been coming to the Bay for a couple of years. Like one or two others, he's stayed the whole summer. I can't imagine him forcing his way into your house."

"How well do you know him? Have you dated him?"

"Tom's good looking, but I only got involved with a visitor once. He took off when he found out I was pregnant."

"You have a child?"

"Richard. Ricky. He's nearly five."

"Meg never told me. You can't have known his father very well."

"He came for a holiday and stayed on to work at Plas Mawr. They were doing renovations and he was a builder by trade, so I thought it would all work out."

"But he left when he heard you were pregnant?"

"He never even said goodbye. I had his granddad's address in Liverpool, and Dat went up to see the old man. He said he had no idea where Mike was. The last he'd heard, he was working at Derwen Bay."

"He might have been lying."

"I doubt it; staunch Catholics they were, not that it means much these days, but Mike always wore a cross and chain. I took Ricky to see the old man soon after he was born. I've been up a couple of times since, always on the hop so he had no idea I was coming. I never saw any sign that Mike was around."

"How did your father take it?"

Dilys chuckled. "If you'd been here, he'd have blamed it all on you for leading me astray. We had a few tough months until he held Ricky. He's the spitting image of Dat. Dark blond hair and blue eyes; he has none of Mike's colouring. Mike was very dark, black hair and brown eyes. One of the blokes in here referred to him as Black Irish."

"They say Liverpool is full of Irish people."

"His granddad spoke with a brogue."

"I'm sorry for your trouble. If there's anything I can do."

"Wait until you see Ricky; you'll fall in love with him. It's the best trouble I've ever had." Dilys looked up as several people entered the bar. "Bring your drink out and I can chat to you between serving them."

Beth rose with the glass in her hand and stepped closer to the painting. "So this is Tom Rowland's work."

"Dat's sold a couple of his paintings after hanging them in here. Tom's a lot nicer than some of the stoppers we get."

"Stoppers?"

"The last couple of years, we've had visitors who've stayed weeks or months, and at all times of the year. You wouldn't think anyone would want to be here in winter, would you, but come they do."

"Stoppers . . ." Beth mused as she followed Dilys out. The man on the cliff said he came to paint the spring flowers and now it was almost June. He'd be one of the stoppers.

Davy nodded to Beth as she took a stool at the bar. "Sorry about your aunty. If you need anything . . ."

"Thanks." Beth nodded. The parents of the children she played with always warned their offspring against playing with a townie. She was surprised Davy would even acknowledge her.

While Dilys and her father took care of their customers, Beth looked around the room. As a child, she came into the bar once, when she coerced Dil into getting them a bottle of pop one hot afternoon. They snuck out to drink it hidden behind the sea wall before smuggling the empty bottle into the crates at the back of the Anchor. She supposed she had been a bad influence.

Ashamed of the way she had behaved, she looked down and studied the contents of her glass. Had anything she'd done ten years ago been bad enough for someone to bear a grudge against Meg? Who killed Meg?

"Have you taken up your auntie's witching ways, then?"

Beth looked up at the man who took the stool next to hers. "Emrys Morgan." Oil washed off, aftershave splashed on, and clean clothes, black grease still rimed his fingernails.

"I thought it was you looking for Gwyn this morning, but I didn't think you recognised me."

"I wasn't sure it was you."

Emrys offered her a cigarette and took one when she refused. "What're you drinking?"

"Baileys."

Emrys waved to Dilys. "Another for the lady and half of my usual, *cariad*." He lit his cigarette and dragged an ashtray closer. "So how have you been, Bethan?"

"I've been okay, until I heard about Meg."

"*Diawl* that was a bad, I'm sorry. You'll be all on your own now, will you?"

"My mother is somewhere in Africa with her new husband. My letter about Meg's death should have reached her by now."

"Don't they have telephones out there, then?"

"I rang the place where they were staying, but they'd gone out on some expedition or other so they were going to get the park rangers to radio them."

"Your stepfather's an explorer, is he?"

Beth laughed. "Nothing so romantic; he's a vet. They do regular treks onto the veldt to tend sick animals. Sometimes they're gone for weeks."

"So you've come to live in your auntie's house?"

"I don't know if I'm going to stay but I'll be here for a few weeks."

"That's good. You can get Dilys to go about with you like when you were children."

"I'm sure she has plenty of friends. Is she seeing anyone?"

Emrys shook his head. "That to-do when Mike left turned her off men, I reckon. She's brighter tonight than I've seen her for a long time. It must be because you're back."

"Is this charmer trying to chat you up the way he did in the old days?" Dilys placed their drinks before them. "I bet his wife will have something to say about that."

"You're married?" Beth eyed Emrys.

"To a visitor, would you believe?" Dilys said. "Her car broke down, and the next thing you know she's married the garage owner."

"Your dad isn't—?"

"Dead? Is he heck. He came up on the Bonds and decided to retire. He gave me the garage, and he and Mam bought a house near where you live, the other side of Ianto Williams."

"So you and your wife live in the house behind the garage?"

"Aye, Julie. You'll have to come over and meet her."

"I'd like that."

"Perhaps you can witch our twins into acting themselves. Little sods, they are, but I love them to bits. Roger and Jennifer."

"What makes you think I'd be able to get them to behave themselves?"

"Megan used to do it. She'd fix them with those eyes of hers, and they'd sit side by side on the sofa without a peep out of them. Julie said she witched them and she was forever asking your aunty to come for tea."

"Your Aunty Megan had a way with her, all right," Dilys said. "Remember how we used to go round there and she'd tell our fortunes, Emrys? She told you you'd have twins."

"Aye, she did and all."

"You used to go there?"

"You were off in London, and she wanted a bit of company. We had a lot of fun."

"It was more than fun. She told us things that all came true. She said that French yacht would get smashed on the Witch, remember?"

"I didn't know Aunty Meg told fortunes." When had she ever spent any time listening or talking to Meg? She was always off out, getting into mischief.

"She didn't do it much in the summer; too busy with the guests. But in the off-season, she had people in her house every day asking what the cards said about something they had on their minds. Everybody swore by her. She told your father not to buy that house the O'Malleys bought, didn't she, Emrys. The next thing you know, they had to redo the foundations or the house would have come down. It must have cost a fortune." Dilys raised a hand to acknowledge a customer and went to the other end of the bar.

"What Dilys said was right. Mind, my dat and your aunty got into arguments about the cottage. If anybody else had told him not to buy it, he wouldn't have listened, but he set great store by what Megan said." Emrys gave a quick laugh. "He said there were times he heard Megan's voice warning him when he was asleep. Proper nightmare, he said."

"I don't remember the O'Malleys. When did they move here?"

"About three years ago. They must have bought the cottage sight unseen, and we wondered if they would try to sell it right away, but there were big cracks in all the walls any interested buyer could see. There's Sean O'Malley sitting at the other end of the bar with Doug Amundson, one of the stoppers."

Beth cast a quick glance at the two men standing at the far end of the bar. One was the painter she met on the cliff earlier; the other had fiery red hair, and freckles swarmed over the square face and snub nose. He might be the driver of the lorry she had seen earlier. "I take it they repaired the cottage."

"They borrowed some of the men working on Plas Mawr and got the place standing again."

"They're renovating Plas Mawr, are they?"

"They've been working on it for ages. Lorries are in and out all the time, either bringing in stuff or carrying out rubbish. Mind, no local has seen inside the house. You know what they're like up there—snobs, the lot of them. None of the workmen hereabouts were good enough; they brought men in from England and Ireland."

"Is Old Griff still working there?"

"No, no, retired he did. They sold Plas Mawr about five years ago. The new owner is Reginald Plews. Not that he spends any time in the village, except to buy petrol from me. He might as well live in London like the owner before him."

"I was up at Plas Mawr today. The garden is full of rubble. Are they digging a new cellar?"

"Could be for all we locals know."

"Is it possible the underground weakness that damaged the cottage also damaged the foundations of Plas Mawr?"

"Like a crack running down through the cliff? It's possible, I suppose. Mind, if that's the case, we might see a whole piece of the north cliff fall into the sea, and Plas Mawr along with it."

"How far is Plas Mawr inland from the cave?"

Emrys paused with the glass halfway to his mouth. "You think the Witch's cave is caving in?"

"That's not what I meant, but the cave goes a fair way back into the hill."

"Not far enough back for it to be under Plas Mawr."

"Is this a private discussion, or can anyone join in?" Tom Rowland stood behind them.

Emrys grinned at the other man. "Tom, *bachgen*, you're back again."

"Can't keep away," Tom said, signalling Dilys and laying a hand on Beth's shoulder. "We have to talk," he whispered.

Beth shrugged free of his hand. She drained her glass and slid off the stool. "I'll leave you two to it. It's time I was on my way."

"I'll ask Julie to call you," Emrys said. "She'll want to meet Megan's niece."

"I look forward to meeting her." Beth turned to Dilys. "We'll get together another time when I can meet Ricky." Without looking at Tom, she left the pub.

P L Crompton

CHAPTER SEVEN

Beth made towards the blue glow lighting the corner opposite the garage. Most people would be finishing dinner. Gwyn Thomas would be eating, too. Beth knew as soon as she entered the police station and took a breath.

He came from the back, shirtsleeves rolled up, and a tea towel in his hand. "Miss Davies."

"I've come at a bad time."

"Is it urgent?" He stood behind the stout oak counter.

"I . . ." This would be old news to him, but someone told her only that day he thought Meg was murdered. "Yes, I think it is; to me, anyway."

"You'd better come through." He lifted a flap in the counter. "That is, if you don't mind. I was about to have dinner."

Beth walked past him and then waited for him to precede her.

Gwyn led the way into the kitchen and hurried to the stove. He opened the oven, wrapped the tea towel around the handles of a roasting pan, and took it out. "Did you eat yet?"

"I'm not hungry." Beth eyed the roast beef he placed on the carving board.

"Are you sure? There's plenty here." He spooned roast potatoes onto a plate and glanced at her over his shoulder. "You look hungry to me."

"Is it part of your job to feed the hungry, PC Thomas?"

"Only if they're young and pretty." He placed another plate on the table. "Sit down, Miss Davies."

Beth sat as he took a bowl of peas and carrots from the oven and knifed a slab of butter on top. "I came to ask—"

"Eat first, talk later." Gwyn sliced beef onto her plate then fetched a pan from the stove. "Sorry. I broke the gravy boat last week." He ladled some onto the meat. "Help yourself to vegetables but, mind, the bowl is hot."

Beth felt awkward but hungry, and spooned a potato and portion of peas and carrots onto her plate. She looked up once and saw the smile of satisfaction on his face. For lack of anything else to say, she asked if he did all his own cooking.

"A man's got to eat, and when there's no woman . . ."

"You're not married?"

"No. Are you?"

Beth shook her head. They ate in silence for a while, and then she asked, "How long have you been a bobby here?"

"Five years," Gwyn answered. "I took over from Elwyn Rogers. Do you remember Elwyn?"

She nodded. PC Rogers seemed to be everywhere she hadn't wanted him to be. Like the time she and Dil—

"He retired to live with his sister in London. Which part of London did you live in?"

"The East End."

"Where about?"

"Not close to the markets, but near enough for developers to want the street." They'd given her a month to move out of the flat above the shop, offering her a place in the block of flats they would build where the shops once stood. She'd left without qualms, but it hadn't been easy for the bookseller next door who'd lived there all his life. She turned the conversation back on him. "Where did you live before you came here?"

"In Carmarthen. When I joined the force, I had to move to another place."

"It must be easier keeping the peace here than in Carmarthen."

"Not when you're a one-man-band."

"I suppose you're on duty twenty-four hours a day."

"I take my days off. If they need a police officer, they can always ring HQ. Someone can be here in less than an hour. During the summer months, they send someone to help out." He placed his knife and fork side-by-side and rose. "Would you like tea or coffee?"

"What are you having?"

"Coffee, but it's instant. I get my fill of tea during the day."

"I'll have the same." Beth picked up their plates.

He plugged in the kettle. "You don't have to do that."

"Yes, I do, and I'll do the washing up."

"But you're a guest!" he protested.

"An uninvited guest." She reached past him to place the dishes on the worktop.

"Not so." He chuckled, a deep rumbling sound erupting from the broad chest. "I invited you."

"Because I'm young and pretty."

"That, too, but you came with a problem, didn't you?"

"Today, someone told me . . ." Beth gulped. "Someone said my aunt . . ." The tears came from nowhere, tears she didn't think she had left.

"Bethan *fach*." Gwyn drew her to him and she went gladly.

Strong arms held her as she sobbed against his shoulder. He thrust a big white handkerchief into her hands and she held it to her face. "I'm sorry."

"No need to be sorry. You were fond of your aunty, and now she's dead."

"But how did she die?" She felt him stiffen. Beth pulled away and looked up into his face. "Someone told me she was murdered."

"Oh, *arswyd*! You mustn't listen to gossip."

"I have to know."

He released her. "All right. Let me make the coffee and we'll go into the other room."

Beth dried her eyes and studied him. Was he playing for time, putting together a story to tell her? "Some people say she was caught by the tide."

Gwyn spooned coffee into two mugs, poured in boiling water, and then placed the sugar bowl and milk jug next to them. "Help yourself."

Beth's hands shook as she poured milk into her coffee. "I came to you because . . . You have to tell me the truth, don't you?"

"Always." Gwyn took the mug from her. "This way." He led her into the sitting room, carrying both mugs, and placed one on a small table next to the sofa. "Why don't you sit here?"

Beth rubbed her nose with the handkerchief, sat and reached for the coffee. She took a mouthful and raised her head to look at him. Long legs extended with ankles crossed, he took the chair next to the bookcase. A book lay on the table beside him, the cover depicting a ruined castle. She had no idea what it was about, because the title was in Welsh. "I don't believe my aunt was caught by the tide."

"Why not?"

"There was a storm that night, they tell me. Who would go onto the beach on such a night?"

"There was a storm; a horrendous storm."

"And?" she pressed.

"We found Megan on the sand with her cardigan snagged on the Witch."

"Who found her?"

"Ishmael. Do you remember him?" Gwyn took a drink of coffee. "He was combing the beach as he always does after the tide goes out. He found her and came to fetch me."

"So you and he were the first ones there?"

"By the time I arrived, a few others had gathered. People walking their dogs, others were jogging."

"Did you think the tide caught her?"

"The medical examiner said she'd had a heart attack."

"So she died before she fell in the water." Beth watched him closely, looking for clues to show her he was telling the truth. "What condition was she in?"

"There was no water in her lungs. She had several cuts and bruises which were to be expected if the sea tossed her against the rocks."

"Yet they found no water in her lungs."

Gwyn put his cup down and leaned forward, elbows on his knees. "Her fingers were raw, her nails chipped and broken, and her palms scratched. The medical examiner said it looked as if she had tried to climb the cliff to get away from the tide."

"You're saying she died of natural causes. That is possible, but she would not have been tossed against the rocks because she would not have been on the beach."

"The tide comes in fast."

"But it doesn't come without warning. It isn't something that happens in a minute or two."

"She had a head injury. She might have tripped and knocked herself out."

"But she would not have been walking on the beach during a storm," Beth insisted.

"No one was about, so no one saw what happened." He hunkered before her. "You mustn't listen to the gossips. No good ever comes of gossiping."

"You checked the beach that morning, didn't you?"

He placed steadying hands on her forearms. "Nothing pointed to someone murdering Megan."

She looked into his blue eyes, aware her own were tear-filled. "How can I be sure?"

"You can be sure I checked very carefully."

"If there had been anything, the tide would have carried it away."

"What sort of thing would there be?"

Beth shrugged. "I don't know—footprints, or something they could have used to hit her."

"They?"

"I feel . . ." She bit back a sob. "Everybody thinks I neglected her."

"I doubt anyone thinks that. You had your own life to lead, and Megan was quite happy. She had many friends."

"Even so, I want to be certain I'm not neglecting her by ignoring the way she died."

"Don't let people saddle you with guilt. I know what this place is like—everybody knowing everybody else's business. You are young—"

"I'm twenty-four!" she said indignantly.

He stood and smiled at her outburst. "And old enough to help with the dishes." He dragged her to her feet.

"I thought you said I was a guest."

"I've changed my mind." He walked to the door and called over his shoulder. "Bring the mugs."

CHAPTER EIGHT

She was different tonight. Learning how Megan died had knocked the stuffing out of her. Thank God she hadn't seen Megan—a mess and barely recognisable. Considering how upset he'd been when he saw her, Gwyn couldn't believe how calmly he'd been able to discuss it. What would she say if he told her Megan had been missing for at least a day before they found her body? Though it went against the grain, against everything he felt about Megan's death, he wanted to allay Bethan's suspicions, give her a bit of peace. Without proof, he could say or do nothing, and stirring it up again would do no good.

Of course, the change in her might be because he wasn't wearing his uniform jacket or helmet. It could be, too, that he was up to his elbows in dishwater. It wasn't an image people had of police officers.

He wondered if she would stay in Derwen. He loved the place. This was his village, his patch. The locals gave him little trouble, thanks in part to Powell-Pritchard. Narrow-minded the minister was, and intolerant, but he shepherded his flock like a vigilant Rottweiler. The locals were law-abiding enough. That made it hard to understand why there were prowlers around Megan's house. No one else had mentioned such a thing.

The visitors were a different kettle of fish. The day-trippers weren't too bad, except for the occasional drunk and children stealing from the shops. It was the holidaymakers who came for a week and got bored once the sun went down.

Fights broke out among the men and the women held screaming matches. If a visitor started paying attention to a local girl, the village lads would get territorial and start a brawl, nothing he wasn't able to handle.

But the others, the stoppers. They came at all times of the year and stayed for months. Much as Gwyn loved Derwen Bay, he wouldn't choose to spend a winter holiday here. There had never been any trouble with them, but something raised flags in his mind.

"Penny for them," Beth said, interrupting Gwyn's thoughts.

"I was just thinking how much I like living in Derwen Bay." Gwyn pulled the plug to let the water out of the sink.

"It must be deadly in winter." Beth folded the tea towel and hung it from the oven door to dry.

"Oh, no, winter is the best time. It's quiet then, even at weekends, but we get the odd visitor out for a Sunday drive."

"Aunty Meg said the place came alive in winter."

"It does. It's a time when the locals get to know each other again. There's always something going on, things to get people together and busy."

"But it must be colder here than inland." She handed him the dried dishes and he put them away.

"When the wind is off the sea, it doesn't bear thinking about." Gwyn closed the cupboard on the last plate. "I'd better get you home."

"There's no need. This is Derwen Bay. Nothing happens around here."

"Not like in London?" Gwyn noted the sudden shift of her glance away from him. She was hiding something. Whatever it was, she didn't want him to see it in her eyes. Oh, no, she didn't want him to see it at all. "I've got to do a round of the village anyway so I can walk in the same direction as you."

He put on his tie, rolled down his sleeves, slid into his uniform jacket, and placed the helmet on his head.

She was waiting for him outside, huddled against the wind. "It's cold," she commented as he emerged.

"You'll need this." He handed her a jacket. "Once the sun goes down, not too many people brave the Front at this time of year. Mind, at the height of the season, it stays warm late into the night. You must remember that from when you came to stay with Megan."

"Some nights, Aunty Meg took me walking around the village and up into the hills. Often it was her first chance to get out of the house. After eight o'clock, she told the guests to fend for themselves. On those strolls, she told me of my father's escapades, and told me she wasn't married because the man she loved was lost in the war; now Meg is lost to me."

Gwyn heard a catch in her voice. "Your father isn't—?"

"He was killed in a car accident when I was ten. My mother remarried four years ago."

He noticed her hesitate as they turned onto the road to Derwen House. He slowed his pace to match hers. "Are you worried your intruder will come back?"

She glanced up at him. "So you do believe me."

"As I've made a note of it in the Day Book, I suppose I must."

"I found proof of someone being there after you left this morning. There was a footprint on the window ledge in one of the bedrooms. He might have jumped from there into the oak."

"I'll add it to my report, and I'll come to look at it tomorrow." He paused and turned to her. "Afraid he'll be there now, are you?"

She shook her head. "There's a paying guest in the house, so it's doubtful he'd come back if he knows I'm not alone."

Megan had said much the same thing. "Who is staying there?"

"Tom Rowland. Dil said he's one of the stoppers."

They resumed their walk. "I know him. Will he be in, do you think?"

"I don't know. Last I saw, he was in the Anchor."

"Tom isn't much of a drinker, so I expect he'll be back by now." He halted at the low wall outside the garden. "There's a light on in the sitting room. Will you be all right or shall I see you inside?"

"I'll be all right." Beth stepped through the open gate onto the path and headed for the door. She looked back once to give Gwyn a small wave of her hand before turning to the door. It swung open at her touch. "Gwyn!" Her frightened cry had him at her side in a few quick strides. "The door was open." She ducked behind him and peered around his shoulder as the door opened wider.

"Megan never locked it until midnight, when there were guests. This is not unusual, but I'll check." Gwyn took a step into the hallway. "Anybody here?" he shouted.

Tom poked his head out of the sitting room. "Is that you, Gwyn?"

"Tom?" Gwyn moved to one side so Beth became visible. "This one had a fright when she found the door open."

"I'd forgotten about the door, that's all," she said. "And after this morning . . ."

Gwyn stood in front of her, his back to Tom. "Least said, eh?" he said in a low voice.

Beth nodded.

Gwyn smiled. "Clever girl," he muttered under his breath then called to the other man: "I'll be on my way, Tom. Goodnight to you both."

* * *

Beth watched Gwyn walk along the path. He was tall, powerfully built, and good-looking. *He's a policeman. He's a bloody policeman, for goodness sake!*

If people had told her a week ago that she'd have dinner with and walk home next to a bobby, she'd have called them idiots. However, in the dark pools between the lamp standards, she was grateful for his presence.

Mentally, she shook herself. This was Derwen Bay, not London, but she would never forget that night in London when she walked home from a club. It happened so quickly. If she hadn't stopped to fasten the strap of her sandal, the burglars would have seen her when they ran from the house. The ring one of them dropped led to trouble. If only she'd left it lying against the railing. If only she'd gone home and forgotten what she'd seen.

"You're late." Tom looked up from the book he was reading when Beth entered the sitting room. "Is that the new fashion in London?"

Beth looked down. Gwyn's jacket hung to her knees. "I didn't know if you'd come back or if you were still at the Anchor."

"I never stay there long, just long enough to say hello to a few people." He stretched and yawned. "I'd go to my bed, but you've locked my room and hidden the key. Is that your coy way of telling me I'm not welcome?"

"You know you're not welcome." Beth went out to the kitchen and opened a drawer. She took out the keys, selected the one marked for Tom's bedroom, and handed it to him.

"Are there other guests?"

"No."

"But all the doors are locked up there, except for yours and the bathroom."

She glared at him. "What business did you have trying the other doors?"

"I didn't know if you were going to be out all night. I was going to kip in one of the other rooms."

"I prefer you to keep to your own room."

"Of course. Earlier, before you ran out, you said something about Megan being murdered. What was that about?"

"You're a paying guest. It's none of your business."

"I see." Tom left the kitchen. At the foot of the stairs, he called out, "I take it breakfast will be at nine, as usual, with tea and biscuits at eight?"

"Yes, sir!" Beth retorted. She heard him laugh as he climbed the stairs. Overhead, his footsteps crossed the landing and paused while he unlocked the door before entering the room above the kitchen.

Beth looked around and felt contrite. He'd washed the dishes and cleaned up. She opened the fridge to get a glass of milk, and saw the delivery boy had brought the things on the list she'd given Daniel Jones. She doubted the boy had put them away. Tom was making himself at home.

After drinking the milk and rinsing out her glass, she locked the back door and put the key in her pocket. She checked all the windows, then went to the front door and locked that, too. No one would get in tonight.

Beth unpacked and put her few things in the wardrobe, the action so bittersweet with memory it jeopardised her fragile composure. She changed into her nightgown, switched off the light, and opened the curtains to let in pale moonlight before curling up on the window seat, Meg's favourite place. She often sat here, staring out.

Beyond the streetlight, Beth's view extended past the lighted car park and deckchair booth to the sea. Between scurrying clouds, the moon bathed the water to a mellow background for the black rock. She had always considered the Witch evil but, if the rock caught and held Meg from the outgoing tide . . .

What happened that night? Why did Meg go out in the storm? The answers Gwyn gave her didn't satisfy Beth. Ishmael found Meg. He'd been the first one there. She'd have to question him. However, would he be able to answer her?

He was a strange man. Beth remembered him as ancient and scrawny. Some said Ishmael washed up in the bay, riding a waterlogged plank of wood. Others said he came for a day trip, missed the bus home and, being dim-witted, decided to stay.

He lived in a cottage he built himself. Seated out of the wind part way up the north slope, the walls consisted of stones he'd gathered. Into an outer skim of clay, he had pressed shells and chips of broken china collected on his jaunts around the village. The door and the shutter on the small opening forming a window consisted of rough wooden boards washed up on the shore. The roof was part wood part ridged metal going rusty. From somewhere, he had scrounged enough tree branches and driftwood to weave into a fence around his small plot. The gate bore a warning sign: *Beware of the Dog* in uneven white lettering.

He'd had a dog once, a stray a visitor dumped in the village. Beth pictured the scruffy ball of fur following Ishmael around, but the dog was long gone, buried in Ishmael's garden with a wooden cross as a marker.

She and Dil made Ishmael's hovel into the witch's lair from every scary film they'd seen and every fairy story they'd read. They dared each other to sneak in when he was busy at the other side of the village. It was neat and tidy, his clothes hanging from pegs, his food stored on shelves suspended from the warped rafters. Two planks made a table, another two a stool. His bed consisted of more planks resting on barrels, and sacking stuffed with straw made the mattress.

The first time they went was an adventure. After that, they made regular visits when Ishmael wasn't home. They left posies of wild flowers in a jam jar on the table and sometimes they left slices of pie or baking filched from their homes. Once, Dil brought a shirt of her father's—a new one, still in the packet—but they never saw Ishmael wear it.

If he knew who was invading his home, he gave no sign. He never spoke to anyone, least of all children, but he knew every inch of the village. People said Ishmael could smell a chipped plate sitting on a rubbish pile, and he carried the trophy back to his cottage. Some gave him odd jobs. Dil's father had Ishmael whitewash the back of the Anchor one summer, and he did a good job. He tended not to be around when the village filled with visitors. He combed the beaches early in the morning, and then hid away until late at night when Derwen settled for sleep.

Would Ishmael know what happened to Meg? Would he be able to tell her? Beth leaned her head against the window frame and let her tears fall unchecked.

* * *

The sound of a motorbike woke Beth. In the distance, the horizon was a paler grey, but the Witch stood an ominous black, seeming to float on the water. Beth untangled her legs, shivered with cold, and arched the stiffness out of her back.

She heard a grating noise and glanced out. A light flashed across the bay followed by a muted clang. The sounds didn't come again, and the light was gone so quickly she thought she'd imagined it. It couldn't be lightning. The flash shone horizontally from the cave across the surface of the water to light the Witch's skirt. Face pressed against the window, she watched for a long time but the light didn't shine again. She may have imagined it, or it may have been a fisherman late in or heading out early. Yachts sometimes anchored in the bay. It may have been a reflected light from one of them.

She eased off the window seat and crossed to the bed, convinced she'd seen the light shine from inside the cave.

P L Crompton

CHAPTER NINE

She'd be safe enough tonight, Gwyn thought as he followed Peartree Lane up the hill on his beat around the village.

He paused. Why would he think she was in danger? Was it because he knew someone was prowling around the house? Megan said the prowler never came when she had guests. When had Megan first noticed someone lurking outside the house? Had it been October or November? Not December because Tom was there for three weeks. He'd check his Day Book because he had a feeling the date was important. He was disobeying the order from HQ that Megan's death didn't call for further investigation, but something wasn't right in the village, and she had known what.

Damn the storm that delayed him that night, and damn the Witch. One legend said the Witch brought storms because of the way children clambered around her skirts. They scraped themselves on her rough rocks and stained her with their blood so she craved more, but the beach was empty on the blustery day preceding the storm.

He liked this last self-imposed duty of the day. He chose to walk rather than drive, and it often paid off because no one knew he was around; petty thieving and many other crimes occurred in silence.

It was quiet enough away from the sea front. Most of the houses were dark but, here and there, he saw evidence of someone up late watching telly. Megan liked taking a stroll in the evening, too. Sometimes, when he paced the beat earlier than he was tonight, he'd come across her inhaling the quiet, resting after a day of rushing about seeing to her guests.

The graveyard lay silent in the shifting moonlight. He hadn't visited Megan's grave that day because he'd been too busy, and he'd better not go in now. The last time he went at night, old Patty Pen Tir glimpsed him from her window and started a rumour the cemetery was haunted. Gwyn had trouble suppressing a smile when he heard, but he let it be because it kept the gossips busy for a while. In his opinion, gossips proved more dangerous than did thieves. Thieves took possessions, but gossips stole lives.

At the top of the hill, Gwyn cut across the field towards the north road, scattering sheep as he went. A magnificent view; at night, there was no colour other than the languid glow of street lighting along the Front. It looked best in winter, when snow was on the ground. All black and white then, and the sea like silver with the Witch cloaked in snow. The incoming ocean splashing against her skirts tossed spray into the air that glittered like earth-bound stars, like the sparklers on a child's birthday cake. If he could paint, this is what he would put on canvas.

Behind him, over the next rise of land, lay Upper Derwen. Developers were building a row of bungalows close to the church with a bigger house going up by the bend in the road. They discovered it was a Celtic settlement at one time; out of sight of the beach, safe from Viking marauders.

Outsiders came, like Reginald Plews, buying up property to use at weekends. More recently, an archaeologist visited.

It was Ieuan-the-Grave's fault. While digging at the edge of the churchyard, he found bits of pots and arrowheads. Howell Hopkins, the vicar, got all excited and contacted Aberystwyth University. The next thing they knew, a professor arrived with a handful of students. They were there all last summer, in the field next to the churchyard wall, on their hands and knees scraping and brushing with tools small enough for a baby.

Caradog Bowen wasn't too happy about it because he held the gymkhana every year in that field. He almost came to blows with Howell Hopkins and the professor, but he was mollified when he learned the artefacts dug up would have plaques naming his farm. They took photographs and Caradog framed them to hang about the farmhouse. He invited Gwyn to view them and informed him another team of archaeologists would be arriving this summer. They would be centring their dig close to the well bubbling out of the side of the hill to form a little stream that laughed its way down to the sea.

Close to the top of the north road, darkness shrouded the campground except for a couple of dying fires, embers a mere glow. Gwyn stood at the entrance, listening to the night sounds. In the distance, an owl hooted and a fox barked. Something rustled at the foot of the hedge. Then, from below in the valley, came a muffled clang. Ears straining, he concentrated, but the sound didn't come again. He started walking along the road, stopping now and again to listen. Whatever the noise—metal on rock, rock on rock—it wasn't repeated. He continued his beat, wondering who or what could have made a noise so out of place.

In the moonlight, hedges defined the road and Gwyn had no need to use his flashlight. When he reached the entrance to the narrow lane up to Plas Mawr, a lorry trundled out and made its noisy, belching way up the hill laden with building rubble. He'd have another talk with Reginald Plews now he'd witnessed the ruckus for himself. It might be something that happened often, but this was the first time Gwyn had done his beat so late; talking to Bethan and seeing her home had held him up.

Seeing her home . . . He hadn't walked a girl home in years, not since he was a lad and couldn't afford a car. He missed the intimacy, that time of winding down a date and the feeling of protectiveness it gave him to escort a girl home with his arm around her waist. Driving her home took it away. In his opinion, kissing a girl in a car was out. He'd shone his flashlight into too many and seen more than kissing going on. Old fashioned perhaps, but kissing a girl in a shadowy corner, noses and lips cold from the night air, seemed far more romantic.

Gwyn remembered he hadn't rung Linda in a couple of days. He'd make it up to her and take her out on Sunday. It would be his last free Sunday for a while, now that summer visitors were filling Derwen.

Almost without thought, Gwyn turned onto the lane to Ishmael's cottage. Since Megan's death, Ishmael's friendship became doubly precious. Candlelight flickered through a gap in the rickety shutter, so he hadn't gone to bed. Gwyn opened the gate, his hand on the *Beware of the Dog* sign to keep it from falling askew as it often did. In the moonlight, the china chips and shells pressed into the clay came alive. To many it looked to be a random pattern but, as seen now, mosaic fish swam around under the rusted roof.

He raised his hand, prepared to knock on the door, and heard Ishmael speaking to someone in a low voice. Surprised, for he never knew anyone to visit the man, he stopped to listen. The words were indistinct, and although Ishmael paused between the eruptions of speech, Gwyn could not hear another voice. He tapped on the door. "Ishmael? It's Gwyn." At Ishmael's invitation, he opened the door and went in. A quick look around showed him the man was alone.

Ishmael sat at the table, a whittling knife in his elegant fingers. "Please sit."

Gwyn sank onto a log beside the table. "How is it coming?"

"I would appreciate your opinion."

Ishmael turned the bust he was working on and Gwyn's breath caught in his throat. The shanty overflowed with carvings that would sell easily if he ever offered them, but this was his masterpiece. "Megan," he breathed. "It's her to a T."

"Are you saying so to appease me? Friends can be generous in their praise."

Gwyn swallowed hard. Life sized, the carving seemed to smile at him in the flickering light. The eyes, sometimes sharp and penetrating, sometimes soft and gentle, looked straight into his. *Tell me, Megan. Tell me what you were going to tell me that night.* "It's as if she's still with us."

"She will always be with us. Friendship does not end with death."

"Bethan heard somebody murdered Megan."

Ishmael nodded. "Gossip has a way of surfacing. I doubt they would have told her the shops closed and the whole village attended the funeral."

"Probably not." Gwyn couldn't take his eyes from Megan's likeness.

"What did you tell the young woman?"

"What could I tell her? That I had suspicions that had no grounding in fact?"

"Are you still convinced Megan came by her death by other than natural means?"

"Aren't you?"

"Yes." Ishmael spoke with conviction.

Gwyn looked at him quickly. "Is there anything you haven't told me?"

Ishmael shook his head.

"Talk to me, man!"

"We have discussed this many times. I will say nothing until I am sure."

Gwyn sighed and got to his feet. "Like Megan, you might carry what you know to your grave."

"Nevertheless, I will die secure in the knowledge I have not carelessly besmirched another's character."

Gwyn left. Angry with Ishmael, and worried for the man's safety, he strode fast along the Front on his way back to the police station.

In the Anchor, a light showed somewhere in the back and the faint sound of voices reached his ears. After-hour drinkers, he left them alone. There were times when it paid to ignore the breaking of a law if it hurt no one, especially in a small place like Derwen Bay.

CHAPTER TEN

No one deactivated Meg's alarm clock. The low beep designed not to disturb guests woke Beth at six. She stretched and walked to the window to look out.

Although still dark in the Bay, the first sunrays were creeping over the horizon. In the bathroom, she splashed water on her face and dressed quickly. To catch Ishmael, she had to be on the beach before he finished combing along the water's edge.

She jogged down the back lane to the beach. Once there, dry sand crept into her trainers. She stopped to take them off, and hung them around her neck by their laces. She continued walking, and shuddered when she stepped onto hard sand still damp and cold from the night tide. Ahead, the Witch stood as if waiting. Drenched in dew, the age-old rock glittered hard and indefatigable.

Ishmael wasn't in sight so Beth made her way towards the north beach, crossing between the Witch and the cave set into the cliff. They'd played in the cave, as children, she and Dil, making out they were pirates burying treasure. It wasn't the safest place because the tide could come in and trap them if they weren't careful. The waterline at high tide marked the cave walls high enough to be over a man's head, even a man as tall as Gwyn—not Gwyn—the Police Officer. She had to remember. Gwyn was a policeman.

Hardly any seaweed settled on the beaches, but Ishmael was picking his way through the flotsam brought in on the tide. If he noticed her walking towards him, he made no sign.

Beth had never spoken to the man, never seen him up close. Before, she'd thought him ancient, but now she realised he couldn't be more than mid-fifties. A half-wit, they said. How could she make him understand she wanted to learn what he knew of Meg's death? How could he tell her what he'd seen? What he'd found?

"Ishmael?"

He straightened with a twist of driftwood like a piece of modern sculpture in his hand.

"I don't know if you remember me. I'm Bethan, Megan Davies' niece."

Ishmael nodded.

Good. He could understand her. "I came to ask . . . I wanted to know . . . You found my aunt?"

He nodded.

"They say the tide caught her."

Again, he nodded.

"I don't believe it. They say there was a storm that night. She would never have come onto the beach during a storm."

Ishmael shook his head.

"Was there anything . . .? Did you see or find anything that might point to what happened?"

He raised a hand and indicated the sea.

Beth worked out what she thought he meant. "Are you saying the tide would have carried it away?"

He nodded.

Beth studied him for a moment before her frustration spewed forth. "I don't believe you! You know something. You won't tell me now, but you will eventually. I'll haunt you until you do. Aunty Meg was not a stupid woman. She would not have come to the beach in a storm. She lived here all her life and knew the tides. She recognised how dangerous they could be." She paused when she saw him smile. "Why are you smiling?"

"You are like Megan."

People said Ishmael either stared at them blankly or gave them a silly grin, but he'd spoken, and with an upper class English accent, as if he had a plum in his mouth. "So you can talk."

"When there is something to say."

"Then tell me what you know. You know something, don't you?"

He shook his head.

"Don't start playing dumb. You were the first on the scene. You went for Gwy—Constable Thomas. I'm asking you what you saw. Were there footprints? Signs of a struggle?"

He passed her, carrying the driftwood. At the Witch, he stopped and pointed to a jagged finger of rock. "She was caught on this."

Beth let out a sob and swallowed hard, fighting tears. Was the Witch Meg's killer or did the Witch stop the ocean from washing her away so they'd find no trace of her? Did the Witch want questions asked about her death?

Ishmael was watching her with sadness in his eyes.

Beth turned away. The black mouth of the cave yawned in front of her. It was in line with the jagged rock of the Witch's skirt. In line with the flash of light, she'd seen the night before. Without turning around, she asked, "Have you anything else you can tell me?"

"No."

Beth covered the beach in long angry strides, heels digging into the sand. He knew something. He damned well knew something! He'd tell her. She'd hassle and pester him until he did, but how long would that take? How long would she have to stay in Derwen Bay?

* * *

Beth spent the afternoon with Julie, Emrys' wife, and Dilys showed up with Ricky. In contrast to the four-year-old twins who romped about the place, the little boy was solemn, appearing older than his four years.

"Do your magic, Bethan," Julie said when the twins became particularly loud and busy, "like Megan used to do."

"I don't know . . ." Beth looked at the two making a tent of the blanket draped across the back of the couch.

Roger was the first to notice she was watching them. He fell still and silent. Jennifer noticed only when she realised her brother no longer pummelled her with a cushion. She too stopped what she was doing.

"Why don't you put the cushions back and sit quietly," Beth suggested. No one was more surprised than she was when the twins obeyed.

"I knew you'd have Megan's touch," Julie said.

Ricky sidled up to Beth, leaning against her knee as he whispered in English, "Showing off, they were. Roger says you're pretty, and Jennifer wants her hair like yours."

Awe made the twins behave themselves, not magic. Beth smiled and hugged Ricky. "I love your son, Dil. I want to take him home with me."

"I'll pay you to take my two as well," Julie said with a laugh.

Emrys made a brief appearance to hug the twins and earned a comeuppance from Julie for getting oil on their clothes. While she took the twins to change, Dilys said, "They're a handful."

"Give me Ricky any day." Beth glanced to where the boy sat with a picture book open on his knees. "I didn't expect him to speak English."

"We live in a pub, so he hears that language often. It worries me sometimes that he's so quiet, but when I come here I know I'm blessed." Dilys called to Ricky, "What's that book you're reading?"

He flipped to the cover and traced the words with a finger, "Snow White and the Seven Dwarfs."

"He can read?"

"That's your auntie's doing. She'd babysit him sometimes, and she taught him."

Julie came back with the twins freshly scrubbed and in clean clothes.

"Why don't you let Ricky read to you?" With shy looks, they did as Beth suggested.

"How much money do you want to come here every day, Bethan?"

Beth laughed. "I think my kind of magic would wear thin in quick time."

"Don't say that." Julie poured fresh tea into their cups. "You've got Megan's ways about you. What do you say, Dilys?"

"The Bethan I knew had nothing of Megan about her, but I haven't got to know her since she came back."

Julie sliced cake for the children. "Megan was special. She had a gift."

You're a witch, Megan Davies! Powell-Pritchard said once. He never said it again, not after his ears burned all the way back to his chapel.

"Come over tonight," Dil said as they walked home.

"I was planning to make a start on the garden after dinner."

They stopped at the door to the Anchor. "It's got to be tonight. Tomorrow is Saturday and the place will be packed so I'll have no time to talk."

Beth nodded. "Do you need a babysitter for Ricky tomorrow night?"

"It's all arranged." Dilys hugged her. "You come tonight, all right?"

"Of course, I'd like to talk to you, too." Beth crouched before Ricky. "Can I have a hug?"

He came into her arms, hands tight about her neck. She felt the fragility of his body, smelled the fresh scent of his hair. "He's gorgeous, Dil."

"I told you you'd love him. Megan was his godmother. If you'd been here, if I could have got a hold of you . . ."

"I'd be honoured to take Meg's place." Beth stood up when Ricky released her.

Dilys smiled. "That's settled then. You are now responsible for seeing that Ricky is brought up as a Christian."

"What does that mean?"

"It means you have to see that he gets to Sunday school and goes to chapel when he's older."

"With Powell-Pritchard? Not on your—" Beth saw the quick glance of warning Dilys shot in Ricky's direction.

The boy was looking at her with wide eyes. She bent and stroked his cheek. "For you, I'll even brave Reverend Powell-Pritchard." Nevertheless, she'd have to swallow a lot of pride.

* * *

As Beth prepared the evening meal, she heard Tom moving around upstairs. She'd taken him his tea and biscuits early that morning; then he left soon after breakfast with sandwiches and a flask of coffee, and she dusted his room and made the bed.

She couldn't say he was much trouble, and she'd avoided verbal skirmishes by setting breakfast for one in the dining room. She'd eaten in the kitchen, a piece of toast she managed to get down as she fumed over Ishmael's lack of information. He surprised her by being able to speak and, now she'd seen him up close, she realised he was clean. Somehow, she always imagined he would smell bad.

Beth was in the dining room setting the table for dinner when Tom came down the stairs to stand in the doorway. "You're making a lot of unnecessary work for yourself."

"I prefer to eat in peace without any reproaches from you," she retorted. "And another thing—if I decide to stay out late, or even stay out all night, it's not your concern."

"I was worried about you, that's all."

"You don't even know me, so you have no cause to worry. You are a paying guest, nothing more. As long as I'm here to cook and clean, it's all you need to know."

"Point taken." He pulled out a chair and sat. "Have you had a bad day?"

"None of your business." Beth returned to the kitchen to finish cooking the meal. She served Tom in silence, then took him a pot of coffee. He hadn't even picked up his knife and fork. "Is anything wrong with the food?"

"I don't particularly like ham." he answered.

"Then eat your vegetables like a good boy." She slammed out to the kitchen.

Still not hungry, the image of the Witch's jagged finger of rock fresh in her mind, Beth picked at her portion. Lost in thought, she jumped when Tom came in. "You shouldn't be in here!" she shouted.

Tom placed his dishes on the worktop. "What is it with you? You're as prickly as a hedgehog."

"I wouldn't be if you remembered your place."

"Pardon me." He made for the door. "I'll be watching the news, if that's all right with you."

Beth didn't answer but went to fetch the rest of the things from the dining room. She heard him switch on the television as she piled the tray and carried it to the kitchen. As she washed the dishes, snippets of news came her way. Princess Diana visited a children's hospital, an American film star was getting her third divorce, then—police had made an arrest in connection with the murder of Amanda Parsons. A plate slid from Beth's hand and smashed on the floor.

She dropped onto a chair. It was from Amanda Parson's house the three men ran. She'd read in the paper that somebody murdered Amanda Parsons at her country estate and that the robbery took place in her London house while it was empty. One reporter suggested a connection between the murder and the robbery. The newspaper headline was clear in her mind:

REWARD PAID FOR INFORMATION LEADING TO THE RECOVERY OF JEWELLERY

Beth took the ring to the nearest police station and gave a statement. More fool her! If only she'd kept her mouth shut, better yet, if only she'd left the ring where it fell.

They didn't believe she wasn't involved with the robbery. They kept her in an interview room all day with nothing to eat or drink. She sat on the hard chair for hours, on her own most of the time, and when they thought she was in a weakened state, they questioned her. Good cop, bad cop, like on television. Repeatedly. Different people. Even a police psychologist. They released her but followed her around. Plain-clothed policewomen posed as customers in her boutique, frightening off genuine shoppers.

Three times, they took her in for interrogation. Three times, they bombarded her with the same questions, checking the answers against earlier statements she'd signed.

"How could I slip up?" she asked. "The truth is the truth."

"Why did you keep the ring for over a week before bringing it in?" they challenged, accusation evident in their eyes.

She blushed; mumbled that she hoped to be able to keep it if no one reported it stolen.

They took her fingerprints and checked for previous convictions or records that hadn't led to convictions, and Daniel-the-Shop's report floated out of the past; a minor stealing sweeties.

To Beth it was laughable once she was over her anger, but not to them, not to the boys in blue with their shiny buttons and their plain-clothed comrades with the accusing eyes, and not to Meg. *You mustn't steal, my girl. Nothing good ever comes of a thief.* Daniel was all for calling the police, but Meg told him Beth would go away and never come back. Daniel reported her to the police anyway, damn him.

The Metro police took her descriptions of the three men. Showed her so many photographs she had trouble focussing. Then they told her she was deliberately refusing to identify her accomplices. Accomplices! She didn't know the men.

"Where did you get the ring?"

"It fell out of the bag when one of the men tripped and dropped it."

"Is it your cut?"

"No!"

Her protestations of innocence meant nothing. They needed evidence to hold her, but they suggested she get a solicitor. She refused. Little remained of the money her father left her. She told them she'd be damned if she'd waste any on a solicitor when she hadn't committed a crime except for keeping the ring for a week. "If I was guilty, why did I come forward and offer information?" she asked.

Their only answer was to tell her she could go.

Beth went, face awash with tears of anger and frustration, and ran into Jerry. She'd seen him in discos and clubs; even danced with him a few times. After what she'd been through, he was a familiar and welcoming face.

Jerry took her to a pub and bought her a brandy, waiting patiently until the sobs subsided. She didn't tell him what the problem was. How could you tell a handsome man the police were convinced you were a thief?

They started dating. Although the police didn't harass her, she became aware they were watching. In the middle of all that, she had to deal with the sale of the boutique. She had to move out of the flat above it and it seemed natural to move in with Jerry.

"I'm off out." From the doorway, Tom eyed the broken plate on the floor.

"You don't need to tell me. I'm locking the door at midnight, as usual. Be back before then."

"I'll try, but Megan often gave me the extra key if I thought I'd be late."

"I'm not Megan." Beth got out the dustpan and brush.

"That's obvious."

Beth clamped her lips together and concentrated on sweeping up the pieces of china. Then a thought struck her. If they were both out, what was there to stop anyone getting in if the door was open?

"Wait!" She ran after Tom with a spare key to the front door. It was old fashioned and heavy. It might be time to see about putting in a new lock. "I'm sorry. It hasn't been a good day for me and I didn't mean to bitch at you."

He took the key without a word, slid it into his pocket, and left.

Beth finished cleaning the kitchen and wondered what it was about Tom that made her so angry? Was it just the way he made himself at home, or the way he reproached her for neglecting Meg? Was it because he reminded her of one of the Metro officers who questioned and accused her? Whatever the reason, she'd be rid of him in a week.

In her room, she noticed Gwyn's windbreaker hanging on the back of the door. Only a step or two to the police station from the Anchor, she could take the jacket back before going for a badly needed drink.

As Beth stepped into the shower, the phone rang. She fought down a tremor of fear. No one in London knew she was here. Of course, it might be somebody wanting to make a booking. It could be Dil checking to see if she was coming. Either way, she had no need to rush to answer it. She wasn't accepting guests, and she'd see Dil in half an hour.

Hair dried, makeup applied, she took a silk dress from the wardrobe. Black, with a barely discernible dark green design, one of the originals she stocked at the boutique. Each time a customer admired it, Beth held her breath. She didn't want to sell the dress. Finally, she kept it for herself even though it ate into her profits.

"I'm not wearing this dress for PC Plod," she told her mirror image as she put on a pair of sheer black pantyhose and slipped into black high-heels. "I am wearing it because I've worn nothing but jeans this past week and I'm tired of them."

Moreover, she needed something to lighten her spirits. She seemed to have reached a dead end regarding her investigation into Meg's death. If she must, she'd talk to every gossip in the place. Sometimes idle talk had a kernel of truth.

Beth shrugged into the soft white-wool jacket too expensive for her customers, and checked the back door and windows. Certain everything was secure; she was heading to the front door when the phone rang again. She hesitated before answering, but told herself no one knew she was here except the locals. "Yes?"

It was the telephone company: They were sorry to call so late, but they failed to get an answer during the day. They understood Megan Davies was deceased but the period they agreed with the solicitor to keep the line active had now passed. Did she wish it activated in her name?

"Yes," Beth affirmed.

"In what name?" the disembodied voice asked.

She dare not give her own name. Without hesitation, Beth lied. "In the same name, I am also Megan Davies."

They would send someone along to get her signature and deposit. Would she be at the same address as the late Miss Megan Davies?

"Yes," Beth answered. "When will your representative be coming?"

"Sometime next week," the voice informed her. "Do you wish him to call first?"

"Yes." What if Tom answered the phone and told them she was Bethan, not Megan? "This is a guest house. If you call, and a man answers, I'd be grateful if you would not speak to him. He is a paying guest."

That was it, then. A lie that would hurt no one and it would keep her safe from anyone tracing her via a phone directory. She locked the front door and dropped the key into her handbag.

Would Jerry look for her? Would he be free to look for her? The police would have questioned him about Beth's involvement but would he guess she'd informed on him? He knew her parents were Welsh but not from which area. Nothing among her things had mentioned Derwen Bay. She had Meg's address in her memory and not written down. Beth's birth record, if he ever had the gumption to look it up, would show her born in Manchester, her father born in London, and her mother in Cardiff. It was doubtful Jerry would bother going back a generation and learn her grandfather came from Derwen Bay. Davies was a common name in Wales so finding her wouldn't be easy.

She'd covered her tracks well. She'd made no calls to Meg's solicitor from Jerry's flat, and they disconnected the phone in the boutique when she sold out. Still, she dared not open a new bank account or take out a credit card, and she certainly couldn't have a phone in her own name.

Lucky for her, the shame she felt about the police thinking her a thief meant she never mentioned it to Jerry. She never told him how they harassed her and popped up when she least expected. They made no effort to hide from her. The women officers were the same ones who haunted the boutique, and she recognised two of the men who were present when they questioned her. That had Beth confused, until she began to suspect they were keeping an eye on Jerry more than they were watching her. It made her doubly cautious of what she said to him.

The first real clue came a week after she moved in with Jerry. She took a job in a clothing store but came home early because of a migraine. She went to bed in a darkened room and woke a couple of hours later to the sound of voices. Jerry and two other men were in the living room. They were discussing the murder and the robbery at Amanda Parsons' house. They were worried because they heard a woman had come forward to say she witnessed the robbery and could describe the men. As she listened, Beth learned Jerry drove the getaway van. The two strangers in the living room were two of the three she'd seen. During their conversation, they mentioned two names—Danno and Peachy. Terrified they would find out she'd overheard them, and ashamed of being so easily duped by Jerry, Beth hid under the bed until all three left.

She had information the police needed, but she was reluctant to tell them after the way they treated her. She realised she dared not approach a police station or be seen talking to an officer, because one of the robbers might see her and recognise her as Jerry's girlfriend. She had only a vague idea what the other three looked like and she didn't even know the name of the fourth. She wondered where she could go without Jerry or the other men tracing her. Derwen Bay was the obvious place.

Beth gave notice at her job, applied to the bank to withdraw her money in cash, and closed the account. It was a large amount and she had to wait. Three days later, as she carried the money home, she bought fish and chips wrapped in *The Times* and saw the announcement to Meg's creditors.

While waiting for the train in Paddington Station, she made an anonymous call to the police to give them the names of the two who were involved in the robbery.

CHAPTER ELEVEN

Gwyn was dealing with a complaint when Beth walked in. He nodded to her. "Good evening, Miss Davies."

"You're Bethan, aren't you?" The man filling in a form turned to study her. "Megan's niece, are you?"

"That's right. Who are you?"

"Ianto Williams. I live next door to you."

"Hello." She passed the windbreaker to Gwyn. "Thank you, Mr Thomas. Goodbye, Mr Williams." She gave him a vague smile and left.

Gwyn watched her go, liking the way her skirt swished about the legs. Dressed up tonight, it looked as if she was going on a date, but what man around here was eligible, apart from him? There was Tom Rowland, of course. An outsider, but so was she in a way.

"Nice looking girl, if a bit on the thin side," Ianto commented. "Right age for you, too, *bachgen*, and you'd soon get her with a fat belly, eh?"

Gwyn gave him a look that threatened thunder.

"Oh, like that is it." Ianto chuckled. "She only just got here, but I can see she's made an impression on you already."

Gwyn said nothing as he took the form to check it. "You've left a few blanks, Mr Williams. Fill them in before you leave." He rose and went into the back of the station. From the window, part of the sea wall and the Front were visible. He liked the way the wind whipped Bethan's skirt. The second gust offered a glimpse of her thighs and she huddled into her jacket. He waited until she walked out of sight, sighed and went back to the office where Ianto had completed the form.

"You've heard about her, haven't you?"

Gwyn fixed him with a cold look. "Heard what about whom?"

"Bethan, of course. Like her aunty, she is. Witched them two of Emrys and Julie the same as Megan did."

"Oh?"

"Aye, aye. You remember the old woman. Bit of a witch, she was. Always knew things before other people did, see. My Bessie went to her regular like, to learn her fortune, and Megan was always right. Mind, I didn't go myself; not sure if I believe in it. Do you think this one will take up where the old one left off?"

"As far as I know, Miss Davies hasn't decided to stay on at Derwen." Gwyn's mind was in turmoil. He wanted Ianto to leave so he could think.

"Well, while she's here, she's put a spell on some people." Ianto grinned. At the door, he turned to look at Gwyn and chuckled. "And I'm looking at one of those people right now."

After Ianto left, Gwyn plopped onto the hard chair on the business side of the counter. While Ianto spoke in jest, he raised questions in Gwyn's mind. He'd known Megan well. He knew her skill, or gift as some called it, was genuine. She told him she used cards or a person's palm as props, but they were nothing more than a place where she could look when she gave a reading. With him, she fixed him with piercing eyes. She helped him more than once with his enquiries, often telling him where to find stolen goods or gave him a description of who had committed a certain crime. She told him personal things, too, like the way he'd fall in love with a local girl with black hair. Gwyn thought that was Linda, a dietician at the health farm, but now this other one with black hair had turned up to confuse things.

Feeling guilty, Gwyn rang Linda and arranged to meet her on Sunday. They'd have a day out, away from Derwen and its distractions. Somewhere he could forget he was an officer of the law.

* * *

Disappointed that Gwyn hadn't been alone so she could question him again about Meg's death, Beth walked into the Anchor. "Is Dilys about?"

"She's just settling Ricky for the night," Davy answered. "She'll be down in a minute. What will you have, Bethan?"

"Bailey's." She waited while he poured her drink.

He brought it to her then fixed his gaze on the doorway. "Would you look at that! There's Geri and an under-aged chum."

Beth froze. "Jerry?"

"Used to be Geraldine before all those American telly shows. Now it's brief names to go with brief skirts." Davy's voice rose to carry to the front of the tavern. "Out with you girls till the ages on your cards match your make-up!"

Beth threw a glance over her shoulders at two scowling schoolgirls costumed like streetwalkers. She resumed breathing.

Davy stared at her. "Are you all right? You look as if you'd seen a ghost."

Beth gave a weak smile and changed the subject. "You've got a wonderful grandson, Mr Rees."

He warmed visibly and took her money. "Aye, he's a treasure, right enough. He took to you, too; couldn't stop talking about you at supper."

"Oh?"

"Said you were Little Megan." Davy laughed. "Megan *fach*, that's what he called you." Davy answered a call from the other side of the bar and went to serve. When he came back, he said, "Dilys tells me you've agreed to be Ricky's godmother in place of Megan."

"Yes, but I'm not sure what a godmother does."

"Nothing more than be there to guide him." He was quiet for a moment. "I'm not altogether sure you are the right choice, Bethan. You were a tearaway when you were here before, and we don't know what you got up to in London."

"Did you make your views known to Dilys?"

"God help me, I did. I've never seen her lose her temper like that. She says the scrapes you two got into were harmless. By her reckoning, if we had to leave Ricky for some reason, she'd rather he be with you than anyone else."

"I would never do anything to hurt Ricky."

Davy nodded. "All right, but make sure you keep your word."

"What word is she going to keep?" Dilys asked as she joined them.

"Nothing for you to worry about," Davy said before walking away.

"So?" Dilys asked. "How are you settling in?"

"I'm not. And I'm not accepting more guests, even if you double book them and send them to me."

Dilys looked puzzled. "I'm not sure I know what you're talking about."

"Tom Rowland. You double booked him once. That's how he ended up staying with Aunty Meg the first time."

The confused look didn't leave Dilys' face. "Really? I don't think . . . Dat!" she called along the bar. "Come here a second."

Davy strolled over to them, polishing a pint glass.

"Do you remember double booking Tom Rowland and sending him over to Megan?"

"When was this?"

"Two years ago, I think," Beth answered.

"I don't think so," Davy said. "The last time we had a double booking was when you were in hospital having Ricky and we left Willy in charge. He double booked that family from Scotland and had to give them my room."

"Who told you this, anyway?" Dilys asked Beth.

"Tom Rowland. Perhaps I got it wrong."

"Must have," said Davy and moved away.

"Well, look who's here." Dilys looked past Bethan towards the door. "Off duty are you, Gwyn?"

"For an hour or two." He eyed Beth. "Mind if I join you?"

"Be my guest." Beth took her purse from the stool at her side and placed it on the bar. A quick glance showed her Gwyn wasn't in uniform and the phrase *scrubs up well* crossed her mind. She hid her smile, wondering what he'd say if he knew what she was thinking.

"My usual, Dilys, and another for the lady." Gwyn sat. "Thanks for bringing the jacket back."

"Thank you for lending it to me." She waited until Dilys brought their drinks and went to serve someone else. "I talked to Ishmael this morning."

"Oh?"

"He knows something. I'm sure of it."

"Knows something about what?"

"Aunty Meg's death."

"I've told you what the verdict was. I can let you read the file, if it'll make you more settled in your mind."

"Isn't that against the law?"

"It is, but I can bend the rules once in a while, if it hurts no one."

Beth wasn't sure if she could take reading the cold, hard facts in an impartial file. The people who compiled the report hadn't known Meg. "If I decide to take you up on the offer, I'll let you know."

"I've given you the gist of what it contains. I don't think you reading it for yourself would throw any light on the matter." He took a drink from his glass. "I made a thorough investigation at the time. If you can come up with new facts, I'll be glad to reopen the case."

"I intend to make Ishmael tell me what he knows."

"How will you do that?"

"I'll be his shadow until he gets so sick of seeing me that he'll tell me everything just to get rid of me."

"You could be charged with harassment or stalking."

"You wouldn't do that to me, would you?"

Gwyn shrugged. "If Ishmael makes a formal complaint, I'll have no choice but to follow up."

"But I know of no other way to get him to talk!"

"You've asked him, haven't you? You've told him who you are. And I suppose you told him he knew something he wasn't telling? Why don't you let the man alone with his conscience? In time, he'll say what he has to say."

"But I don't have that much time!" She noticed Gwyn's hand tightened around his glass.

"You're leaving Derwen?"

"I hadn't planned on staying." She saw his grip loosen.

"So your departure isn't imminent."

"No. For a start, I'd have to put the house up for sale, unless I leave it to a solicitor to handle. Even then, there are Meg's personal things to deal with, and the furniture."

"That could take weeks. At least until the summer's over."

"At least."

Gwyn swallowed a mouthful of beer. "I heard something today . . . About you."

A flicker of fear forced a sharp breath before Beth managed a cautious: "Yes?"

"They say you witched Julie's two."

Beth felt her eyes widen with disbelief. "That's ridiculous! Where did you hear that?"

"From Ianto Williams, the man who was in the station when you came in. He was the first. I've heard it a couple of times since."

"But—"

"News travels fast in this place."

"Well, you can put a stop to it as soon as you like. The twins were in awe of me, I think, so they behaved themselves. That's all it was." Beth's laugh faded when she saw the serious face he turned to her. "Don't you believe me?"

"Megan had a gift."

"And you believe I inherited it? Well, I can tell you I have never had a psychic episode in my life. As for reading the cards, I can't even play Snap." Beth raised her glass to her lips.

Not psychic, perhaps, but what happened the night when the police raided Jerry's flat? For no reason, in the middle of watching Coronation Street, she had an urgent need to leave. She ran out, saying she'd forgotten to get milk for the morning. As she reached the corner, she looked back and saw two police cars pull up outside the building. They found nothing, Jerry was too clever for that, but they took him in for questioning. She'd barely escaped joining him in the police car, but that was intuition not psychic phenomenon.

They sat without speaking for a while, each directing a concentrated gaze on the drinks they held until Beth looked up and saw Tom in conversation with the red-haired man she knew to be Sean O'Malley. "There's Tom," she said, breaking the silence. "Isn't that funny? Last night the other stopper, Doug Amundson, was with Sean, and now there's Tom with him."

"Leave them be." Gwyn spoke in a low voice.

She gave him a hard look. "I beg your pardon?"

"Ignore them. There's a good girl."

Good girl, indeed! "Don't patronize me!" Beth hissed and downed the last of her drink. "Dilys?" She waved to the other woman. "I'm off. I'll talk to you tomorrow, all right?"

"You're going so soon?" Dilys looked from Beth to Gwyn. "I'll come with you to the door."

Without a glance in Gwyn's direction, Beth picked up her handbag, swivelled around on her stool, and hopped down. Her heel skidded against the stool leg and threw her off balance against Gwyn. He steadied her.

"Thank you," she said stiffly.

"Don't mention it," he replied.

With as much dignity as she could muster, Beth stalked to the door beside Dilys. Once outside, she relaxed and muttered: "Men!"

Dilys giggled in the way she had when they were children. "I think Gwyn is sweet on you."

For a fleeting second, Beth felt a surge of something inside that seemed to lighten her heart. She fought it. "Don't even think about it, Dil."

"Why? Because he's a small-town bobby? Used to flash London men, are you?"

"Dil!"

"You'd never find a better man than Gwyn, I can tell you."

"Then have a go at him yourself!" Beth stomped away.

* * *

"Will she be all right?" Gwyn asked when Dilys returned.

"You don't need to worry about that one. Tough as an old boot, she is."

"I thought you were her friend."

"So I am, and I love her to bits, but I know how she can be. She's got a temper on her."

"She's outspoken, like Megan."

"But without Megan's veneer of civility, eh? And I'll tell you what, Gwyn *bach*." Dilys gave his hand a quick squeeze. "I think she likes you." She gave him an impish smile and walked away.

Gwyn nursed his pint. What had he said? What in hell had he said? Whatever, it was doubtful she'd speak to him again. Women were funny creatures, well, some women. Take Linda now. She was easy to get on with, always pleasant and eager to please, always falling in with whatever plans he made. A woman should be like that, not get mad at something a man said in total innocence.

Diawl, hadn't Bethan dismissed him from Megan's kitchen as if he were a schoolboy. A woman like that would keep a man forever on the hop, beating his brains out and rehearsing every word. Even then, after all that, she'd take offence. There would never be any peace. But hell and damnation, she made his pulse race, her and her expensive clothes and London ways. With a sigh, he lifted his pint and took a drink.

What about the rumour Bethan had Megan's gift? True or not, the damage was done. More and more, as Gwyn thought about it, he felt Megan's fortune telling had something to do with her death. Someone believed she knew something she shouldn't have, and whomever it was thought she'd written it down. That's why he or she was searching the house. Now people were claiming this girl had the same gift. If his assumptions were correct, the gossips could be placing her in danger.

A sliding of his gaze took in the reflections in the mirror behind the bar. Sean O'Malley and Tom Rowland were still in conversation. Whatever they were talking about wasn't private because Ifor limped to join them. Davy put in a word or two between serving and then Ianto joined the group.

"Another drink, Gwyn?" Davy stood before him.

"No, ta, Davy, but a word to the wise," Gwyn said, lowering his voice. "You had a bit of a party here last night after closing." He saw a wary look creep into the landlord's eyes. "I'll be away on Sunday, and the one who takes my beat might not be so hard of hearing. You get my drift?"

Davy opened his mouth long enough to say, "Thanks."

"I never mentioned it. Right?"

Davy nodded.

Gwyn left the Anchor without any feelings of guilt. The Sergeant would put him on charge for tipping off Davy, but the Sergeant didn't have to live here. If ever the people in Derwen turned against him, his job would be impossible.

Gwyn passed his sergeant's exam two years earlier but leaving Derwen to take up a higher-ranking position somewhere else didn't sit easy. Then he began to realise not everything in the Bay was as it should be, and he turned down the promotion. It was just a hunch, something he couldn't even mention to the Sergeant, but Gwyn started looking more closely at the people around him. He took note of who spent time with whom, and who avoided him. He made cryptic notes about the thoughts that wandered this way and that, none of them tying together or making any sense. Something under the surface tugged like an undertow and, so close to the sea, Gwyn knew how dangerous that could be.

Megan hinted at something. A few of the things she mentioned echoed what he'd been feeling for months. He was angry with her for not being more explicit, but she was afraid of someone branding her a gossip and refused to speak until she was certain.

Then that last phone call. *I'm ready to tell you.* Her words haunted him, and he felt sure Megan died because of something she knew. However, where had she gone that day she was missing?

A three-page fax was waiting when Gwyn walked into the station. The Town Planning information confirmed

Reginald Plews had permission to enlarge the cellar at Plas Mawr, which was disappointing.

However, in his request for information on Bethan, Dorothy Driscoll exceeded his expectations. Randall and Toomis, a large firm specializing in building residential blocks of flats, bought out Bethan's boutique, B D Modes. They paid Miss Bethan Louise Davies by cheque, which cleared the Royal Bank. The bank's report was on the third page and it retained confidentiality. They would disclose no sum unless a court order authorised them to release detailed information. Miss Davies had closed the account and withdrawn her money in cash.

Gwyn frowned. Could she be carrying the cash with her? That much money would tempt any thief, and Megan's small safe wouldn't present much of a challenge. He didn't know how to broach the subject. It was none of his business anyway.

P L Crompton

CHAPTER TWELVE

Beth's temper hadn't waned by the time she reached the house. Good girl, indeed! Who did Gwyn Thomas think he was! No one had called her that since—well; actually, nobody had ever called her that. She didn't think she was a bad person but, when she was angry, she let people know.

She was too much like Meg. Her mother kept telling her that, and now people here were saying the same for a different reason. Well, she had nothing but admiration for Meg. If she was becoming like her aunt, she could think of worse things to be. However, had Meg's habit of speaking out been the cause of her death? Had she upset someone enough to make him or her kill?

Beth fought the idea aside and stomped up the stairs to unlock the door to her room. She changed into jeans and a shirt. It was still daylight, the sun low over the sea. A stint in the garden might lighten her mood.

The potting shed was cobwebby. As she pushed the door open, Beth remembered the day she and Dil hid in there to smoke the two cigarettes snaffled from Davy's packet. They were giggling and coughing when the door opened. Meg ordered them out and stood over them, forcing them to smoke the rest of their cigarettes. Dil was the lucky one. She had a fit of coughing and vomited over the hydrangeas. Beth, on the other hand, felt ill for days, but it cured her of ever wanting to smoke.

Wary of spiders, Beth took two steps inside. Two shoulder-high shelves ran the length of one wall holding pots next to a bag of grass seed and a box of fertiliser. On the floor next to the mower, rakes, spades and hoes stood like soldiers at attention. The hand tools Beth was looking for were at the far end on the worktable. Beth crossed to it and studied the things spread out on the sheets of newspaper. Meg had been preparing geranium cuttings. They looked like sticks of wood now, shrivelled and dried. Pots filled with soil stood ready for the cuttings. Someone had moved them recently, because they were at least an inch away from the dust-free circles on the paper. The hand tools didn't appear to be where Meg left them either. Someone had searched the shed.

Beth turned to face the door. Although several footprints surrounded the mower, farther in only one set of prints mingled with hers. She bent to examine them more closely. They matched the imprint left on the windowsill.

What did the intruder want in Derwen House? What did he hope to find in the potting shed? Suddenly, the half-dark place held menace. Beth gathered the hand tools and a basket and rushed out.

She was on her knees, clearing the weeds around the primroses when Mrs Williams came to lean on the low wall separating the two gardens.

"Now then, you're making a start on the garden, Bethan."

"It will take a lot of work to get it as Aunty Meg had it."

"Yes, indeed. Gwyn Thomas came around to cut the grass, but he didn't know enough about plants to do any weeding, he said."

"Gwyn did that?"

"He came every week, when it wasn't raining."

Beth tried to think of something to say rather than be rude and ignore the woman. Meg said Mrs Williams was a hypochondriac. As a child, she thought it was because the woman was enormous, as wide as she was tall. Hippo and hypo sounded alike. "I heard you tell Tom Rowland you hadn't been very well."

"Oh, fair to middling, like always." The woman plucked at the moss growing between the stones. "Always good to me in that respect, your Aunty Megan was. Used to make me up a drink to help with the digestion and wouldn't take a penny for it."

Beth bent to the weeds to hide her smile. The potion Meg made up was a mixture of ginger and honey in water with a touch of green food colouring. "I'm afraid I have none of her abilities, Mrs Williams."

"Oh? Well . . . Now then . . . I hoped . . . See, they told me you could do what Megan did."

The gossips had been busy. "Perhaps you misheard what was said."

"But—the twins . . . You made them quiet down, girl."

"They were a bit shy with a stranger, that's all." Beth raised grimy hands, soil rimmed around and under her nails. "Look at these, Mrs Williams. From what I recall, Aunty Meg looked at a weed and it withered. Do you think I'd be in this state if I could do the same?"

Mrs Williams gave a coy smile. "Oh, ho! I've seen your aunty with her hands in the same state. Weeds never grew in her garden because she kept at them all the time."

"You saw her, did you?" Meg used to say *that blasted woman is watching me again!*

"I see everything that goes on around here."

"You didn't happen to see anyone in the shed, did you?"

"Only Gwyn Thomas getting the mower out and putting it away. Oh, here he is now. Good evening, PC Thomas."

"Good evening, Mrs Williams. Good evening, Miss Davies."

Beth struggled to her feet, her knees stiff, and saw he had changed into his uniform. "Constable Thomas. What brings you around here?"

"I believe you had something to show me in the house."

For a moment, Beth was puzzled, and then she remembered the footprint on the window ledge. "Yes. You'd better come in." She placed the hand tools on top of the weeds, picked up the basket and led the way into the house through the back door.

When they reached the bottom of the stairs, Beth said, "Wait here. I'll get the key."

"You keep the rooms locked?"

"I feel safer with them that way." She took him to the upper floor. "The footprint is in here." She unlocked the bedroom door and paused for him to pass her. Instead, he stopped, the two of them forced into close proximity in the doorway.

"About earlier . . . I don't know what I said or did to offend you, but I'm sorry."

"Forget it." Beth edged into the room and crossed to the window. She opened it and stood back. "If you check outside, you'll see the footprint and the leaves and twigs under the tree. They must have broken off when he leapt into it."

Gwyn leaned out to check the ground below, and Beth watched. One thing about a policeman's uniform, it fitted like a glove. Tight at the waist, it showed off Gwyn's broad shoulders, narrow hips and long legs. Not bad. Pity he was a bobby. When Gwyn glanced over his shoulder, Beth swung away and felt her face begin to burn.

"Someone has been in the shed, too," she mumbled.

"That was me, getting the mower." Gwyn closed the window and locked it.

"There are other footmarks, prints, I mean. Footprints like the one up here." When he left the room, she followed and locked the door. "I asked Mrs Williams if she'd seen anybody."

"Had she?"

"Only you." Beth stepped to the top of the stairs.

"While we're up here . . ."

"Yes?" Beth paused, one hand on the bannister.

"Megan had a small safe in her room. Has anyone tried to open it?"

"I forgot about it."

"Let's look now."

"All right." Beth walked past him and opened the door.

"You don't keep it locked?"

"Only when I'm out." Beth crossed to the old-fashioned oil painting above the heavy desk and grasped one edge of the frame. The painting swung away from the wall. "Oh!" The door to the safe also swung open, the lock drilled through and useless.

"Let me." Gwyn pushed past Beth. With a handkerchief, he fingered the safe door wider. "There are papers inside."

"Let me see them."

Using the handkerchief, he took the papers out. "I'd rather you didn't touch them. There may be fingerprints." He spread the papers on the bed.

"A copy of her will . . ." Tears pricked behind Beth's eyelids. "And paid invoices for repairs to the house. I don't know what's in the envelopes."

"I'd like to take these with me to have them examined. I'll give you a receipt." Gwyn looked up. She was staring at the documents, tears running down her cheeks. "It's all right, Bethan." He stepped towards her and drew her into his arms. "Cry, if you want to." He thrust the handkerchief into her hands.

He held her, stroked her hair, and murmured soothing words until her grief eased and she drew away.

"I'll find something to put the papers in." She all but ran to the door.

* * *

Thankful she had pulled away, for he could never have, Gwyn wondered if she was upset because someone stole the money she withdrew from the bank in London. Had she placed it in the safe? If not, where was she hiding it? Of course, she could have deposited it in a Carmarthen bank, he supposed. He crossed to the safe and gingerly pushed it closed, touching only the tip of the door, before putting the painting back against the wall.

On the desk, a row of photographs caught his eye. Valuable antique silver frames, they weren't what the thief was after. In one snapshot, Bethan wore a princess costume with Megan beside her dressed as a witch, probably taken at the carnival they held in Derwen each summer. Bethan was riding a donkey on the sands in another. An older photograph, black and white and faded, showed a young man in a soldier's uniform.

"That's the man Aunty Meg was to marry," Beth said quietly. "She said he was lost in the war. He gave her the brooch she always wore, the one shaped like a heart."

Embarrassed to be caught snooping, Gwyn reached for the brown envelope Beth held out. "I'll need something to stop me getting my own fingerprints on the papers."

His sodden handkerchief was in her pocket. Beth opened a drawer in the dresser and took out a scarf. "Will this do?"

"Great." Gwyn took it. Silk and expensive. He caught each document and small envelope by the corner and dropped it into the larger envelope. "I'll take them to Carmarthen on Monday to get them checked."

"I don't need a receipt. If I can't trust—" She stopped.

"A policeman?" Gwyn suggested.

"You," Beth said, turning away. "I'll show you the shed now."

Gwyn followed her down the stairs; his heart a bit lighter than it had been a minute ago. She trusted him. Not the damned uniform—him. Megan said the same thing. *It's the man I trust, Gwyn. If I didn't trust you, I wouldn't tell you what I think is going on.* Why hadn't she told him her suspicions then? She might still be alive.

At the back door, Beth opened it and Gwyn touched her arm to halt her. "If you're working on the front garden, anyone could enter through the back and you wouldn't know. It's wiser to keep it locked."

White faced, Beth looked up at him. "Are you trying to frighten me?"

"Only advising you. Someone has been in the house. He may come again." Gwyn reached out to place a comforting hand on her shoulder but she moved away towards the shed. Sighing, he followed.

"See here?" In the narrow confines, they stood shoulder to shoulder.

"These are my footprints." He pointed to the marks left by plimsolls so worn he'd have to replace them soon. Gwyn took another step into the shed. In the shaft of light from the doorway, other footprints led towards the far end. He crouched beside the closest. The ridged pattern matched the one on the window ledge upstairs.

"They're the same, aren't they?"

"Yes." Gwyn straightened. Staying clear of the prints, he took the few strides separating him from the table.

"You can see how someone moved the pots," Beth said. "What could they have been looking for? There's nothing here, only gardening things."

Although someone had moved the pots, the pages of newspaper on which they stood hadn't been touched. Perhaps someone disturbed the prowler or something caused him to leave before he finished his search. "Give me a hand here."

Gwyn stood the envelope on a shelf and began taking things off the table.

"What are you doing?" Beth took two pots and placed them on the floor.

"He was looking for something, but he didn't check under the newspaper. I want to see if there's anything there."

Together they cleared the table and Gwyn removed the newspaper page by page. He didn't find anything underneath. Next, he tipped the soil out of each pot onto the newspaper, still nothing.

A shadow broke the shaft of light and the girl beside him gave a startled cry. Gwyn spun around; tense until he recognised the man who stood there. "Tom."

"Are you here again, Gwyn? What is it this time? Did someone leave the shed open?"

Gwyn placed an arm around Beth's shoulders to steady her and took the envelope from the shelf. "There's nowhere you can take a girl these days without somebody creeping up on you."

Tom chuckled. "I can think of better places than a shed." He stepped back as Bethan and Gwyn emerged.

"Think it through, man." Gwyn released Beth and closed the shed door. "Where better than a cobwebby place when the girl's afraid of spiders?"

Beth pushed between the two men and walked to the house, anger evident in the stiffness of her back.

He'd done it again; said something to upset her. What the hell had he said?

"So you're not going to tell me what you two were doing in there?" Tom teased.

"We'll never kiss and tell, eh girl?" Gwyn called after her.

"You like trying the impossible, do you, Gwyn?" Tom asked with a laugh as Beth entered the house.

Something hard and nasty gripped Gwyn's heart as he studied Tom. "Tried it, have you?"

"Not on your life," Tom answered. "She's a piece from hell, if you ask me."

Gwyn relaxed. He hadn't liked the idea of the two of them all cosy in Derwen House. Then another thought crossed his mind. Tom would have access to the house and the shed. Nobody would question his going in there, not even the nosy parker next door. "Shall we see if she'll make us a cup of tea?"

"If she won't, I will. After eight, we guests get to fend for ourselves. At least, that's how it was in Megan's time." Tom led the way into the kitchen.

Gwyn stood in the doorway, unsure of his welcome. Beth was slicing a slab of pound cake. "Is that for us?"

"It is. Sit down."

Tom sat, but Gwyn took no more than a step into the kitchen before stopping to tuck the envelope under his arm and remove his helmet. He was brushing the cobwebs from it with the cuff of his sleeve when Beth came to stand before him. "I'm sorry if I said . . .," he whispered.

Without a word, she reached up and picked a cobweb from his shoulder. Their eyes met in a searching glance before she smiled and moved away.

A piece of hell, was she? On the outside, perhaps, but inside she'd just shown him she was like Megan. She was all he had loved about Megan.

Gwyn put the envelope and helmet on the table beside Tom who sat with his legs crossed. On the pretence of brushing cobwebs from the bottoms of his trouser legs, Gwyn studied the sole of the other man's shoe and saw the imprint of a star. It hadn't been Tom in the shed, unless he had another pair of shoes. He pulled out a chair as Beth brought a pot of tea and a plate of cake to the table. "I don't suppose the place has changed much since you were here last year," he commented to Tom.

"I was here at Christmas," Tom answered.

"Oh, aye, so you were." It was the first Christmas Gwyn's name hadn't come up on the duty roster, and he'd spent the day in Carmarthen with his parents. "I remember it rained a lot, and we had some sleet. Did you get much painting done?" Gwyn was aware of Bethan taking a chair across from him.

"Not a lot. If it had snowed, things would have been better." Tom took a piece of cake.

"Derwen is very pretty when it's covered in snow."

"I'll have to try to get back here sometime again in winter."

"Where do you go, when you're not here?" Gwyn watched him intently over the rim of his cup.

"I was in Scotland after I left here. There's snow and plenty in the Highlands."

The answer came too pat. "I didn't mean that," Gwyn said. "Where is your base? Where is your home?"

"A little place in North Wales you've probably never heard of."

North Wales? With a London accent? Well, so did Reginald Plews. "Try me."

"Ruabon."

"Outside Wrexham? I have a mate policing in Wrexham. We were in training together." A tightening of the other man's jaw was his reward. "I'll have to tell him to call in on you to say hello."

Tom nodded. "You do that, but I'm hardly ever home."

"No dogs or cats or plants to look after?"

"No. Do you?"

Tom had turned the tables on him, and Gwyn knew further questions would be useless. "A man who lives on his own tends not to collect anything that needs nurturing." Before she rose to begin clearing the table, he saw the puzzlement on Bethan's face.

"I'll help with those," Tom offered.

"No need," Beth replied. "You did them last night so it's my turn."

"Then I'll watch the news and leave you lovebirds alone."

When Tom had left the room, Gwyn carried the rest of the dishes to the counter.

"What's going on?" Beth whispered.

"We need to talk." Gwyn shot a quick glance at the door leading into the hallway and heard the television. "Can you get a look at any other shoes Tom may have?"

"I can check now."

"No, not now; sometime when he's out of the house."

"Were they his footprints in the shed?"

"Not unless he has another pair of shoes. That's what I want you to find out."

"He didn't bring much, only a small bag and his painting things."

"He came here often and may have left a pair behind for when he came back."

"I'll do it tomorrow." She removed a cup from the water and handed it to him. "Since you're here you might as well make yourself useful."

Gwyn grinned and grabbed the tea towel. Even washing dishes was a pleasure in the right company.

* * *

Envelope in hand, Gwyn left Derwen House and made his way to Ishmael's cottage. The carving of Megan was almost finished and Ishmael was working on the base, fashioning the heart-shaped brooch she always wore.

"I hear Bethan talked to you." Gwyn perched on the log.

"Had I closed my eyes, I would have believed it was Megan talking to me; without the Welsh accent, of course. In this girl it is muted, but it is still there."

"She lost her temper, did she?"

"She promised to haunt me until I told her something she thought I knew about Megan's death." Ishmael grinned. "No young lady has threatened to pursue me in many a long year."

"But you do know something, don't you?"

Ishmael shook his head.

Gwyn bit his lip in frustration. "I'm worried about Bethan; that something might happen to her while I'm gone. I'll be away all day Sunday."

"Bethan has assumed Megan's role as Godmother to Richard," Ishmael informed him. "No doubt she will take him to Sunday school and then take him home and stay for lunch as did Megan. I think her morning will be quite safe. I will stroll past Derwen House in the afternoon and evening if you wish."

"I'm wondering . . . Bethan's working on the garden . . . I don't suppose you could see your way clear to helping her, could you?"

"Of course. Is there anyone or anything I should be watching for?"

"I think you know that better than I." Gwyn studied Ishmael. "You know you're taking a risk by not telling me what you think you know."

"And you are aware I will not speak out until I am certain of my facts."

"I don't want to lose you, too."

"I survived the battering of the ocean and have always believed I am living on borrowed time. Do not worry about me, my friend, but watch over the girl. Warn her to be careful."

"I would if you would tell me what she has to be careful of."

"Loose lips sink ships," Ishmael said quietly.

He studied Ishmael, waiting for him to say more. When he didn't, Gwyn left with a brief: "Good night."

One story bandied about was that Ishmael arrived in Derwen on a piece of driftwood. Was there truth in it? What was there in Ishmael's past that made the man wary of voicing his suspicions and drawing attention to himself?

P L Crompton

CHAPTER THIRTEEN

It seemed to Beth that Tom dawdled over breakfast. At length, he went up to his room and she heard him moving about as she cleared up and prepared his lunch. He was still up there when she brought out the vacuum cleaner and ran it over the hallway and stairs. In the sitting room, she dusted and she was vacuuming the rug when Tom came down. She went to fetch his sandwich and flask of tea.

"Are you working on any particular scene today?" she asked as he took the lunch from her in the hallway.

"I might try the north cliff, to get a different perspective on the bay."

From the window, Beth watched until he walked through the car park; then she got the spare key from the kitchen and hoisted the vacuum cleaner up the stairs to his room. As she made the bed, she kept glancing out of the window. Eventually, Tom climbed the cliff walk and disappeared into the morning mist.

His wardrobe was almost empty. Two shirts and a jacket hung on hangers and a small pile of clothes lay on the floor. She recognised the shirt he'd worn the day before. A pair of plimsolls lay beneath the laundry. She turned them over to examine the soles and saw a maker's pattern carved into the rubber. Disappointed, she replaced them and piled the laundry on top.

Three boards with mounted paintings stood propped against the wall under the window. Curious, she flipped through them. The first was a view from the south cliff, with

115

Plas Mawr in the distance and fishing boats in the foreground. A second encompassed the shoreline itself, the Witch black and prominent against a sparkling sea and an equally dark cave yawning behind the rock. The third was of the south cliff. In the foreground, a girl with black hair looked out to sea. The painting the other artist had done the day she went onto the cliff.

Why did Tom have it? She looked for a signature but found none. Puzzled, she studied the canvas. Unmistakably the same scene, she sat close to the edge of the cliff. In the water outside the bay and beyond the south headland, a yacht rode the swell as though anchored there. It was all black, as if the artist hadn't finished working on it. As she angled it to the light, she could make out the furled sails and the detailing on the deck. Nothing shone, as if someone painted over the brass fittings common to most yachts. Perhaps he'd add the details once he was sure the paint was dry.

She must ask Tom about it. If she said she'd knocked over the boards while cleaning, would he accept it? It was worth a try. However, she'd have to contain her curiosity until that evening because he said he would be out all day. To back up her story of having to move the canvases, she vacuumed the room.

Beth planned to be out, too. She hadn't forgotten how Daniel Jones reported her to the police all those years ago, and she was loath to give him her business. She would go to Carmarthen for groceries, where the prices were better and offered more choice. A bus went to Carmarthen from the Front, but the idea of sitting for an hour in the company of somebody like Mrs Williams made her squirm. She'd drive, have lunch in town, and take her time. She made a casserole, left a note for Tom that it was in the oven, set the timer and left.

* * *

Gwyn was giving directions to a visitor when Beth drove by. *Stop her!* The voice filled his head with sound and urgency. He jerked as if shot.

"Are you all right, Officer?" The driver eyed him from inside the car.

"What?" Gwyn brought the man into focus. "Just a minute."

Bethan's car rounded the corner on its way up the hill. He began running. When Gwyn reached the corner, she'd accelerated out of earshot. He stood in the middle of the road and waved his arms but a lorry-load of rubble came out of the lane to Plas Mawr and trundled in her wake. Even if she looked in her mirror, she wouldn't see Gwyn.

A horn blared behind him and he stepped smartly to one side to let the car pass. "Emrys!" he shouted and ran to the car as Emrys slammed on the brakes. "Bethan's just driven up there. Catch up with her and tell her I have to talk to her right now."

"Constable!" the motorist shouted impatiently.

"Urgent, is it?" Emrys asked.

Was it? *Yes!* The voice screamed through his head. "Go quick now, Emrys, there's a good boy."

"I'll try." Emrys took off and Gwyn watched him speed up until he was behind the lorry. The road was too narrow for him to pass, and the lorry was making heavy weather of it. Even at the top of the hill, where the road was wider and he could pass, Gwyn realised Emrys wouldn't know which direction Bethan had taken.

Why was it so important to call Bethan back? There had been a voice; the same voice that had him out of bed the other morning. Megan's? He hadn't thought his job stressful, but it was obvious something was getting to him because it was the second time he'd heard the disembodied voice.

"Constable!"

Gwyn went back to the tourist's car. "Sorry about that."

Gwyn hurriedly gave the directions the motorist wanted, and crossed to Beach Road. Without Bethan's car parked in front of the house, everyone would know the place was empty because he, like anyone else about, had seen Tom walk up to the north cliff. As fast as he could without raising suspicion, Gwyn made for Derwen House.

Nosy Mrs Williams had left for Carmarthen on the early bus, so no one was around to question Gwyn as he walked around outside and checked the doors and windows. Bethan had everything locked up tight but someone always managed to get in. Though he'd checked carefully each time, he never found any sign of forced entry, so whoever it was had a key or was a damned good lock picker.

Gwyn rushed down the back garden and out onto the lane, heading for Ishmael's cottage. "She's gone out," he said over the driftwood fence when he saw Ishmael in the garden. "The house is empty."

Ishmael rose from his weeding. "I believe you speak of Bethan. Did she tell you where she was going?"

Gwyn shook his head. "Once up the hill, she could go in either direction." He faced the bay and saw how the car park was filling up. "You can see Derwen House from here."

"And I assume you wish me to keep watch?"

"Would you do that?"

"Of course."

"Good lad." Gwyn retraced his steps. People often saw Ishmael sitting in the grass on the hill. No one would think anything of it.

He'd examined the documents taken from Megan's safe, handling them carefully even though he wore protective gloves. Two of the envelopes held love letters to Megan from the man who had died. They caused a lump in his throat. Those wouldn't go to Carmarthen; they'd stay locked in his safe until he returned them. The rest of the documents contained nothing of note beyond a copy of the will that left everything to Bethan. There were Property Rate papers, a few Premium Bonds, and a letter Bethan had written years earlier to say how much she'd enjoyed her holiday and how much she loved Megan. Gwyn listed all the items, but did not mention the love letters. If Carmarthen didn't come up with a fingerprint match on their computer, he'd have the onerous task of getting prints from one or two of the men who made him uneasy, and he'd start with Tom Rowland.

Several times that day, Gwyn made a point of passing in front of or behind Derwen House, and saw Ishmael on the hill huddled over his whittling. By noon, a few more day-trippers arrived despite the cold of early June. Dressed in their anoraks, the children made sand castles while the adults sheltered behind windbreakers. Had they asked, he could have told them that the best place to be out of the wind was on the flat rocks at the foot of the south cliff.

A scuffle outside the Anchor grew calm as Gwyn strolled towards the group. By the time he reached the door, the men had gone back inside. Gwyn gave them a moment to sit themselves down before he went in and walked up to the bar.

"Is everything all right, Davy?"

Davy nodded. "I knew you had to be about somewhere. Everything is fine now."

"Is there anything I need do?"

"They had a bit of a squabble over a darts game, that's all."

"Fine." Gwyn looked around and recognised the men he'd seen. He fixed them with a long look, and then left. All in all, it had been a quiet day. It was too early in the season for coaches to arrive for the day; anyone who'd come in a car would be long gone by dinnertime because it was still too cold to sit on the beach. He made one last tour past Derwen House before going back to the station.

P L Crompton

CHAPTER FOURTEEN

Beth was late leaving Carmarthen. After a leisurely lunch, she spent the afternoon wandering around the shops and the marketplace. She dawdled for an hour at the Heritage Centre and checked if the Roman-built quay wall was crumbling yet. She debated about, then decided against visiting the castle, and had a cup of coffee while she waited for what the locals called the rush hour to end. In early evening, she began the drive back.

That morning, she passed through a huddle of houses and saw a sign at a pub offering food. *Cegin Gwlad*. She had no idea what the name meant, something like Country Kitchen she thought, and decided to stop there for dinner on her way home. Beth parked at the side of the fieldstone building. As she entered, two men left. One was red haired, one of the O'Malley brothers she thought, but the man with him was older and well dressed in a navy blazer and grey slacks. The pub was filling up with a small after-work crowd but Beth found a table in a corner and studied the menu. It offered what Meg called *home cooking*. She ordered Welsh roast lamb and looked around the room.

The decor was old Welsh with horse brasses and dark beams. The curtains drawn across the windows and the coverings on the padded seats depicted a foxhunt with red-coated riders galloping after a pack of hounds. In London, she'd visited a pub where a decorator tried to achieve the same effect, but everything had an air of being new, costly, and unnatural. This was the effect he was trying to achieve, this that had grown together over the years and came across as real. She relaxed and ordered a half bottle of wine to go with the meal.

When Beth left the restaurant, treed hills hid the sunset. Although still relatively early, only the glow from the dining room windows lit her way to her car. Most of the traffic was coming from the coast, but even that petered out by the time she reached the health farm and the road down to Derwen Bay.

The sun was low on the horizon and in her eyes as she topped the hill. She dropped a gear in readiness for the sharp incline and braked often as she followed the winding road. Half way down, the brake didn't respond. She pumped the pedal but there was no answering pressure. Breath locked painfully in her chest; she shifted to the lowest gear and pulled up on the hand brake as the gears ground in protest.

The car veered to one side and Beth lost control. She screamed as the car glanced against a bank, the crunch of metal against wet earth and stones unnerving. She jerked the steering wheel away from the embankment and fought to keep it on the road. It was picking up speed and she reminded herself not to panic. There! Ahead was a runaway lane, cut roughly through the bank of earth. She gripped the wheel and steered towards the field run in, praying the car wouldn't overshoot the access. As she angled the car upward into the field, it finally came to a halt with a judder. She shoved the gear stick into park, switched off the engine, took a deep breath and sat there shaking. In the silence, she heard a car coming up the hill from the bay. Beth threw the car door open, ran out onto the road on wobbly legs and flagged it down.

"What are you doing up here, then?" Emrys drew to a halt alongside and two faces pressed against the rear window to stare at her. "You're shaking like a leaf."

"I—" Beth doubled over and rested a hand on the fender. She was trembling so hard she could barely speak. She pointed into the field. "I . . . the brakes—"

"*Duw mawr!*" He jumped out and ran across to her car, skimming his hand along the gash on the side. "There's lucky you managed to stop, girl."

"C—can you—?"

"Give you a ride? Course I can. I have to drop them two off at the health farm, but you'd better come with me. I'll only be a couple of minutes."

Beth eyed the lovebirds in the back of the car. "I can wait."

"No you won't." Emrys opened the front passenger door. "In you get."

Beth climbed in and sank into the passenger seat. Hands clenched in her lap to steady them, she finally felt safe enough to acknowledge she could have been killed if she'd failed to pull into a field.

She'd never owned a car before, but she'd driven all types. When she went out with friends for the evening, she was always the designated driver. She'd driven fancy sports cars and beat-up jalopies, mini buses and campers, and never with any trouble, but this car, bought from a reputable dealer, nearly killed her. If it hadn't been for the run in . . . If she'd continued down the hill out of control . . . There were houses at the bottom, and people, and she'd never manage to navigate the bend at speed so she'd have ploughed into the sea wall. If she was travelling that fast, the car might have launched itself over the wall to end up against the Witch.

She was calmer by the time they dropped off the couple and Emrys had driven back to the run in.

He stopped at the field entrance. "I'm thinking . . . If you are up to it, it will be safer if you stay by the car while I fetch the tow truck."

"You want me to hang around here?" It was getting darker by the minute.

"It's safer. Just in case somebody comes by—kids you know—and decide to hot-wire her. They won't know about the brakes. You're sure it's the brakes, right?"

"The pedal lost resistance on the way down the hill."

"Sounds like the brakes. I won't be more than five minutes."

Beth climbed out and watched him disappear around a bend as a motorbike sped up the hill. It stopped beside her.

"You all right, love?"

She recognised Doug Amundson and shouted above the bike's roar: "The tow truck is on its way."

Doug cut the engine and wheeled the bike off the road as she explained what happened. "It's getting dark, and you don't want to be out here on your own. I'll wait with you until Emrys gets here."

"You don't need to, I'll be fine."

He ignored her. "You're not from Derwen Bay, are you?"

"I'm staying here for a while." Beth was uneasy in his company, even though he kept the bike between them.

"You're the woman I met on the cliff, aren't you; the one in my painting."

She almost asked him why his artwork was in Tom Rowland's room but thought better of it. This was a lonely spot. "Where are you off to?"

"I'm leaving Derwen. I'll probably come back next spring and see if I can catch better light. This must be the tow truck." Doug got back onto the bike and kick-started it. "You'll be okay now."

"Thank you for stopping." Beth watched him roar up the hill.

"Who was that, then?" Emrys asked after he'd turned the tow truck around. "One of the stoppers, was it?"

"One of the artists. He's leaving Derwen to go home."

Emrys pulled the chains from the truck and attached them to the back of the car. "I'll give you a ride down, but stand to one side until I've got her hooked up."

He climbed into the cab, winched up the car and aligned the tow truck with the exit to the road. "We'll have to take it easy; we'll be holding her back rather than towing her." He wiped his hands on a rag. "You can get in the truck now, *cariad*."

"I was lucky you happened along."

"Lucky for you I got a call for a taxi."

"You run a taxi service?"

"Most nights during the summer, I'll take somebody up to the campground or health farm. After a night in the Anchor, half of them can't walk straight, let alone drive. Those two work at the health farm. Julie doesn't like me going out but the money's good."

Beth began to relax as they approached the bottom of the hill. "Will you be able to repair the brakes?"

"I'll take a gander at her tomorrow. It sounds as if one of the lines had a leak or worked loose. Did you have any trouble earlier?"

"No, not until I was half way down the hill."

"That's when you'd be braking the hardest. It puts a lot of pressure on the lines." He drew into the forecourt. "If you'll give me a minute to unhitch her, I'll drive you home."

"I've got a few groceries in the boot."

"We'll get them out. Leave your keys with me for the morning."

"You work on cars on Sundays?"

"Powell-Pritchard can't see what goes on inside the garage, if I keep the door closed. And anyway, he works on Sundays, doesn't he?"

Beth waited as Emrys lowered the car. He unhitched it from the truck and she helped push it inside the garage. In the boot, most of the groceries had fallen out of the plastic bags. She began repacking things as Emrys reversed the taxi. "I can walk, you know."

"Not while I can drive you. Now, hop in, there's a good girl, before anybody sees you and starts a bit of gossip."

"What would they have to talk about? You run a taxi service so you're bound to have women in the car from time to time."

"But not one who could witch me."

Beth climbed into the car. "You don't believe that rubbish, do you?"

In the glow of the streetlight, he smiled. "Oh, I don't know. You did a pretty good job on me when I was a boy."

"Emrys!" Beth laughed as the memories rose from the past. He was the boy she'd given her first kiss to in the shadows behind the deckchair store. A brief peck followed by a rush of heat to her face. Beth had run home and dived into bed, pulling the covers over her head for fear Meg would know what she'd done.

"Here we are then." Emrys drew the car to a halt outside Derwen House. "Do you want any help with the bags?"

"They're not heavy." Beth opened the car door. "What do I owe you?"

"I'll send you a bill," he said with a grin as she got out and closed the door. "I'll give you a ring when I've seen what's what."

The house was dark and silent when Beth entered. She put the groceries away and made herself a cup of tea. Tom hadn't been back, because the casserole she'd left had gone cold in the oven and the note was still on the table. Unconcerned, and too tightly wound to sleep, Beth took the toiletries she'd bought to her room and gathered her laundry to put in the washer. Gwyn's handkerchiefs went in with the whites. As the washer chugged away, she poured more tea and mulled over her day.

Small town Carmarthen echoed the rush and bustle of London, except for the lilting voices. Because the shop assistants switched from Welsh to English when they saw the mystified look on Beth's face, she felt like a visitor.

When the washer fell silent, Beth transferred the clothes to the dryer and put in a load of darks. She rinsed her cup and the teapot and left them on the counter before checking the doors and windows and heading up the stairs. The memory of rushing down the hill with no brakes haunted her as she prepared for bed. In years of driving, she had never come close to having an accident. That could have been her first and last. She shivered at the thought, turned out the light, and went to sit on the window seat.

The darkness beyond the window was soothing. No wonder Meg sat here most nights and let the day wash from her. As she had the night before, the Witch stood dark and eerie, seeming to move as moonlight settled on the undulating water. It would be easy to believe she walked.

Then it came again—the grinding and a shaft of light extending horizontally across the water followed by a clang. It wasn't her imagination; this time she was wide-awake. Beth dressed hurriedly, left the house by the back door, and ran down the lane.

The tide was in and ready to turn. It grasped with feeble fingers at the narrow strip of dry sand, pulling at the fishing boats as if it would take them with it. Beth lowered herself into a corner where steps broke the sea wall and watched the expanse of water between the Witch and the cave. It was from there the light had come, from inside the cave.

As she strained to hear any sound, she heard a soft swish as someone plodded across the sand. She turned her head and saw a man making his way towards her. Beth felt a quick surge of fear until she recognised Ishmael. He approached the steps and climbed them, seeming not to notice her huddled in their shadow, and then his footsteps faded into the night.

With a last glance at the Witch, Beth rose and went back to the house. She undressed in the dark, watching out the window, but the flash of light did not reappear.

In the middle of the night, noises in the next room woke Beth. She looked at her clock. It was almost three-thirty. In an odd way, the noises were comforting. Tom was back. She reminded herself to tell him off for making so much racket, rolled over and went back to sleep.

CHAPTER FIFTEEN

The Sunday papers dropped through the letterbox as Beth walked downstairs. She took them through to the kitchen, made coffee, and spread the papers on the table. On page four of *News of the World*, she found the report. Police had arrested four men in connection with the theft of jewellery and valuables from the London house of Amanda Parson. The article suggested a connection with the woman's murder.

Beth felt a release of the tension building since she left London. When Dilys rang to remind her that Ricky had to be in Sunday school by eleven, her friend commented on how happy Beth sounded.

"I'll come with you," Dilys said, "and we can have a chat while we wait for him."

Annoyed at the way Tom banged around during the night, Beth neglected to take him tea and biscuits at eight. She clattered around the kitchen beneath his room, surprised when it didn't wake him. When she heard no sound from upstairs as she prepared breakfast, Beth went up to tap at his door. "Tom? Are you awake?" He didn't answer. She tried the door and found it unlocked. "I hope you're decent, because I'm coming in."

The room was empty and the bed didn't look slept in. Tom had been back and he'd removed the paintings and the rest of his painting gear. Beth checked the wardrobe. It was empty. Surprised he would leave without saying anything; she crossed to open the curtains and stepped on something squishy. Gingerly, she raised her foot and found a burst tube of blue acrylic paint. Beth removed her smeared slipper, took it to the bathroom to clean, and returned with a wad of toilet paper to scrub the floor. She flushed the paper, took another length to wrap around the paint and carried it down to the kitchen. She placed it on the counter, intending to carry it out to the bin later. Although glad he'd left, Beth wondered why he would leave in such a hurry and in the middle of the night. Perhaps he made a lot of noise because he thought he'd wake her to tell her. Nevertheless, he could have left a note.

Perhaps he didn't think she was home, because her car wasn't sitting out front. Beth placed half the bacon she'd cooked into a container and dished up her own breakfast, her mind on what to wear to take Ricky to chapel.

Meg always said people should dress in dark clothes for chapel, as if God didn't want to see any bright colours or clothes depicting the flowers He'd created. For Ricky's sake, she'd wear her cream linen suit, the jacket patterned with soft rose and green flowers. Let's see what Powell-Pritchard makes of that, she thought as she shampooed the stained patch of carpet in Tom's bedroom. Beth ironed Gwyn's handkerchiefs, folding them to take over later. She didn't have to and realised she sought an excuse to speak to him. About nothing in particular, just to see him.

But he's a policeman, a small voice cautioned.

Dilys arrived at ten minutes to eleven with Ricky. She'd dressed the boy in a suit, like a miniature man.

"Oh, he's beautiful, Dil." Beth bent to kiss Ricky's cheek.

"Mam says you're my godmother," he said. "Will you teach me to read, like Aunty Megan?"

"I will," Beth vowed. "I'll be here to help you whenever you want."

"Don't make promises you can't keep, Beth," Dilys said quietly and Ricky looked from one to the other. "Aunty Beth might not be staying in Derwen much longer," she said to her son. To Beth, she said, "Isn't that what you've been telling people? You don't know if you'll be staying on."

"I haven't made up my mind." Beth placed her hand on the boy's rounded cheek. "But if I do go away, I'll be back for visits." She took Ricky's hand and they walked up the hill towards the chapel.

Powell-Pritchard stood at the chapel door. With a smirk on his face, he stared at Beth as she led Ricky up the path between the graves. "I hate that bloody man," she muttered under her breath.

"Language," Dilys hissed, glance swivelling towards Ricky.

"Good morning, Richard. I'm glad you are here on time." Reverend Powell-Pritchard shot Beth a meaningful glance.

"We'll be out here waiting for you," Dilys said as she bent to straighten Ricky's tie.

"And Aunty Beth, too?" he asked.

"I'll be here," Beth promised. She watched Ricky enter the building before she collared the minister. "If you ever treat him the way you treated me, I'll make sure you won't ever do it again to anyone."

Tight lipped, Reverend Powell-Pritchard turned without a word and entered the chapel.

Dilys smothered a smile as they made their way around the side of the chapel. "You don't forget a thing, do you, Beth?"

"I'll never forget the way that man blighted my life." Their steps led them to Meg's grave where someone had replaced the wild flowers. "Who put up the gravestone, Dil?"

"Mostly it was Gwyn. He held a collection for the funeral and headstone. Big friends with your aunty, he was. People around here knew if they couldn't find Gwyn in the police station, he'd be visiting Megan. They got on like a house on fire."

"He told me they were friends."

"So what are you going to do? Stay or go?"

"I haven't made up my mind."

"If you left, where would you go, back to London?"

She wouldn't dare. Even though Jerry and his chums were in prison, they wouldn't be there forever and there might be others involved. Wherever she went, she'd have to lie low.

"Beth?"

Beth looked up and found Dilys smiling at her.

"You were miles away, girl. Thinking of London?"

"In a way." If—when—she left here, she dare not let Dil know where she was going. It was safer that way on the chance Jerry traced her to Derwen Bay.

"Megan said you had a shop. Is somebody looking after it for you?"

"I sold it. That's why the solicitor had trouble finding me when Aunty Meg died. I'd moved out." She took a deep breath. "Dil, with incidents like the prowler the other night I'm sure somebody murdered Aunty Meg." The word made her flinch.

"I wish I could set your mind at rest about the way she died. I don't think anything was stolen from the house that I could tell when I went there with Gwyn."

"You went to Derwen House?"

"Because we'd played there as children, Gwyn and the solicitor, and the Sergeant too, thought I would notice if anything was taken."

"But nothing had?"

"No. The place was upside down. Gwyn said it looked like somebody had rummaged through everything, but the Sergeant pooh-poohed that idea. He tore a strip off Gwyn for even thinking such a thing."

"Did it look to you as though somebody had been searching for something?"

"Yes. Megan always kept the place like a new pin. When we went there, some drawers were open and their contents rumpled. Even her clothes brought out of the wardrobe and thrown on the bed."

"The place was tidy when I arrived, so who—?"

"Gwyn and I put everything away when the police investigation finished."

"So they did investigate."

"Yes. We had police all over the place."

"But they decided it was an accidental death."

"There was a question of suicide, but everyone who knew Megan put a stop to that. She wasn't the type."

"No, she wasn't." Meg was feisty. What if she'd been in a fight with someone? Would that account for the bruises and cuts, and the ragged nails? Had she disturbed a burglar? Whoever rummaged through Derwen House was still looking for something. What could it be and where would Meg have hidden it?

Briefly, Beth wondered about the money hidden under the floorboard. Meg was cautious. She was unlikely to tell anyone she had that much money in the house, and who would know if she planned a holiday on the continent? "Did Aunty Meg mention going abroad on holiday?"

"Megan? Going abroad? You know she'd never go farther than Carmarthen."

"I found French money in the house. She didn't mention a holiday in France to you?"

"She'd never go there. Megan told us about an old war when the French tried to land somewhere on this coast, Fishguard, I think, and the British army was too far away to get there in time to stop the invasion. The village women put on their red cloaks and marched down the hill. The French thought it was the Redcoats and sailed away. No, she'd never go to France."

"I remember her telling me that story."

"Perhaps a guest paid her in francs and she hadn't taken it to the bank yet."

It was too large an amount of money for it to be payment for staying at the guesthouse. And— "Dil? Have you noticed a strange flash of light in the bay at night?"

"What sort of light?"

"I'm not sure. I've seen it twice now. It comes out from the cave."

Dilys chuckled. "I remember when you swore there were vampire bats in the cave. Is this another of your fantasies?"

"I only said that about the bats to keep Emrys from following us. This is real, Dil. It's only one flash each time. Very bright, it comes horizontally from the cave and hits the Witch."

"I've never seen it and no one has mentioned it in the bar. What time did you see this light?"

"Both times about one o'clock in the morning. The first time, I thought I'd imagined it, but I saw it again last night."

"It was probably the light from a yacht."

"Not coming from inside the cave; at high tide there wouldn't leave enough ceiling for a yacht to enter."

"A boat, then."

"Why would a boat go into the cave? Anyway, I went down to the beach last night after I'd seen the light, and the fishing boats were on the sand next to the police launch and your dad's speedboat."

"Well then, I have no idea what you saw." Dilys looked over her shoulder. "They're coming out."

Suitably chastened for the rest of the week, Ricky looked around and spotted them. He began running in their direction until a stern voice called, "Richard!" and he slowed.

"He hasn't changed, has he," Beth said, inclining her head towards the minister.

"Neither have you, Beth," Dilys pointed out as she bent to hug her son.

CHAPTER SIXTEEN

Gwyn picked up Linda soon after ten in the morning. At her request, they went along the coast to Aberystwyth. Surprised she had made a suggestion, Gwyn was happy to agree. With a laugh, he said, "Just what I need, another day at the seaside."

"You don't mind, do you?" she said quickly. "We can go somewhere else."

"Aberystwyth is fine," he answered. "There's a little pub on the way. We can stop to have lunch and then walk it off on the beach."

"If you like."

Gwyn glanced sideways at her. Linda was always happy to fall in with any plans he made. He doubted Bethan would be so amenable. The only thing Linda was adamant about was meat. She refused to eat it, although she made no sign of disapproval when Gwyn tucked into the roast beef he ordered for lunch.

They'd been dating for four months after Linda bumped into him as she left the post office. She grabbed for his hand as she fell. She wrenched her ankle and Gwyn carried her to the police station to bandage it before driving her back to the health farm. Linda was pliable, eager to please, as if she had no will of her own. Sometimes it rubbed him the wrong way and he wanted to shout at her to voice an opinion. He never did because he imagined she would burst into tears. Gwyn had little patience for women who cried at the drop of a hat.

He hadn't felt that way when Bethan cried, but Bethan had good reason. Although he'd never admit it to a soul, when Megan died he shed a few tears himself in private.

Who made the rule that men couldn't cry anyway? Gwyn remembered an incident during his time in Llanelli, after combing the area for the baby, they found . . . Even the sergeant, a twenty-year veteran, had turned away, a handkerchief pressed to his face. A seasoned officer, things like that would always bring an emotional reaction. Any man who said it didn't was a liar in Gwyn's book.

They strolled along the front at Aberystwyth and he puffed with pride as the men they passed ogled Linda. Once or twice, Gwyn glanced back and found men had stopped and turned to watch her. Lovely, tall and slim, her dress floated about her long legs like a cloud as she strolled at his side in shoes with, what seemed to him, impossibly high heels. How she could walk in them was a mystery but he liked the way she leaned on his arm when the ground grew rough.

He pondered what Bethan was doing. Gwyn tried to talk to her on Saturday, to see if she'd checked Tom's room for another pair of shoes, but she was gone all day. When he passed the house on his last beat of the day the car wasn't outside as he expected. He'd driven by that morning, taking the long way around to pick up Linda, but again the car wasn't there. He wondered if she'd get back in time to take little Ricky to Sunday school and have lunch at the Anchor. She'd be safe until then, but what about the afternoon? Would she work in the garden where Ishmael would be able see her? Would Ishmael keep his promise and offer help?

If Linda noticed his silence, she said nothing. Gwyn took advantage and let his thoughts wander but, after a while, he began to feel guilty. "Fancy an ice cream?" he asked.

"Not for me. But you go ahead."

"I can leave it. Maybe have one later, eh?"

Linda nodded. "If you like."

Gwyn sighed. Linda wouldn't stroll along eating an ice cream cone. Bethan would probably order a double scoop with any side orders that came with it. "I think I will go for that ice cream. Are you sure you don't want anything?"

Linda shook her head. "I'll wait here."

Gwyn lined up with the children and observed how the men around paused to admire Linda. She faced the sea, one hand raised to hold her sun hat in place as the breeze whipped her dress against her body. Even the old codger with the flat cap and cane was watching her. Aware he was the envy of every man, Gwyn thought she was too nice, too accommodating. Even in bed, he didn't know if he pleased her.

As he turned from the ice cream van with the cone in his hand, two lads stopped beside Linda. No more than eighteen or nineteen, they obviously fancied their chances. One of them said something and Linda turned, fury on her face as she snapped an answer. Gwyn grinned. There might be hope for them yet, if he found out what the lad said to get sparks flying. When he reached her, the same serene, compliant woman smiled at him.

"Did those lads bother you?" he asked innocently.

"Those children? Oh, no."

Children! She was twenty-seven last March. Gwyn ate his ice cream as they continued along the promenade and Linda held her skirts away from any drips that might fall. He finished and was wiping his hands when they came level with a bookshop. "Mind if we go in and have a gander?" he asked, knowing her answer would be *if you like*.

"If you like."

Linda veered to a display of fashion magazines and Gwyn headed deeper into the shop. He'd been in here loads of times to root through the used-books section. He'd made a few rare finds in the past, books no longer in circulation.

The owner of the shop smiled to show he remembered Gwyn. "How are you today, Mr Thomas?"

"I'm well, Mr Evans. Any books I should be looking at?"

"Funny you should come in today. I had a couple of boxes delivered from an estate two days ago and I was just pricing them. It's history you are interested in, yes?"

"Local history." Gwyn followed Edwin Evans to a desk at the back of the shop.

"This should interest you. It's about New Quay. Only a few miles along the coast, but I glanced through it and learned a lot."

"I've been there. A quaint little place." Gwyn leafed through a few pages. "I'll take it."

"You'll remember that Dylan Thomas hated the place, and no doubt you'll recall what he called it in *Under Milk Wood*: Llareggub."

"Llareggub?"

"Spell it backwards," Edwin said with a chuckle as he headed for the till. "Now then, seeing as you're a regular customer, I'll only charge you two pounds."

"And if I wasn't a regular?" Gwyn handed over the coins.

"One pound twenty. Do you want a bag?"

Gwyn shook his head and glanced at Linda. "Is there anything you want to buy?"

"No thank you." She stood beside the display of magazines with an air of one who would wait there all day if Gwyn had a mind to stay longer.

When they emerged from the bookshop and continued their walk, Gwyn read bits and pieces on the history of New Quay. "They used to build ships in New Quay back in the eighteen hundreds."

"Oh?" Linda eyed shop windows they passed.

"And I'd forgotten about the dolphins. We'll have to go to see them one of these days."

"If you like."

"And . . ." Gwyn turned a page. What he read brought him to a halt.

Smugglers. New Quay had been a centre for smuggling contraband back in the 1800s. He knew the harbour. It was secluded and ideal for smugglers to get in and out, much like Derwen Bay. The headlands curved in either side of the entrance and placed much of the bay in darkness at night. Anyone bent on smuggling would hardly show lights, and a rowboat could easily creep ashore on dark water.

Linda moved on a few paces. She stopped and came back. "Gwyn?"

Gwyn dragged his attention back to Linda. The glint of anger in her eyes disappeared when he looked at her. "Oh, sorry."

"You were miles away." The indulgent smile on her lips didn't quite reach her eyes.

"Just thinking."

"Thomas!" A voice boomed from behind him. "Is that you, Thomas?"

Gwyn turned and quailed. Sergeant Dorothy Driscoll. Unmistakably a police officer even with her broad shoulders covered in denim. He waited as she strode towards him. A man half her size and inches shorter trotted to keep up with her.

"Having a day out?" Dorothy spared a quick glance at Linda. "I need to talk to you."

"Yes?"

Dorothy caught his arm and tugged him to the edge of the paving. "Something I don't want the stick insect to hear."

Gwyn glanced at Linda and saw her blush. "There's no need to be rude."

"Pish-tosh. Listen! That girl you asked me to check on. Bethan Louise Davies. There's something fishy there."

"How do you mean?"

"It was something I didn't want to put in the report, see. Something I wasn't sure how."

"Get on with it."

"The information I sent you, about her selling the boutique and taking the money out of the bank, it was all I could find."

"But you think there was more?"

"There's a file on her, but it's restricted. I couldn't gain access and word came from higher up that I was to leave it alone. A right bollocking I got because of you, Thomas. You owe me. And that's not all. After I checked the planning permission you wanted, the Chief Inspector questioned me about it and told me to channel any future requests through him. Hasn't he been in touch?"

Gwyn shook his head.

"What the bloody hell is going on in that patch of yours?"

"I don't know, Sarge."

"Then bloody find out!"

Gwyn nodded and returned to where Linda had her back to Dorothy Driscoll's man friend.

"You owe me, Thomas. Don't forget!" The booming voice echoed from the shop windows and bounced along the pavement at Gwyn's heels.

"Who was that horrible woman, Gwyn?" Linda asked.

"She's a sergeant in HQ."

"I didn't like her."

"Few people do."

Gwyn urged Linda to enter a shop to try on a dress she saw in the window. He took the opportunity to be alone to think, and waited outside, staring blindly at the horizon.

Why would there be a file on Bethan and why would it be restricted? He remembered the first morning he met her. She'd been afraid of something other than the intruder in the house, and been wary of the uniform. What in her past made her nervous? She'd taken her money out of the bank in cash. A person would do that if she wanted to disappear; if she didn't want anyone to find her.

Then there was Reginald Plews and the Planning Permission. Why would the Chief Inspector be interested? His superior hadn't been in touch, so perhaps Gwyn wasn't supposed to know they would channel future requests for information. The odds of him meeting the sergeant in Aberystwyth were astronomical so there would be little chance of Gwyn finding out.

Someone was keeping things from him. He was the man on the spot and he had a right to know. Well, he intended to go to HQ with the documents from Megan's safe so he'd ask. He'd make an appointment with the Chief Inspector and find out. Whatever it was, it might give him a lead on what was going on in Derwen Bay.

Was Bethan involved? Had her arrival been a coincidence? He'd seen her up on the north cliff the morning after she arrived. Had she been to see Reginald Plews? Was there a connection? And why was Tom Rowland back again?

Linda emerged from the shop with the dress in a bag, the drawn look fixed on her face by Sergeant Driscoll's comment gone. "Let's take the train to the top of the cliff," she suggested as she took his arm.

Gwyn endured. They took the train and admired the view; they did more window-shopping and stood for a while to watch children playing in the amusement park. They walked around the ruined castle and stopped for coffee at a French restaurant. On their way back to the car, it grew cold and clouds swept in over the sea. Gwyn viewed them with delight. "I think it's going to rain. We'd better make a run for it."

She ran with him, heels clicking like castanets on the paving, one hand holding the broad-brimmed sun hat in place. He opened the car door for her and she swept in like a duchess.

"That was close," Gwyn said as he took his place behind the wheel and rain spattered the windshield.

"Yes," Linda agreed.

They stopped at one of the hotels for dinner and Linda ordered trout. Not wanting to cause a rift with the evening looming, Gwyn ordered the same with a bottle of wine the waiter recommended. He was a beer man but Linda enjoyed wine. He ate the cherries-in-brandy Linda ordered for dessert and paid the bill without any qualms. On the drive back, Linda laid her head on his shoulder.

"It's been a lovely day, Gwyn. Don't you agree?"

"Yes," he replied, concentrating on his driving. Was it worth it for an hour in bed?

As he drove down the north road to the Bay, he slowed as he passed the entrance to Beach Road. There was no car parked in front of Derwen House.

CHAPTER SEVENTEEN

On her way back after lunch with Dil and Ricky, Beth saw Daniel Jones inside his shop. Although closed on Sundays, except during visitor season, the doors were glass. She tapped and motioned to him to open them for her.

"We're closed," he mouthed.

"I'm not here to shop; I came to talk to you."

"What about?" He opened the door for her to enter and then closed and locked it behind her.

"What you said the other day—about someone murdering Aunty Meg. Why did you say that?"

He moved behind the counter, as if to place safe distance between them, and gave his attention to a speck of dust. "It's what a lot of people said when they found her."

"Why?" she asked, aware he was the biggest gossip in the village.

He looked up at her. "Your aunty wasn't silly. She wouldn't go out in a storm that bad no more than any of us would."

"I agree. But there must be something else to make people say it was murder."

"Well . . . See, Megan used to walk around the village at night, and sometimes on the beach."

"I remember. I used to go with her."

"Then she stopped."

Beth thought for a moment. "Why would that lead anyone to consider murder? She may not have been feeling well. Or she may have been too tired."

"That wouldn't make her afraid."

"Afraid?"

"You could see it in her eyes. Always looking over her shoulder, she was; always in a hurry to get home. Didn't even go to choir practice, and Patty Pen Tir said she didn't go to the Women's Institute either."

"Do you have any idea what frightened her?"

Daniel shook his head. "She never said anything, not even to Eleri-the-School, and you remember what good friends they were."

Eleri! She'd forgotten Meg's friend. "She lives on Peartree Lane, doesn't she?"

"The third cottage: the one with the wishing well in the front garden."

"If something frightened Aunty Meg, why didn't she go to the police?"

"I can't answer that, Bethan. Perhaps she did. Gwyn Thomas would be able to tell you."

When Beth talked to Gwyn, he said nothing of Meg being afraid. "I'd better go to ask him."

"He's not there today. I saw him drive by earlier."

"Then I'll talk to Eleri." Beth moved towards the door.

Daniel came out from behind the counter. "Are you investigating Megan's death, then?"

Beth paused. "Yes, I suppose I am."

As she walked past Derwen House on her way to Peartree Lane, a motorbike erupted from Mrs William's garden and roared away. Beth turned to watch as the boy with spiked, purple-tipped hair screamed the bike around the corner by the public toilets. It sounded like the bike that disturbed her the night she first noticed the flash of light from the cave.

Pixies painted in bright colours peeped from cascading trails of roses and surrounded the mock wishing well in front of Eleri's cottage. She stayed clear of the thorns threatening to take over the path and made her way to the front door. Half hidden behind climbing roses, it came as something of a surprise. The oak surface was barely discernible beneath what appeared to be a doorway cut into a tree trunk. As a child, she'd seen something similar in one of the *Wind in the Willows* books. She couldn't find a doorbell or knocker but a length of rope hung from the thatch. Beth tugged it and a school bell clanged somewhere in the depths of the house.

She looked around as she waited. What she had first taken to be flowers planted against the whitewashed walls turned out to be a painted backdrop for real flowers. From the depths of her memory, Beth dragged up an image of the woman who sometimes came to spend an evening with Meg, and she remembered Meg's words: "Artist, Eleri is."

When no one answered, Beth trotted around the side of the cottage to the back door. As she prepared to knock at what looked to be a dungeon door, a man shouted from over the hedge.

"She's up at the church."

Beth looked around but saw no one. "Thank you," she called in reply. The church was in Upper Derwen, a fair hike up the hill but Beth had nothing else to do on a Sunday afternoon.

Beth recognised the elderly woman standing beside Reverend Howell Hopkins: Eleri-the-School. Grey hair tied at the nape of her neck, even on Sunday she ignored convention and dressed in jeans and an oversized sweater. Eleri and Meg spent little time together during summer when the guesthouse was full, but Meg talked about her quite a bit, laughing over what they said and did during the winter.

As Beth approached, Eleri gave a small cry and ran to her.

"Bethan? Is it you? They told me you were back."

"It's me." Beth returned the woman's hug.

"It's a sad time for you, my girl; for all of us." Eleri slipped her arm through Beth's. "Come and meet the professor and his wife."

With a shy smile, the vicar mumbled a greeting when Eleri introduced them. "And these are Professor Lowndes and his wife, from Aberystwyth University. They've been staying at Ty Goch."

Beth nodded to the couple. "I'm sorry to interrupt . . ."

"We're just finished." Professor Lowndes placed an arm around his wife's shoulders. "I'm sorry we can't spare time to examine your work today but we'll be in touch, Mrs Edwards."

"I'm sure they will be," Howell Hopkins said as the couple left. "Nobody could do a better job than you, Mrs Edwards."

"I hope you're right, Mr Hopkins, for it would help out with the pension. Now, I'm going to take this girl home for a cup of tea." With that, Eleri drew Beth away.

"What are you going to do for them, Mrs Edwards?" Bethan asked when they were clear of the graveyard.

"Please call me Eleri. Professor Lowndes is an archaeologist. He and his team will be excavating alongside the well in Caradog Bowen's field. Howell heard them mention they would need to bring in an artist to sketch and record the finds so he told them about me. I was in church and so were they. We've just had our first meeting."

"I'm pleased for you. Aunty Meg always said you were a great artist."

"They might not hire me. I must show them examples of my work first but they had to rush back to Aberystwyth for a grandson's christening. They won't be back for a couple of weeks, so it will mean a trip to Aberystwyth for me. Ned-the-Milk will probably give me a lift there when he's done his rounds and I'll have to stay there overnight and come back with him the next morning."

"My car is here and I can drive you," Beth said impulsively.

"Would you? I'd pay for your petrol of course."

"The only thing is my car is in for repairs. Emrys said he'd get it ready for me by tomorrow so you make the arrangements and let me know."

"Well, that's a load off my mind. I didn't fancy going all that way in Ned's lorry with all the bottles rattling away at the back."

"Then it's settled."

"Thank you. Now, how about you; how long are you going to stay? Will you come to live in Derwen House?"

"I haven't decided yet." How could she tell someone who'd lived in Derwen all her life that it wasn't everybody's idea of heaven? "I expect I'll be here for a little while."

"Then you must visit me often. We'll set up a regular day and get together."

Beth agreed, noticing how Eleri clung to her arm as they navigated around a slippery patch. "I came to ask . . ."

"Yes?"

"It's awkward . . . I . . ."

"Out with it, girl; there isn't much you can't ask me. Mind, I don't promise to have the answer." They reached Eleri's cottage and she led the way to the front door.

"It's about Aunty Meg. Daniel-the-Shop said somebody murdered her."

Eleri dropped her key and Beth bent to retrieve it. When she looked up, Eleri's face was white as the walls of her cottage.

"Is it true?" Beth asked.

"You'd better come in." Eleri unlocked the door and headed towards the back. A white cat came to rub at Bethan's legs as she followed.

"From your reaction, I'd say the rumour has some truth." Beth stood uncertainly in the kitchen doorway.

"Many unanswered questions surrounded Megan's passing." Eleri busied herself filling the kettle and taking out cups and saucers. She kept her back to Beth.

"Gwyn Thomas said the verdict was accidental death. He didn't tell me there'd been any dispute about it."

"Gwyn nearly lost his job."

"So he didn't think it was an accident?"

Eleri faced Beth. "None of us accepted the verdict, but it was better than the alternative of suicide."

"Aunty Meg would never kill herself."

"I know that. Gwyn knows that. Are you going to look into the matter?"

"Yes."

Eleri sank into a chair. "I'm not sure what good will come of it, but I'll help you all I can. Mind, Bethan, you'll have to be careful."

"What do you mean?"

"Sit down, girl. Now, funny things have been going on in this village what with Megan's death and people disappearing. I suppose Dilys told you about Ricky's father, Mike. Well, he's one of the ones who went missing."

The cat jumped onto Beth's lap and she stroked it. "Dil said he ran away when she told him she was pregnant."

Eleri shook her head. "I talked to him the night they say he ran away. He lodged two doors up with Mrs Jones, Daniel's mother. I'd been for a visit with Megan, and Mike was on his way home from seeing Dilys, so we walked up the road together. He was that happy. He told me he had a secret; he was going to marry Dilys. I told him they were very young to think of getting married but he said there was a baby on the way. I wasn't to tell anyone because they hadn't mentioned it to her father yet. So, Mike did not intend to run away."

"Did you tell Dil?"

"Of course, but she wouldn't listen; said I was making up stories to make her feel better."

"Who else is missing?"

"Ardwy Williams. He lived in Upper Derwen so you might not have known him. His brother, Ianto, lives next door to you. Widower, Ardwy was, so when he disappeared his boy, Sammy, went to live with his uncle and aunt."

"The boy with the motorbike."

"That's right."

"Did Ardwy and Mike go away at the same time?"

"Near as I can remember, it was a couple of weeks apart. Ardwy liked to do a bit of poaching. He used to go out after dark and catch a few rabbits for the pot and to make a bit of money selling them here and there. Nobody knew where he'd gone. A few of us were afraid he'd fallen somewhere in the hills and broken a leg. Poor Sammy was in tears, sobbing his little heart out. They got up a search party and scoured the hills, but they never found Ardwy. Sammy was about thirteen at the time."

"So, two people have vanished."

"Four." The kettle began to whistle and Eleri rose to make the tea. "A woman artist came here about three years ago. She rented Ty Goch for the summer. Wilhelmina Tingle, her name was. Funny name but one easily remembered. Because we were both artists, we talked about our work a few times. When she wasn't around anymore, we assumed she'd gone home." Eleri carried the teapot to the table and poured the tea. "Weeks later two people from London came looking for her because she'd never arrived home."

"Someone could have attacked her on her way to London," Beth pointed out as the cat deserted her in favour of Eleri's more familiar lap.

"But she wouldn't leave all her clothes and paintings at Ty Goch." Eleri eyed Beth through the steam rising from her cup. "Then Megan went missing."

"What? Gwyn didn't tell me that."

"She was missing for at least a day before we found her body. As I said, Bethan, you'll have to be careful. Whoever is involved might come after you if they hear you're checking into things."

"Do you think the missing people are connected with Aunty Meg's death?"

"I'm not sure what to think. This is a small place for so many things to happen."

"I heard the tide caught her on the beach."

Eleri made a derisory huffing sound. "I knew Megan for forty years, ever since I came to teach here, and I never saw her out during a storm. There was a storm to beat all storms that night. Patty Pen Tir had half the slates blown off her roof and I had leaks all over the place. Snowy and I had buckets everywhere, didn't we, Snow?" Eleri stroked the cat. "Megan would no more have gone out in that kind of weather than Snowy would go for a swim."

"Gwyn Thomas said she was covered in cuts and bruises, and there were blows to her head. The coroner said she'd been thrown against the rocks by the waves."

"Blows to the head can be caused by other things." Again, Eleri looked hard at Beth. "Don't be misled by commonly drawn conclusions."

"Do you think someone murdered her?"

"I don't know and that's the truth. What will you do now?"

"Ishmael found Aunty Meg and I've questioned him. I'm sure he knows something but I haven't been able to get it out of him yet. I don't know whom else to talk to."

"Gwyn Thomas is the obvious choice."

"I've spoken to him but it didn't help."

"Talk to him again. He and Megan were very close and he didn't like the verdict they pronounced. Gwyn's a policeman so he might not be willing to open up. You've got to gain his trust, girl."

"But he was clear about it. He said it was death by misadventure."

"That doesn't mean he accepts it. You go to him again. You tell him what I've said. Tell him about the others disappearing, two of them not long after the time he came here. If he hasn't made the connection yet, you make him. Moreover, you be very careful to whom you talk. If some people know you're checking into things, they'll spread it around. That's the last thing you need if you want to stay safe."

* * *

Aware people walked past the front of the house on their way to chapel, and anxious not to antagonise those she might have to question about Meg's death, Beth concentrated on the back garden. She was clearing the weeds around the herb patch when Ishmael arrived. Without a word, he got the fork from the shed and began turning over the vegetable patch.

"Do you have anything to tell me?" she asked.

"No." he answered.

It was the only conversation between them until Beth brought two glasses of iced tea and he thanked her. When she went in to prepare the evening meal, through the window she saw him digging away. At one point, he used the outside toilet before getting out a rake to level the patch he'd dug. It wasn't too late in the season to plant something fast growing like lettuce. Beth caught herself planning the garden and shook the thought away. She didn't intend to be here long enough to harvest what she planted.

When the meal was ready, Beth invited Ishmael in. He came nervously, flat cap turned around and around in his hands. He scrubbed his feet on the cocoa mat outside the back porch before stepping inside the house.

"Tom isn't here," Beth said. "I thought we'd eat in the kitchen to save work." She hadn't spared Tom a thought all day. Well, she'd wanted him out and now he was.

Ishmael held out his hands to show how grubby they were.

"There's soap by the sink and I'll get you a towel."

Back in the kitchen, she handed Ishmael the towel and began dishing up. "I hope you like chicken."

"Yes. Thank you." He stood beside the table and sat when she indicated a chair. "This is kind of you."

Beth shrugged. "You helped me with the garden. How much do I owe you, by the way?"

"This is sufficient."

"No, it isn't. I insist on paying you."

"I have no use for money."

Beth was on the point of saying everyone needed money but Ishmael was different. She reached for the bowl of vegetables and saw him bend his head over his hands. Contrite, she did the same. The only grace she remembered was the silly one she'd said as a child that made Meg laugh. *Thank you for the food we eat. Don't let us drop it on our feet.* When she looked up, Ishmael had taken the napkin to spread over his knees.

"Help yourself." She passed him the platter of meat. He took each portion onto his plate and used his knife and fork with unexpected refinement. What an odd man he was. So different from the way she'd imagined him. They ate in silence until she asked if he would like tea or coffee.

"I would enjoy coffee, if it is not too much trouble. May I help clear the table?"

"If you wish." Beth filled the kettle and took mugs from the cupboard as he moved behind her with the dishes.

"Did you say Tom would not be in for dinner?" Ishmael asked as he returned to his chair.

"He's gone." Beth informed him. "I heard him rummaging about in the early hours. When I went to call him this morning, I found he had left and taken his things." Her eyes strayed to the tube of paint lying on its bed of toilet paper. She mustn't forget to put it in the bin.

"I trust he remitted his board."

"That's the strange part. He paid for a month in advance, to Aunty Meg." Beth carried the mugs to the table and sat. "Did you know Tom?"

"He asked to paint me once but I refused." Ishmael drank his coffee quickly. "I believe it will rain later. I would like to finish out there, if you have no objection."

Beth shook her head. "Go ahead. If you won't let me give you money, I shall find another way of paying you."

"It is not necessary. Thank you for an excellent meal."

Beth cleaned up the kitchen and saw him working away like a demon. Without his help, it would have taken her weeks to get the back garden into shape, even if she could do the heavy digging. Perhaps she would get him a couple of shirts because the one he wore was threadbare and faded. Not in bright colours, though. The one Dil gave him all those years ago had been bright red chequered with yellow but they'd never seen him in it. Beth had the feeling Ishmael liked to fade into the background.

The phone rang in the hallway and she hesitated before answering it, but Jerry and his friends were in custody or in prison. It was Emrys letting her know one of the brake lines had worked loose. He wanted to replace it before he handed the car over, but she could pick it up the following day, any time after ten.

When Beth went back outside, Ishmael had left. It started to rain while she gathered up the tools to take back to the shed. A cloudburst drenched her before she got under cover. She shivered and took a deep breath. She'd forgotten how fast the storms came on and how violent they could be in Derwen.

At the other end, close to the worktable, a steady drip drew her attention. Meg had never bothered to find the hole in the roof and kept a bucket there to catch what fell. Next to it were the mounds of earth Gwyn had tipped out of the pots. Beth decided to put the pots back on the worktable and sweep up the soil.

Beth groped for the brush Meg kept behind the door, brought it out and swept the floor clean, emptying the earth into a container under the worktable. When she half-closed the door to replace the brush she found Meg's slicker and wellingtons, just what she needed to battle the torrent hammering against the shed. She exchanged her shoes for the boots and held the slicker over her head. Shoes under her arm, she stepped outside, closed the shed door, and strolled to the house through the pummelling rain.

She showered for the second time that day, the water from the showerhead in unison with the rain lashing the window. People would be racing from the beach, some with newspapers over their heads and the women holding their skirts tight against their knees. They'd parade in skimpy swimsuits but they would be mortified if their skirts blew up an inch.

Beth returned to her room and put on fresh jeans and a sweater. From the window, she could barely see the Witch behind the blanket of rain. The soft glow surrounding the houses in the row told her the streetlights had come on down on the Front. Even mechanical things recognised how dark it had grown.

Her raincoat was a fashionable gabardine; it wouldn't stand up to the wind-whipped rain along the sea front and her car was still in the garage. In the back porch, she slid her feet into Meg's wellingtons and buttoned the slicker to her neck. As she drew the matching fisherman's hat from a pocket, a piece of paper fell out. Beth picked it up and unfolded it; another French banknote, like the ones hidden upstairs. She wondered why Meg would keep one in her pocket, then placed the money beside the tube of paint before going in search of a plastic bag for Gwyn's handkerchiefs. After locking the back door and windows, she left.

Beth got as far as the garden wall when she stopped. She looked down. She was wearing Meg's boots and slicker. If Meg went out in the storm that night, why was her rainwear in the shed?

Beth ran. Bent against the rain, she raced along the deserted Front; one hand holding the fisherman's hat to her head, because the wind insisted she should wear it lop-sided. Around the corner, she bolted up the steps to the police station door only to find it locked. Around the side, she found another door next to a lighted window with the curtains closed. She banged on the door with her fist. "Gwyn!"

It was a few moments before Gwyn opened the door, his shirt unbuttoned and his hair rumpled. "Bethan?"

"I've got something to tell you and these are yours." She fumbled in her pocket and held out the handkerchiefs. Behind Gwyn, a woman dressed in a man's robe peered at her.

Beth sized up the situation and felt her face redden. "I'm sorry. I didn't realise you had company. I'll talk to you another time." She turned away and flew around the corner, hearing Gwyn call after her.

How stupid! How silly to think a man like that wouldn't have a woman around. She'd made a fool of herself by going there, a silly, stupid mistake. Beth faltered when she reached the Anchor but company wasn't what she needed. She wanted to run home and hide under the covers. Silly, silly, silly.

P L Crompton

CHAPTER EIGHTEEN

Beth locked the door and returned the slicker and wellingtons to the back porch. Still embarrassed, she plonked onto the sofa in front of the television and watched without seeing. Sometime later, the doorbell rang. She checked her watch: ten-fifteen. Who could be calling at this time of night? She crept to the window to peep through the curtains and saw Gwyn on the doorstep. "Go away!" she shouted.

"Let me in, Bethan," he called above the wind and rain.

"I don't want to see you."

Gwyn thumped the door. "This is the police!"

"Bugger off!"

There was a second's pause before he called back. "What did you say?"

"You heard!" Beth turned up the volume on the television, went back to the sofa, and concentrated on the political debate on the screen.

"They say loud noises can make you deaf and blind," Gwyn said from the sitting room doorway.

Beth leapt to her feet. "How did you get in here?"

"Via the front door."

"You can't have. I locked it."

"The solicitor gave me a key so I could keep an eye on the house."

"I want it back now!" Beth held out her hand.

Gwyn walked across the room to lower the volume on the TV before dropping onto a chair beside the fireplace.

"Megan's will is still in probate so I will retain the key until everything is settled."

"That doesn't mean you can charge in here when I told you to go away."

"You came to talk to me earlier. You said you had something to tell me."

"Tomorrow."

"No, you will tell me now," he said firmly. "Megan called me the night she died and said she had something to tell me. The storm held me up and when I came, she wasn't here. I don't want history repeating itself."

"That was the night there was a storm like this one."

"Worse than this, it brought thunder and lightning, too."

"Would she have gone out in it without wellingtons and a slicker?"

Gwyn flinched as if she'd struck him. "The slicker you were wearing earlier?"

"And the boots. We took the same size."

Gwyn scrubbed at his face with his hands. "That's the missing piece."

"They found Aunty Meg wearing only a cardigan, right? Didn't it occur to any of you that she wouldn't have gone out in a storm dressed like that?"

"It's the simplest things. It's always the simplest clues that are overlooked."

"So where do you go from here? Do you treat it as murder now?"

"I'll be in Carmarthen tomorrow; I'll speak to the Sergeant then. If he won't listen, I'll talk to the Chief Inspector."

"I need a drink." Beth walked to a cupboard beside the fireplace and grabbed a bottle of sherry. "I wouldn't normally drink this, but I don't think there's anything else in the house." In the kitchen, she found wine glasses. The distraught look on Gwyn's face as he followed her into the room prompted her to ask, "Do you want one?"

He nodded. "I've let Megan down. Why didn't I realise she wouldn't be out there without a coat and boots? What a damn fool I've been!"

"I'll second that." Beth handed him his drink. "You said Meg was covered in bruises and cuts. She might have been struggling with somebody. She might have put up a fight to save her life."

"That thought occurred to me, too, but the experts said she'd been thrown against the Witch several times by the tide." Gwyn gulped the sherry and emptied the glass.

Beth refilled it. "Were there scrapings taken from under her nails?"

Gwyn paused in taking a drink from his second glass of sherry. "Forensics checked but found nothing."

"You also checked, didn't you?"

"The case was out of my hands."

"Stop making excuses for your inefficiency!"

"I'm not, I'm telling you—"

"How you bungled my aunt's murder investigation?"

"I'm telling you the top brass come in and take over if murder is suspected."

"So you had no say in how far this was investigated."

"I had nothing to go on."

"But now you do. You're nothing but a village bobby, aren't you, Gwyn?"

"Don't lash me, Bethan. I feel bad enough as it is."

"Lash you? If I had my way I'd kick you and your blasted top brass all the way from here to Fishguard." Beth's voice rose, shrill and accusing. "How many months is it since Aunty Meg's death? How long has her murderer walked around free?"

"Don't."

The agony Gwyn felt was in his voice and Beth didn't know if there were tears on his face or just rain dripping from his hair.

"Aunty Meg was a fighter. If you'd followed it up right away, you might have found someone with bruised knuckles or a scratched face. By now they've healed, and you haven't got a hope in hell of finding him."

"Him?"

"No woman would have got the better of her." Beth took her first gulp of the sherry. It stung her throat and her eyes burned. She went to stand beside the sink, her back to him. "Damn you, Gwyn. Why didn't you check more closely?"

Gwyn went to comfort her. He placed his hands on her shoulders and she jerked away.

"Don't touch me! The first murder here in fifty years, and you bungled it, PC Plod. Get out of my sight! I never want to see you again!"

"Bethan—"

"If you won't find out what happened to Aunty Meg, I will. Now sling your hook!"

After Gwyn left, Beth finished the sherry between sobs and poured another. Anger burned through her with the alcohol. "I'll find him, Aunty Meg," she said to the empty room, "you have my word. I'll get whoever did this to you."

Anger kept her from relaxing. She got the slicker and boots and put them on before letting herself out of the house. Somebody was going to tell her what happened that night, and the person who would know was Ishmael.

With only a suspicion of moonlight and without a flashlight, Beth slipped on the path several times before arriving, mud covered, to hammer on Ishmael's door. "Let me in, Ishmael. It's Bethan Davies." When silence followed her call, she kicked the door and it flew open. There was no sign of Ishmael. Where would he go in such a storm? Why would he even go out? Disappointed, Beth left and pulled the door closed behind her, struggling against the howling wind.

The wind carried a solitary clang, like the noise of metal against rock. She tilted her head to listen, but the sound didn't come again.

She decided to take the shorter, cliff path back to Derwen House. Far off, lightning speared the sea, giving her momentary glimpses of the muddy way, and thunder clapped in the distance. Rain turned the path slick and forced Beth onto the grass. The going was easier, but she had to bend double against the wind. Rain found its way inside her collar and dripped from her hat to blind her. She struggled on, staying upright with difficulty when she reached the top of the cliff. She stayed away from the edge, knowing that somewhere down there the Witch waited.

Far below, the village lights appeared as if through fog, so dense was the rain. On top of the cliff, Beth could see nothing but dark clumps of gorse tossed this way and that in the whining gale. Lightning scored the sky and a clap of thunder echoed around the hills followed by another jagged arc. The brief flash showed her a man standing a few paces away. Beth screamed.

CHAPTER NINETEEN

On Monday morning, Gwyn tucked HQ's receipt for the documents from Megan's safe into his pocket and walked to Sergeant Jenkins' office. He tapped on the door, entered at his superior's bidding and came straight to the point. "I want to reopen the investigation into the death of Miss Megan Davies of Derwen Bay."

The Sergeant looked up from the file in his hand. "Good morning to you, too, Thomas. Sit down." He slid the file aside. "The woman found on the beach, right? Why do you want to reopen the case?"

Gwyn perched on the hard chair. "Further evidence has come to light which point to Miss Davies dying by means other than misadventure."

"And the evidence is?"

"There was a violent storm the night before she was found. Miss Davies would not have gone out without a raincoat. Her niece found the coat in the garden shed yesterday."

"She's pretty, is she, this niece?"

"Her appearance has no bearing on what I want you to do."

"As I recall, you were friendly with Megan Davies."

"Yes."

"After you called me this morning to arrange this meeting, I pulled the file on Megan Davies. The notes I made at the time show I thought you were being irrational regarding the woman's death. You said she intimated she had information, which you said she had been withholding until certain of her facts. I put it to you now as I did then—Miss Davies, an elderly woman, liked to have a young man around to ease her loneliness."

"She wasn't like that!" Gwyn's voice rose.

"I advise you to modulate your tone, Constable."

"I'm sorry." Gwyn lowered his voice. "I told you at the time that Megan Davies was clear minded and not lonely as one or two of her neighbours said."

"They also spouted some rubbish about her being psychic. One old soul called her a witch. Can you believe that, in this day and age?"

Gwyn chose his words carefully. "Megan Davies had a way of knowing things. I felt at the time that something illegal was going on in Derwen Bay. I believe she found out what it was."

"And now you've discovered a raincoat."

"In her garden shed. I also found her safe forced in the house."

"Was anything taken?"

"I don't know. All I obtained were documents. I brought them in for fingerprinting. Her niece, who lives in the house, informed me she'd heard an intruder on the night she arrived. I investigated and observed a footprint on an upstairs window ledge and others to match in the garden shed."

"These are petty thefts. They should be kept separate from the investigation into the woman's death."

"Then you'll reopen the case?"

"No."

"You have to! I think the niece's life is in danger."

"I have to do no such thing. If you can bring me evidence of danger to the niece, I will review the matter. As for opening the original file . . . You are aware I made certain concessions because of your friendship with the deceased. In most circumstances, I would have marked the file Suicide. Instead, it reads Death by Misadventure."

"You're wrong, sir." Gwyn rose.

"If you can bring me proof, I will reopen the case and head the investigation."

"I'll find you the proof. One way or another, I want the case reopened and the murderer brought to justice." At the door, he turned. "Do I have your word that further investigation would take place?"

"It is my duty to investigate crime," Jenkins said. "And Thomas, don't become emotionally involved in this one, will you?"

"I think it's too late for that, sir."

* * *

Chief Inspector Mathews played golf with Gwyn's father. Even so, he could spare Gwyn only five minutes as he walked briskly to his car. Without preamble, Gwyn said, "Sergeant Driscoll advised you were going to call me about my request for information on any planning permission given for the work at Plas Mawr, in Derwen Bay. She said she has to channel future requests through you. Can you tell me why?"

"All I am prepared to divulge is that it is part of a larger investigation." Mathews thrust through the door with Gwyn at his heels.

"What type of investigation?"

"One conducted by another division."

"Out of Carmarthen?" Gwyn ran down the steps after his superior.

"Out of London." Mathews glanced at Gwyn as he caught up. "And you didn't hear it from me. Leave the Plews fellow alone."

Encouraged by the other man's confidence, the mention of London brought the question of Bethan's restricted file to mind and Gwyn pushed on. "There's another matter that concerns me about someone recently moved to Derwen Bay."

Chief Inspector Mathews came to an abrupt halt and turned to face Gwyn. "Who?"

"A young woman: Bethan Davies." As soon as the name was past Gwyn's lips, he read relief in the other man's eyes.

Mathews shook his head. "Never heard of her." He continued walking towards his car.

"The file on her is restricted and I want to know why."

"Is she a juvenile?"

"No, she is in her twenties."

Mathews put the key in the lock and shot Gwyn an enquiring look. "Why is it important for you to know what is in the file?"

"She's the niece of a woman who died a short while ago. At the time I was concerned that it was a case of murder."

"I remember. You got roasted for that, didn't you? I suppose this is another one of your hunches. It is insufficient reason for me to allow access to the woman's file."

Gwyn gulped. "There is another reason, sir."

Mathews opened the door, tossed his briefcase in and eased behind the wheel. "This had better be good."

"I think I'm falling in love with her."

Mathews looked up at Gwyn with a smile, and then he laughed. "And I suppose you don't want to be involved with a known criminal. Is that it?"

"Something like that."

Mathews chuckled. "It's high time Anwen and Edgar had grandchildren. I'll see what I can do. Mind, this is between us, all right?"

"Yes, sir, thank you, sir." Gwyn stepped back as Mathews slammed the door shut and then drove off.

With mixed emotions, Gwyn drove to his parents' house. Why had he mentioned he was falling for Bethan? He didn't even know her. That she made his blood race was no reason to think he was in love and, after the whipping she'd given him the night before, she was unlikely to return his feelings. He wondered if the warmth he felt towards Bethan arose, in part, from his regard for Megan. Better to put her out of his mind.

Gwyn's father was at work but his mother was more than willing to sit and chat over a cup of tea. "You look distracted," Anwen said as she poured the tea. "What's wrong?"

"I slipped up badly, Mam." Gwyn took the tea but ignored the cake she brought out. "I missed a vital clue. Something so simple we all overlooked it."

"If the high-ups missed it, too, there's no reason for you to beat yourself over it."

"There is. They judged Megan's death a misadventure. If I'd noted the clue, they would have investigated it further as a murder case."

"Megan was murdered?" Anwen's cup clattered onto the saucer.

"I've had my suspicions all along but I had nothing concrete to give the Sergeant. I've asked him to reopen the case, but he wants more than I have at the moment."

"You'll find something. I know you will."

"I'm not so sure. I wouldn't have made note of it if Bethan hadn't said something."

"Who is Bethan?"

"Megan's niece. She arrived a few days ago from London."

"Is she a nice girl?"

Gwyn couldn't miss the hope in her voice. "She's like Megan. Not to look at, she's only in her twenties, but in her ways."

"Do you like her?"

He ignored the question. "I don't think she'll ever talk to me again. She blames me for not noticing Megan wasn't wearing a coat when she went out into the storm."

"Perhaps she'll come round. What about the other girl; the one you were seeing? You haven't brought her to meet us."

He didn't want to tell his mother Linda had accused him of seeing Bethan on the side. She knew he'd walked Bethan home. He felt guilty that he hadn't explained how he came to be taking Bethan home or how innocent it had been.

Guilty that he'd taken the easy way out of the relationship, he said. "Bethan and I had a row last night."

"Lover's tiff?" Anwen had a twinkle in her eye. "When you rang and said you were bringing Megan to see us, Dat and I thought you'd finally found the right girl. It was a shock when I saw Megan. She was older than me!"

"There was nothing like that between Megan and me. We were friends and I wanted her to meet you both."

"I liked Megan. She was sharp for her age."

"Not according to Sergeant Jenkins. He thinks she was turning senile."

"Well, he didn't know her; that's all I can say."

"That's what people told him."

"So you're trying to get the case opened again?"

Gwyn nodded. However, the case the brass had made for a verdict of death by misadventure seemed watertight. "I'll need Bethan's help."

"You'll see. She'll come round."

Gwyn shook his head. "I'm not so sure. We've had a spat before and she wasn't easy to win over."

"You said Bethan had only been in Derwen Bay a few days. You've had little tiffs already?" Anwen smiled when Gwyn shrugged. "You know what they say, Gwyn—the path of true love never runs smoothly."

CHAPTER TWENTY

True love, Gwyn thought as he took the north road to the bay. For that, you'd have to know a girl. Being partial to the way she looked, the way her hair smelled of flowers and sunshine, enjoying what the sight of her did to his body wasn't enough. You'd have to talk with a girl and Bethan might never talk to him again. He pulled up outside Derwen House. There was still no sign of Bethan's car. He got out of the Land Rover, stepped onto the path, and Mrs Williams appeared with her broom.

"*Prynhawn da,*" she called.

He nodded. "Mrs Williams."

He rang the bell, aware the neighbour was sweeping in an area where she could see and hear everything. When Bethan didn't answer, he knocked.

"I haven't seen her this morning," Mrs Williams said. "She was working on the garden yesterday but it might be too wet today."

"Thank you." Gwyn went around the side of the house to the back door. He knocked and called out; still no answer. She was angry with him and who could blame her? He'd failed Megan. It was easy to tell himself he was too grief-stricken at her death to think clearly but it was his job and he had to cast emotions aside. Speeding and illegal parking were mere nuisances but a suspicious death was why he was here. He returned to the front of the house. "If you see Miss Davies, will you tell her I have to speak to her urgently?"

"No trouble, is there?"

"No trouble, Mrs Williams." He got back in the Land Rover and took off before the woman had a chance to question him further.

Damn you, Bethan. With everything that's going on, even if you are angry with me, how can you leave when we have to talk!

Gwyn parked at the side of the station and returned to the front of the building.

"Gwyn!" Emrys stood on the opposite pavement. He checked for cars and then ran across the road. "I want a word. Inside."

"What's up?" Gwyn asked when they entered the police station.

"It's Bethan's car."

"I noticed it wasn't outside Derwen House."

"It's in the garage. I didn't want to hand it back to her until I'd spoken to you."

"Oh?"

"It's the brakes, see. They failed on her Saturday night when she came home from Carmarthen. She was driving down the hill. Lucky for her, I was taking a fare up to the campground and saw her. I towed the car down and put it in the garage."

"I'd better take a look." Gwyn turned for the door.

"Not yet." Emrys put a hand on his arm to hold him back. "The thing is, and I haven't told Bethan, the damage to the brakes was deliberate."

Gwyn's breath caught in his throat. Logic told him Bethan was all right because he'd spoken to her since, but the attempt on her life would be enough to reopen the investigation into Megan's death. "Are you sure? Is it something you'd swear to if it went to court?"

"Yes. There's no doubt."

"Show me, and tell me how you can be sure." Gwyn followed Emrys across the road and into the garage.

Emrys closed the overhead door and switched on the light. "You can see for yourself." The car was up on a lift and Emrys shone a portable light underneath the engine. "See here, where the line attaches? It's dirty there and clean closer to the tip. There's a fingerprint smudge on the line itself and that tells me someone grabbed it. They slid the brake hose back so, when Bethan braked hard for the hill, it gave way and she lost fluid." Emrys stood back as Gwyn examined the line leading from the reservoir. "They're new brake lines. I know the dealer where she bought this car and he's reputable. He's known for safety checking every used car he sells."

"It would have looked like an accident."

"Caused by poor maintenance. Whoever did it was smart enough not to cut the line. Who would do such a thing to Bethan?"

"I don't know, Emrys, but keep the car here for now. I don't want Bethan driving it because whoever did this might do something else to it. I'll see if I can get a print to try for a match."

"Lucky she's a good driver. She brought the car to a stop but look at the damage she did." Emrys led Gwyn around to the side of the car. "She ran it against the bank as she steered for a run in. It's going to cost to get it put right."

Gwyn slid his fingers along the scrapes and gouges. "She could have been killed."

"If she'd failed to stop, she could have come down the hill at top speed and killed herself and other people. She could have run me down or Doug."

"Doug?"

"He was on his way back to London and stayed with her until I got back with the tow truck."

"I need you to make a report. Don't leave anything out because my Sergeant will be interested in reading it. The sooner you do it the better, before you forget any details." Gwyn hurried back to the station with Emrys on his heels.

While Emrys made out his report, pressing hard with the ballpoint pen so that it came through to the carbon copy, Gwyn rang Bethan. At the other end, the phone rang and rang, but no one answered.

"I'm done, Gwyn," Emrys said, retracting the ballpoint. "Do you want to look it over and let me know if it's all right?"

Gwyn's hand shook as he reached for the report.

"Are you all right, mate?"

"I've been trying to reach Bethan. I don't think she's home."

"She'll be over with Dilys, I expect. Go back a long way, those two do."

"I'll try Dilys later." Gwyn read the report. When the Sergeant read this, he couldn't fail to take the matter seriously. "This is good, Emrys. I'll fax it to Carmarthen with my own report, so expect a visit from my boss."

"Any time. You know where to find me."

After Emrys left, Gwyn put his own report together, faxed it with Emrys' report to Sergeant Jenkins, and rang the Anchor to ask Dilys if Bethan was there.

"I haven't seen her all day, Gwyn. Isn't she at home?"

"No. I need to talk to her urgently. Do you have any idea where she might be?"

"None, unless she went over to see Julie and the twins. She doesn't know too many people well enough to visit them."

"Thank you." Gwyn hung up and ran across the road to ask if Julie had seen Bethan. He heard the twins running and squealing up and down the hall behind her as Julie replied she hadn't. Gwyn took off along the Front, walking as fast as he could without having people think there was an emergency.

To avoid Mrs Williams, he approached Derwen House from the lane. When no one answered the back door, he slipped around to the front and let himself in.

"Bethan?" he shouted up the stairs. "Tom?" Gwyn checked the sitting and dining rooms. In the kitchen, he took note of the sherry bottle and the two glasses on the counter, the tube of blue paint, and— Gwyn did a double take. A French banknote? Did she plan to leave the country? He went to the back door, unlocked it and walked out to the porch. The yellow slicker and boots were gone. "If you've gone up the cliff the day after a storm . . .!" He swore under his breath, went in and locked the door. He went out the front door, locking it behind him and headed off along the road before Mrs Williams could do more than twitch her curtains.

Gwyn climbed the cliff walk quickly, scanning the ground for a sign of Bethan's passing. The rain of the night before had turned the path into slick clay. He stepped to one side, onto clumped grass and wild flowers. Beaten down, no footsteps showed.

From the top, he could see the fishing boats trawling beyond the headlands, bobbing in the water like ducks on a pond. He followed the path until he reached the track to the north beach. Slipping and sliding, he arrived at the handful of concrete steps built into the base of the cliff. When the tide was in, the sea swallowed the small beach, and the steps offered safety to anyone unable to climb the steep incline. During a violent storm, the waves could wrench someone into its maelstrom. The crags showed where the surging rollers would reach. In a storm, they would crash higher, high enough and strong enough to wash an elderly woman from her perch.

Was that what had happened to Megan? Had Bethan taken a walk in the storm and been trapped here? Would they find—?

No, oh no, he mustn't think of that.

Gwyn climbed back to the top and followed the cliffs until Derwen Bay was so distant he could barely make out the individual houses. He turned and started back. When he arrived at the path down to the bay, he felt the ground beneath his feet tremble. He stopped and stood still. There had never been an earthquake in this part of Wales, but there had been incidents of cliffs falling into the sea. In the silence broken only by the haunting cries of the gulls, he felt rather than heard a rumbling underground. He knelt and placed his ear to the grass. Somewhere beneath him, noises echoed, as if the cliff were hollow. Then there was a sharp clang. The same noise he'd heard two nights earlier.

Gwyn got to his feet, to continue towards Derwen, and a lorry filled with rubble left Plas Mawr to crawl up the north road. Gwyn made for Derwen House, hoping Bethan had returned.

The fax awaiting Gwyn when he reached the police station informed him they had no computer match for the fingerprints on Meg's documents. He picked up the phone, called Carmarthen, and asked to speak to Sergeant Jenkins. After a few moments, the desk sergeant told him the Sergeant was on a case and out of reach unless it was an emergency.

"No emergency," Gwyn said and hung up.

He rang Derwen House, but again no one answered. He checked with Emrys and learned Bethan's car was still in the garage. On edge, he couldn't sit still and eventually he went around the corner to the Anchor.

* * *

Davy was at the bar serving Ianto Williams. He looked up and nodded. "You're in uniform, so I don't expect you'll want a drink."

"No," Gwyn confirmed. "Is Dilys about?"

Davy inclined his head at the back of the bar. "She's giving Ricky his dinner. Go on through."

Gwyn pushed through the rear door and walked along the hallway to the kitchen where Dilys was cajoling Ricky to eat his dinner.

"There now, PC Thomas has come to tell you the same." Dilys shot Gwyn a quick smile. "He won't grow big like you if he doesn't eat, will he?"

Gwyn's mother used to tell him the same thing. He voiced his agreement with Dilys and dropped onto a chair beside the boy.

"You seem worried, Gwyn." Dilys took a forkful of mashed potatoes and urged them on Ricky. "What's wrong?"

"It's Bethan. I can't find her. Did she say anything to you about going away?"

"Not a word and I don't think she'd leave without telling me. You've been to the house, have you?"

"I had to. When I couldn't find her and she wasn't answering the phone . . . I still have the key the solicitor gave me. When did you see her last?"

"Yesterday. We took Ricky to Sunday school and Bethan came back for lunch. She stayed for an hour playing with Ricky."

"Did she say anything? Anything at all that would tell us where she went?"

"Not that I recall."

"What did you talk about?" Gwyn realised his questions perturbed Dilys.

"Just old times, like when she used to come here as a child, and Megan, of course. Oh, and she told me about the brakes failing on her car."

"What did she say about Megan?"

Dilys shrugged. "She's convinced it wasn't an accident."

"And I doubt she'd leave until it was sorted out to her satisfaction."

"You know, Gwyn, I had a feeling at the time you didn't think Megan's death was an accident. Have you changed your mind?"

"The more I think about it, the more convinced I am that somebody had a hand in her death. Things have been happening. Bethan must have told you."

"She said somebody had been in the house but she asked me not to say anything to anyone."

"I'd rather you kept it to yourself, too. By the way, I want you to do me a favour."

"If I can."

"I need to get Tom Rowland's fingerprints. If he comes in, would you keep the glass he uses for me?"

"He hasn't been in for a couple of days. What's he done?"

"Nothing I know of. I'm just checking up on something." Gwyn rose to his feet and ruffled Ricky's hair. "Eat it all up, there's a good boy." He made for the door but paused when Dilys called out.

"Gwyn? Wait. Bethan said something odd. She'd seen some sort of light out in the bay at night."

"From a yacht?"

"No. It shone from the cave onto the Witch. She saw it twice, both times about one o'clock in the morning."

"Flash of light," Ricky said quietly and quailed when they both looked at him.

"What?" they said in unison.

"It shines on the Witch. I've seen it."

Gwyn exchanged a glance with Dilys.

"His bedroom is up in the attic and it overlooks the Front," she explained.

"Can I see it?"

Ricky was off his chair and running into the hallway. "Come on." He sprang up the stairs.

"Anything to get out of eating his dinner," Dilys muttered as she followed with Gwyn on her heels.

Ricky stood beside the dormer window in a room cluttered with soft toys and a train track. "Over there." He pointed out the window.

Gwyn crouched beside the boy. "Does it shine up into the sky?"

Ricky shook his head. "It's quick. Like that!" He clapped his hands together.

"How is it you're up at one o'clock in the morning?" Gwyn asked.

Ricky hung his head. "My bed was wet."

"Oh." Sorry he'd embarrassed the boy, Gwyn hugged an arm around Ricky's shoulders. "How many times does it shine?"

"One time. I told Aunty Megan. She said she'd seen it, too."

Something pricked his neck and cast a chill down Gwyn's spine. "Have you told anyone else?"

"Aunty Megan said not to because it was our secret."

"Aunty Megan was right. You mustn't tell anyone, all right?"

Ricky nodded, clung to Gwyn's hand and whispered, "Have I got to eat my dinner?"

"Maybe not tonight, eh?" Gwyn raised an eyebrow at Dilys. "I think Ricky deserves to be let off for one night, don't you? But only if he promises not to tell anyone else about the light."

Dilys went white. "Is it important?"

"It might be the only real clue to what's going on in Derwen Bay." Gwyn straightened, Ricky still clutching to his hand. "You've got a detective in the making here, Dilys."

"Am I? Am I?" Ricky danced in front of Gwyn and looked up at him with shining eyes. "I know other things, too."

"What other things?" Gwyn sat on the bed and drew Ricky onto his lap.

"There's a boat that comes. Then the light shines."

"A fishing boat?"

Ricky shook his head. "A rowing boat with no lights. I'm waiting for it to hit the Witch."

"Are there people in the boat?"

"Two. Sometimes only one."

"Are you making up stories?" Dilys asked.

Ricky shook his head. "Ishmael's seen it, too. He must have 'cos I've seen him on the sand when the boat comes."

"Does Ishmael talk to the men?"

"No. He hides in the rocks. I think he's afraid of them."

"Is there anything else you have to tell me?"

"Yes. Roger said a bad word today."

Gwyn hid a smile. "I'll have a word with him."

"I don't suppose Roger eats his dinner either," Dilys said with a sigh.

"He doesn't have to," Ricky said, reproach in his voice. "His mam doesn't make him."

"Your mam isn't going to make you eat it for tonight. But remember, you won't grow big and strong if you don't eat. If you're not big and strong, you can't be a detective when you grow up."

Ricky studied Gwyn for a moment then he nodded.

"To think I nearly didn't mention what Bethan said about the light," Dilys said as they went back down the stairs. "What's going on, Gwyn?"

"I don't know, but I'm certain it ties in with Megan's death. It may have something to do with Bethan's disappearance, too."

"You think she's in trouble?"

"I hope not." However, she told him she was going to find out what happened to Megan and that might make some people nervous.

Back at the station, Gwyn filed a missing person's report on Bethan and faxed a copy for Sergeant Jenkins' attention. Normally, there would be a twenty-four hour delay before filing such a report, but there were times when a police officer cut through the red tape. He pocketed the powerful police-issue flashlight and set off for the beach.

* * *

The tide was out, and a few toddlers played on the hard sand. Swaddled against the breeze, they ran roly-poly backwards and forward to catch the ball thrown to them.

At the mouth of the cave, wind and sun had dried the walls. Farther back, they glistened cold and wet in the beam of light Gwyn played over them. Several feet above his head, the tidemark was higher on the back wall where the waves had rushed in and dashed against it. Gwyn directed the flashlight onto what looked like a fissure. Some caves had chimneys, but the opening he studied curved back on itself and ended in the darkness of rock. Slowly, he moved the beam along the roof. Nothing offered a source of light. He could see only rough rock and a narrow ledge. Nothing except—

Farther up, there were marks on one of the rocks. Gwyn held the light steady. A narrow band of rock, about the width of a tethering rope, looked polished. He wedged the flashlight into the hard sand, angling it so the beam shone on the area he wanted to examine, and started to climb.

Twice he fell back, regulation boots sliding on the damp rock, but at the third try, he found purchase and pushed himself up, inch by inch. A foot below the area of smoothed rock, he reached above his head and felt around. A few strands of rope came away in his hand and Gwyn dropped back onto the sand.

He placed the fragments into a fold of handkerchief, picked up the flashlight and examined the wall. He found a sliver of wood caught on a jagged rock. A boat had entered the cave and bobbed against it. A rope would hold the boat, but they'd have to fasten it to something at the other end.

Gwyn studied the area around and above where the rope had been. It didn't look any different from the rest of the walls and roof, not from where he was standing. To do a proper check, he'd need a ladder. Sion-the-Window's ladder wouldn't be long enough; he needed an extension ladder like the one on the lorry going up to Plas Mawr. Gwyn was loath to ask a favour of Reginald Plews and mindful of the Chief Inspector's warning.

If he came in by boat when the tide was high . . . He wouldn't dare bring the police launch into the close confines of the cave but any number of people would lend him a rowboat.

Out on the beach, Gwyn told himself teenagers might be larking about inside the cave after dark. Ricky said he'd seen two people in a boat and one of them might have been a girl. The explanation didn't satisfy him. Why would teenagers do their sparking inside the cave when all they had to do was go to the north beach where no one would see them from the village?

On his way back to the station, Gwyn walked along the road to Derwen House. As soon as he stepped onto the path to the front door, Mrs Williams came out with her broom.

"She hasn't been back, Mr Thomas. I've been watching for her." Mrs Williams came to the low wall separating the two gardens. "Is there a message for Miss Davies, then?"

"Only that I want to talk to her," Gwyn called over his shoulder as he took the path to Ishmael's house.

Ishmael wasn't at home. On the table, the carving sat under its shroud. Gwyn pulled it away and the bust of Megan gazed at him. He dropped onto a stool and leaned his elbows on the rickety table. Nose to nose with the carving, he touched the heart-shaped brooch carved against her throat and stared into the wooden eyes as if he would find an answer there. What was it Megan knew?

I've got something to tell you. What, Megan? What were you going to tell me? You knew about the light. The same light Bethan saw, and Ricky. Were you going to tell me something about it?

For a long time, he studied the carving and his mind raced in circles around a black void that showed him nothing. He was like a blind man; a man swept helplessly around the Witch's skirts.

On his way back to the station, Gwyn paused at the end of the road to Derwen House. Mrs Williams was sweeping the pavement outside her gate. She looked up when she noticed Gwyn and shook her head. Gwyn nodded in reply and walked on.

CHAPTER TWENTY-ONE

In the hours he waited for darkness, Gwyn dealt with one or two complaints about the rumbling lorries from Plas Mawr and entered their grievances in the Day Book. He did what he could to get a fingerprint match off the brake lining on Bethan's car. He doubted it would lead anywhere because it was so oil smudged.

Young Debbie Lewis from the campground brought in a dog caravan renters left when they cleared out. She blushed as she handed him the end of the rope and their hands touched.

Twelve, she was. Gwyn knew all about crushes because he'd had one or two himself. There'd been the Welsh mistress, the chemistry mistress, and the woman who'd lived next door in Carmarthen. He remembered turning red every time they looked in his direction. Now he was at the other end of the stick and he still felt embarrassed.

Gwyn hunkered beside the dog with the bewildered look in her intelligent eyes. He petted the same dog when he went to talk to the rowdies. "What's her name, Debbie?"

"Talia," Debbie answered with a tremor in her voice. "Mam says we can't keep her because Stitch doesn't get along with other dogs in the house."

"Have you got the name of the owners?"

"Mam wrote it down." Debbie took a scrunch of paper from her pocket and handed it to him. "They left the caravan in a mess."

"They didn't just go out for the day, did they?"

183

Debbie shook her head. "Dat checked. They took everything."

"I'll follow up on it." Gwyn patted the dog's head.

"Can you keep her until you find the owners?"

"She seems obedient enough, eh, Talia?" A sad expression met his gaze.

"She's a lovely dog, but they kept her tied up to the caravan all the time."

"No walkies?" The dog's expression brightened. "I won't have much time to take her out. Do you think your mam could spare you to take her for a walk every day?"

Debbie's eyes sparkled. "Yes." Then she turned red faced.

"Good. I'll see you tomorrow, all right?"

"What time?"

"Any time your mam says."

When Debbie skipped out, Gwyn took the dog into the kitchen and placed a bowl of water on the floor. Talia lapped eagerly then sat next to the bowl and eyed Gwyn. "Hungry, eh?" In the fridge, he found leftovers. She wolfed everything including the green balls of sprouts and then stretched out in the corner by the door.

Gwyn forgot about her as he took out the recipe book his mother had sent him—French Cuisine. He'd done a bit of French cooking but this recipe was new. He had the ingredients, even the spices, and assembled them on the table.

He'd always been interested in cooking, hanging around while his mother bustled about the kitchen. Anwen never weighed or measured anything, and Gwyn learned that came only with practice. He tested her once and found the two ounces of sugar she'd put in a bowl came to within a grain of being exact. With familiar meals, Gwyn did as she did, but with new food, he weighed everything. Over the years, he learned not to mix countries. Italians may get along with the

British but you didn't mix their country's spices. A sliver of garlic into a shepherd's pie ruined the whole dish.

Some boys at school made fun of Gwyn's interest in cooking and it surprised them when he joined the police force. He often wondered about their attitude. He'd been in the rugby and football teams, he played tennis in summer and he'd been one of the few who joined the rowing club the town tried to put together on the Tywy but, because he made no secret of the way he liked to cook, they'd assumed him to be effeminate. It didn't make a difference that most of the restaurants in town had male chefs behind their swinging kitchen doors. Did he join the police force to squash any slurs cast on his manhood? Gwyn often asked himself that question.

As he chopped and mixed, blended and stirred, Gwyn mused that putting together the ingredients was a bit like putting together clues. He got rid of a lot of the frustration brought about by his job when he cooked.

Did he want to be a police officer all his life? Did he want to spend the next twenty years inside the damned uniform that stood between him and other people? He was invisible. Apart from the few, like Dilys and Emrys, he was his uniform. It was one reason why his friendship with Megan and Ishmael had been so important. They saw him as a person, a man with foibles and weaknesses, but someone they liked all the same.

He placed the casserole in the oven and set the timer. Two hours of slow cooking, and another half hour to sit before it was ready, the recipe suggested a salad to complete the meal. He'd make it later, adding a few of the spices from the main dish into the dressing to carry the flavours through the meal, a trick Anwen taught him. He cleaned the rest of the kitchen, washed everything he'd used and put it away.

Behind him, the dog moaned in her sleep and twitched. She'd eaten well and she'd likely want to go out. In the fenced back garden, she couldn't run away and there was nothing to damage. Gwyn knew little about gardening, except for cutting grass and tending the few herbs he grew in pots outside the back door. Female dogs didn't lift their legs to do their business, so his pots were safe.

"Talia?"

The dog came awake instantly. Head up, her tail thumped the floor slowly.

"Out? Do you want to go out?"

Talia stood.

Gwyn passed her to open the door. She eyed the garden as he took off the length of rope around her neck. "Go on, then."

She moved cautiously onto the doorstep, nose up as she sniffed the air, and stepped tentatively onto the path and gingerly onto the grass. She went a couple of feet and squatted.

"Good girl!" Gwyn called. At least she was house trained. Mind you, the grass would have a brown patch there unless he did something about it right away. He went to the shed and brought out a bucket, the dog following his movements with her eyes. Every time he peeked at her, she wagged her tail, the white tip a blur.

As he filled the bucket, Gwyn watched Talia sniff around the garden. At one point, she must have found the trail left by a mouse or rabbit. She followed it at an angle across the garden, nose tickling the grass. A tracker, then. A tracker . . .

Gwyn threw the water over the patch Talia used and called her inside. "We're going for walkies," he informed her. She jumped up and down in her excitement and made yelping sounds as he rummaged through the Lost Property box. He found a dog collar, but no leash. "I guess it's the rope for now, girl." He tied it to the collar and bent to brush away the hairs Talia shed on his trouser legs. With a last check on the oven timer, he led the dog out.

Talia followed at his heels, well trained and attentive. When he stopped to talk to Patty Pen Tir, Talia sat patiently. Without a word from him or even a pull on the rope, she paced him. Even when they passed another dog, she paid it no attention. When they reached the road to Derwen House, she halted. The first slight tug on the tether drew Gwyn's attention. He looked to where she stood at the edge of the pavement. "Quite right, girl. Rules of the road, eh?" In his anxiety to reach Derwen House, he'd stepped onto the road without thought for traffic. It took a dumb animal to remind him. "All clear." He walked across without hindrance from the dog.

Well trained, yes. Smart, yes. But was she smart enough? She'd scented a trail across his garden but it didn't mean she could track people.

Mrs Williams was nowhere in sight when Gwyn let himself and Talia into Derwen House and closed the door. He untied the makeshift leash from around her neck and realised it was the first time he hadn't rung the bell or called out. Subconsciously, he accepted Bethan wasn't here.

The dog was curious and followed Gwyn when he went to the kitchen to get the keys. At least Bethan had put them where Megan always kept them. Talia moved from room to room, sniffing here and there, as Gwyn searched for something of Bethan's to give Talia an odour to follow.

When he found nothing in the bedroom Bethan had shared with Megan, he thought she might have moved into one of the other rooms. He unlocked doors and ran in a panic from one room to the other. Every wardrobe and drawer proved stripped clean as if Bethan had never been there. Back in her bedroom, he found tissues wadded into balls in a wastebasket. Wet at one time, they were dry now. Bethan must have cried into them but he couldn't tell how long ago, or if they would retain a scent. He held them under the dog's nose.

Gwyn put the tissues in his pocket and followed as Talia ran helter skelter around the house, dashing from room to room, upstairs and downstairs, nose to the floor. She finally stopped beside the sofa and sat, tail thumping the floor as she eyed Gwyn. Of course! Bethan's scent would be all over the house. It would be strongest on the sofa because she slept there her first night in the house, and she'd been sitting there in front of the telly last night. It was odd the scent hadn't been strongest around the bed. Did it mean Bethan hadn't slept there last night?

He searched every room on the ground floor and sneaked out to the shed to check it. Again, he held the wad of tissues under Talia's nose, expecting her to run to the road or back lane. She ran back into the house and settled in front of the sofa.

"Good girl!" He petted the dog and attached the rope to her collar. Then he returned the keys to the kitchen, locked both doors and they left the house.

On the cliff path, he kept Talia on the rope. Occasionally, he held the tissues under her nose. It was a slim chance. If Bethan came this way on Sunday night, it had been raining hard. The breeze from the sea would have taken care of any scent that remained. Disappointed, he let the dog off the leash. For a moment, she stood stock still, eyeing him with a question. "Go on, then. Run!"

She ran. She rolled in the grass. She followed a scent under a gorse bush and tried digging after whatever it was. Joy lighting her face, tongue lolling, she came back to him.

Gwyn went on one knee and caught the longer fur below her ears. "Good girl, Talia. You're a good girl." She licked his face, and then stiffened. She stood tense, as if she was made of stone, then Gwyn felt it again—a rumbling from beneath their feet, deep in the cliff.

Gwyn dropped onto the grass, drew his knees up and wrapped his arms around them. Beside him, Talia settled with her head on her paws, her eyes on Gwyn. "There's something going on here, girl. I don't know what, but I'm going to find out." Again, the thought of smugglers came to his mind.

Ishmael knew about the light, and he must have seen the boat go into the cave. Ishmael didn't believe Megan's death was an accident, either, but he wouldn't open his mouth. Well, he would now. "He's going to tell me, girl. When I get hold of him, he's damned well going to tell me!"

The dog sat up, alarmed.

"It's all right, girl. I'm not angry with you, only with a fool of a man who deserves to be called dim witted." He patted Talia and got to his feet. "We're going to look for Ishmael. If he's not at home, we're going to comb the village until we find him."

But Ishmael wasn't to be found. Talia took the scent and led Gwyn hither and thither, into the haunts the other man went, but Ishmael wasn't anywhere.

"Don't tell me I've got two missing persons on my hands," he muttered, confusing the dog. He tied her to the gate outside the churchyard and walked to Megan's grave. Ishmael was in the habit of putting fresh wild flowers there every morning. Those standing in the jar now had discarded most of their petals.

"He didn't come today."

"Good afternoon, Mr Powell-Pritchard."

"*Prynhawn da*, Constable. Ishmael hasn't been here today."

"Thanks." Gwyn turned to leave.

"We didn't see you in chapel yesterday."

"No, you didn't." Gwyn kept walking. Powell-Pritchard was always hanging around the graveyard, blighting people paying their respects to the dead. At the gates, Gwyn untied Talia and headed back toward the police station.

P L Crompton

CHAPTER TWENTY-TWO

As Gwyn passed, Eleri emerged from the post office. "I see you've acquired a dog, Gwyn. Police-trained is it?"

"She got dumped up at the campground and I'm looking after her until I find the owner," he explained.

"Nice little thing," Eleri said, patting Talia. "I suppose you've spoken to Bethan?"

"Not since last night."

"Oh, then she told you what I said."

Sunday night's conversation was clear in his mind; word for damning word. "I don't remember her mentioning you."

Patty Pen Tir shuffled towards them. "Will you be at the Women's Institute tonight, Eleri?"

"I will and I'll talk to you then." Eleri clutched at Gwyn's arm. "Right now I'm taking Gwyn home for a cuppa."

Patty entered the post office and Eleri pulled at Gwyn's arm.

"What was that about? Have you two had a falling out?" Gwyn asked as Eleri led him and Talia away.

"Nothing like that, only I wanted to say something without anyone hearing." She let go of his arm. "Fancy a cup of tea, then?"

"I wouldn't say no, but how is Snowy going to react to a dog in the house?"

"Not very well I'm afraid. We'll have to tie the dog outside."

"What did you want to talk to me about?"

"About Bethan. She's in danger, Gwyn. I expected her to go straight to you but, as she didn't, it's up to me to tell you what I told her."

"Bethan's in danger?" A fist that had been hovering in the shadows thrust its way into Gwyn's chest and fastened on his heart. "What danger?"

"She's investigating Megan's death."

"Yes, but—"

"She may end up like Megan."

Gwyn halted and Talia sat. "What do you mean, Eleri?"

"Since Megan died, I've been doing a lot of thinking. Seeing Bethan yesterday brought me to voice thoughts that have since become more valid."

"What thoughts?"

"You know how it is. You get feelings about things. In your job it must happen a lot—you feel something but you can't prove it."

Gwyn knew what she meant, but— "You're not making much sense."

"Good afternoon." Ieuan-the-Grave walked past with a shovel resting on his shoulder.

Gwyn and Eleri returned his greeting before Eleri took hold of Gwyn's sleeve. "Come on in the house. We can avoid interruptions there."

Gwyn tied Talia to the wishing well and followed Eleri into her kitchen. "What's this all about?" He took off his helmet and sat while Snowy came to sniff his trouser legs.

"I was sure Bethan would have told you last night. I expected you around here first thing this morning."

"You tell me now."

"All right." While Eleri plugged in the kettle and put out the tea things, she told him what she said to Beth about the missing people and her suspicions about Megan's death. "You didn't consider it an accident either, did you?"

Gwyn shook his head. "But I had no proof."

"One of those times when you know something's going on but you can't put your finger on it?"

"Something like that. You mentioned three people disappearing. I remember two—the woman who rented Ty Goch and Ardwy Williams, Sammy's father."

"Did they ever find them?"

"No. The files are still open."

"I expect the file is still open on Mike O'Brien."

"Who?"

"Ricky's father." Eleri poured boiling water into the teapot. "He went missing around the time you came here."

"Are you suggesting there's a connection between the disappearances and Megan's death, and the danger Bethan might be in?"

"Is in. The girl is in danger." Eleri brought the pot to the table and poured the tea. "Yes, the more I think about it the more sure I am there is a tie in."

Warning signals set up a screech in Gwyn's head. Eleri wasn't known as a gossip; or Megan would never have made a friend of her, but there was always a first time. "Why?"

"I've lived here for forty years, Gwyn. In a small place like this you know when something isn't right."

"Dilys said Mike took off when he learned she was pregnant."

"No he didn't. I talked to him that night. He was excited about becoming a father. He was going to marry Dilys."

"Ardwy was a poacher. He went after rabbits one night and never came back." Gwyn sipped his tea. The disappearances, if they were connected, shot his theory of smugglers right out of the water. Unless . . . What if the three who'd disappeared, had stumbled upon the smugglers? Someone would silence them, but the bodies would have shown up by now, surely. Was it possible for smuggling to go on for five years or more without someone seeing something? And how did this relate to Megan's death? Did she witness something? Had she gone down to the beach for a closer look at the light? Did Bethan do the same?

"What are you thinking, Gwyn?" Eleri asked quietly.

"Oh, just some of those unsubstantiated thoughts we all get. Did Bethan mention going abroad?"

A puzzled look crossed Eleri's face and she shook her head. "Not to me. Why?"

"I found a French banknote in the kitchen at Derwen House."

"*Arswyd y byd!*"

"What's the matter?"

"It was Megan's, I expect. See, we joined in the search for Wilhelmina Tingle, two old biddies trailing miles behind the main search party. You were heading one group that went onto the cliffs because someone had seen her up there. Megan was afraid of the cliff top so we went up the road to Plas Mawr. On the way there, she picked up a French banknote."

"No one mentioned it at the time," Gwyn pointed out.

"She kept it as a souvenir. We didn't think it had anything to do with the Tingle woman."

"You found it on the road to Plas Mawr?"

"Blowing about. Megan thought it was litter one of the visitors had thrown away like a sweetie bag, and she got upset enough to pick it up."

"Where exactly did you find it?"

"Close to the O'Malley's cottage, I recall. Bethan must have found it among Megan's things. And that reminds me."

"Of what?"

"When I went to see Megan in her coffin . . ." Eleri fumbled in her pocket for a handkerchief and dabbed her nose. "Remember she always wore that brooch; the heart-shaped one given to her by the man killed in the war. She wasn't wearing it and I asked the undertaker where it was. He said it hadn't been on her when they brought her in."

"It could have been stolen or torn off by the Witch."

"Or by somebody else." Eleri raised tear-filled eyes. "She was murdered, Gwyn. I'm certain. Megan was murdered. You find out who did it."

"Don't you think I've tried? I'm as certain as you are that it wasn't an accident but I have nothing to go on." He bent his head. "I'm in the wrong job."

"Don't you ever think that way. If you only knew how much we hated your predecessor, Megan more than any of us."

"Why?"

"Didn't she tell you?" When Gwyn shook his head, she went on: "Daniel-the-Shop caught Bethan stealing sweeties and reported her to Elwyn Rogers. That excuse for a human being allowed Daniel to lay charges. Fourteen, she was; a child's prank, nothing more."

Gwyn was relieved. They'd restrict access to a juvenile's file.

"The worst of it was Megan got so angry with Bethan that she sent her home. I never saw her again until a few days ago. No, Gwyn, don't you ever say you're a bad bobby."

"Yet I let Megan down."

"Yes, you did," Eleri agreed bluntly. "But that is in the past, you can set the record straight now."

"How?" Gwyn asked. "I have nothing to go on."

"Bethan is determined to get to the bottom of it. With the two of you working together, you should be able to find out what happened."

"If I can find her. No one has seen her since last night."

"There was a storm . . ."

"Don't remind me!" He was half-afraid to return to the police station, in case he found a message telling him Bethan's body had washed up somewhere. "Megan was killed during a storm."

"Yes, killed. Not dead by misadventure."

Gwyn got to his feet. "You've given me a lot to mull over, Eleri, given me some clues I should have seen for myself."

"Tish! What else does an old woman like me have to do but stroke Snowy and think?"

Gwyn walked to the door. He was on the path when Eleri called out.

"I know you used to talk with Megan a lot, not that she ever told me what about, but if you need someone to talk to I'm always here."

Gwyn hesitated. He missed talking to Megan. He couldn't find Ishmael and no one in HQ would discuss anything with him except Dorothy Driscoll in her own way. He turned to face Eleri. "Do you mean that?"

"What's the matter? It's something more than what I just told you, isn't it?"

"I think Bethan has left Derwen."

"Without telling me?" Eleri frowned. "She was up here just after lunch yesterday and I saw her working in the garden later in the afternoon. She didn't say anything about leaving."

"I talked to her late last night, about ten-thirty. We said some harsh words or at least she did. Since then she hasn't answered the phone and nobody has seen her."

"Harsh words about what?" At the look on Gwyn's face, Eleri caught his sleeve and drew him back into the house. "Now then, what's all this about?"

Back in the kitchen, Gwyn rubbed his brow. "A damned mess I've made of things."

"What sort of mess?"

"I'm a fool. It took Bethan to see the clue right under my nose. That night, the night of the storm when Megan died, she went out without her slicker and boots. Do you remember the yellow coastguard slicker Megan wore? Bethan found it in the shed."

"You are not the only one to blame. I told the Sergeant that it was strange Megan had gone out without her coat. He didn't seem to think it was important."

"It doesn't make any difference now. If Bethan has left Derwen, I can't say I blame her."

"Why?"

Gwyn told Eleri what Emrys said about the brakes.

"Did she think someone was trying to kill her? Do you?"

"The car is badly damaged. She might have been killed and it would have looked like an accident."

"Two accidents—aunt and niece; your superiors could not dismiss it easily."

"That's not the point! I don't want her dead; I want her alive! Even if she never talks to me again, I want her alive."

Eleri poured Gwyn the tea left in the pot and sat opposite him. "Did she tell Dilys she was leaving?"

"No."

"What makes you think Bethan has left?"

"Her clothes are gone. There's nothing in the house that was hers."

"How do you know?"

"I went there earlier. I still have the key the solicitor gave me. I went through the whole place and didn't find anything of hers." Only the tissues she'd used to wipe her tears.

"There must be some sort of clue to show where she's gone like a bus or train timetable."

"I didn't see any."

Eleri got to her feet. "Come on, we'll take another look. Two pairs of eyes would double our chances of finding a clue."

Gwyn put on his helmet, untied Talia and they set off down Peartree Lane. He talked to Megan. Everybody knew he visited Megan all the time. Did someone get the idea she was telling him what was going on? Were they so afraid that they silenced her?

If Mrs Williams saw them entering Derwen House it was from behind her lace curtains. Gwyn called Bethan's name when they entered. A cursory glance showed them the ground floor was deserted. Gwyn took the ring of spare keys from the drawer in the kitchen and led the way upstairs.

"This is the room Megan and Bethan shared." He opened the door and Talia trotted in.

Eleri walked into the room. "It looks very bare in here."

"I told you—Bethan's things are gone." Gwyn's shoulders sagged. Wasn't it better to believe Bethan had returned to London than to think she was hurt in some way?

"Is it possible . . .?" Eleri's words faltered at the pain in Gwyn's face. "Because this room would hold memories of Megan, could Bethan have moved into one of the other rooms?"

"I've checked them all, every wardrobe, every drawer. They're all empty, even Tom Rowland's room."

"Bethan told Dilys that Tom left rather suddenly even though he paid a month's board in advance."

"She didn't tell me." Gwyn went out onto the landing. "That's it, then. Bethan has left Derwen Bay." He prepared to go down the stairs, but stopped. "Just a second . . ." He went back into Bethan's room, got on his knees to check under the bed and then rose to feel the space above the wardrobe.

"What are you looking for?" Eleri asked.

"Megan's clothes. Dilys and I packed them in two suitcases and put them on top of the wardrobe in this room. They're not there now."

"Bethan may have taken them with her."

"What would she want with Megan's clothes? They wouldn't fit her. The slicker fitted because it hung down to Megan's ankles. She used to look like a yellow tent."

Eleri smiled. "I remember."

"Bethan had no reason to take Megan's clothes."

"She might have given them away to one of the charity shops in Carmarthen."

"It's possible," Gwyn said doubtfully, then, "What isn't possible is that Bethan would leave without a word to anyone, not even Dilys. And she wouldn't have gone until she felt settled in her mind about what happened to Megan." Gwyn checked under the beds and on the tops of the wardrobes in the other rooms. With Eleri and Talia on his heels, he ran down the stairs and into the kitchen to return the keys.

"Oh," Eleri said. "Here's the banknote Megan found. But this is odd."

"What?"

"This tube of paint, Cobalt Blue; it must be part of Tom's painting paraphernalia."

"He must have forgotten it."

"Blue paint? To one who paints seascapes, blue would be vital for all projects. Wouldn't you agree?"

"What are you trying to say, Eleri?"

"Perhaps we are looking for two people."

Gwyn shook his head. "You're making too much of this. Tom probably didn't notice he'd dropped it." He went to stand beside Eleri. "You can see the tube is damaged. Bethan probably found it and brought it down here. She's out there on the cliff. The slicker and boots are gone so she's out there."

Yes! The voice came from nowhere, filling his ears so he felt as if his brain would explode. Megan's voice. He rocked on his heels.

"Gwyn? Are you all right?" Eleri caught at his arm to steady him.

"She's still here; she hasn't left. Bethan is still in Derwen."

"But why would she wear the slicker? It hasn't rained today."

"I've given up trying to guess why women do things."

"But think logically, Gwyn. If Bethan is still here, where are all her clothes? Where are Megan's clothes?"

"I don't know, but I'd better get back to the station and see if there's any news."

"What news are you looking for?"

He couldn't tell her he half-expected a message to say Bethan's body . . . "I still have a job to do."

"Perhaps I should stay here," Eleri offered. "I'll look around the house again. There's a chance we overlooked something."

Gwyn hesitated, but Megan and Eleri had always been close friends so he saw no harm in leaving the woman in the house. "If Bethan returns . . ."

"I will explain how worried you were about her. If she does return before you, I will phone you to let you know."

"Fair enough." Gwyn headed for the front door with Talia at his heels.

"Gwyn?" Eleri halted him at the door. "It is best if we keep cool heads."

Gwyn nodded as he let himself out. As he had with Megan's death, he was allowing his emotions to play freely. It wouldn't help Bethan if she were in trouble. After all, the suggestion Eleri made for Bethan's absence was feasible. Only Gwyn's emotions told him Bethan hadn't left Derwen Bay. He didn't want to believe she'd leave without a word to him. They'd quarrelled, it was true, but it wasn't possible for her not to feel something of the way he was beginning to feel about her.

But the voice that came into his head—*Yes!*—as adamant as if someone had shouted . . .

He was losing his grip; allowing the job to get to him. Trained to be impartial, not to become emotionally involved in his cases, and yet . . .

CHAPTER TWENTY-THREE

Beth woke to total darkness and an overpowering stench. She was cold and her head hurt. Water trickled from somewhere to her right. She remembered being on the cliff. Remembered seeing a man close by when lightning flashed, and the blow to her head that turned everything to brilliant white, then nothing until now.

Something sharp dug into her back. Beth eased away from whatever she lay on and groaned.

"Are you awake?" a voice whispered.

"Who's there?"

"I am Ishmael. Who are you?"

"Bethan." She struggled to sit up and the movement brought on nausea. "Where are we?"

"We are inside the north cliff."

Beth fought the need to vomit as she tried to make sense of his words. "Did you say inside the cliff?"

"Yes. Where did they catch you?"

"The last thing I remember is being on the cliff, then nothing."

"That is all I remember, too. What day is it?"

"They caught me on the cliff late on Sunday night."

"You were unconscious for a long time. Without light, it is impossible to tell how much time has passed. This may be Monday or Tuesday."

"My watch!"

"They took it."

"How long have you been here?"

"Since Sunday night. Tom Rowland is also here. He has been here since Saturday morning."

"A likely story," Beth said, touching the sore lump on her head. "I heard Tom in the early hours of Sunday morning packing his things."

"That could not be Tom. He was here before I arrived."

Beth raised clenched fists to her mouth. If not Tom . . . who had been in the house? The intruder must have come back. If she'd gone to tell him off for making so much noise . . . Emrys had her car in the garage, so whoever it was thought the house empty.

How did they get in? Did Megan give anyone a spare key? Gwyn had a key. He'd let himself into the house when she refused to open the door. Beth didn't want to think Gwyn had anything to do with this, whatever that was, but who else could she suspect.

"Are you still conscious?"

"I'm thinking."

"May I ask what you are thinking?"

"For starters, I'm wondering what this is all about."

"Tom has been able to tell me a few things. He frequently lapses into unconsciousness and has not spoken for several hours."

"Is he dead?"

"No."

"This is all Tom's fault! If he hadn't insisted on staying in my house, I wouldn't be involved in any of this."

"He is not the one who attacked you."

"They must think he told me what was going on."

"They do not."

"How can you be sure?"

"They have been searching Derwen House for months. They are looking for something and you were in the way."

"What were they looking for?"

"No one knows."

"What did Tom say?"

"He is a detective attached to a special branch of the London Metropolitan Police."

An added fear made Beth shiver. "Why is he in Derwen?"

"Because he is badly injured and may not survive, he told me things dangerous for you to know."

"Yes, I suppose things could get worse. Someone knocked me out and tossed me into some sort of cave. What's going on?"

"The police suspect Derwen Bay is the centre for a forgery operation. This is the ideal place. It is quiet. No one would suspect such a thing here."

"Aunty Meg hid a large quantity of French banknotes. If they are forgeries, they might be searching the house for those."

"That is possible. Megan knew something."

"Didn't she tell Gwyn?"

"That may have been her intention. She telephoned him and asked him to go to her, but the storm delayed him. When he arrived at the house, Megan had gone."

"Who's running it?"

"Reginald Plews."

"Bastard. I suppose he is the one who put us in here."

"He or one of his men is responsible."

"You say Aunty Meg was gone when Gwyn got there. I refuse to believe she went onto the beach, but that's where you found her."

"We searched for her for several hours. She was not on the beach during that time."

"Where could she have gone?"

"We do not know."

"Does Gwyn know about what's going on here?"

"No. Tom said the police had no idea who in the village was involved. Their instructions were to tell no one, not even the local constable."

"Idiots!"

"Others work with Tom. They take turns to stay around the village."

"The stoppers. That's why I found a painting by another artist in Tom's room."

"How did you learn the painting was not Tom's work?"

"Because I'm in the painting and another stopper did it."

"Oh."

"Tom has been coming here for two years. Hasn't he been able to find out anything in that time?"

"Somebody is in collusion with them; somebody in the village. Tom used the phrase *tipping them off*. He said whenever they closed in and approached the solution; everything became quiet for a while."

"Won't anyone miss Tom? Doesn't he report to someone?"

"Yes. He and another artist meet at assigned times."

"Doug? But he left Derwen on Saturday night."

"Are you sure?"

"He told me so. But Tom must have contacted others."

"I had the impression only two men or women were here at one time. If others come, will they look for Tom inside the cliff? They did not consider looking for the female officer in here."

Bethan fought the need to cry, but a sob escaped.

"Bethan?"

"I . . ." The need for human contact was overwhelming. "Where are you?"

"You are to the right of me. If you reach out with your left hand, perhaps we can find each other."

Beth rose to her knees and winced; pain and stiffness made moving difficult. A wave of dizziness stopped her moving for several minutes. The rock was damp and cold and a sharp fragment cut through her jeans. "Blast!" Her hand found something round. A football? Harder, and— Beth screamed and fell back.

"What is the matter?"

"I found . . . a . . . is it you?"

"I did not feel you touch me."

"Then . . ." Beth gulped. "I found a body."

"There are several. Two are female. Tom believes one of the women is a London Metropolitan officer who disappeared. Two men from the caravan site are also here. He did not know who they were but one was alive and spoke to Tom. The man had not spoken for several hours so I checked him. He was not breathing."

A hand rested on her arm and Beth screamed again.

"It is I." Ishmael's voice came from close beside her.

Beth huddled against him, her head on his shoulder, and he cried out. Beth pulled away. "Are you hurt?"

"I broke my shoulder when they threw me in here."

"I'm sorry. I didn't mean to hurt you."

"At least I am alive."

"Did they kill the others they put in here?"

"We are not meant to get out."

"Why didn't they kill us?"

"Apart from Tom and the man from the caravan park, the others were dead when they arrived here."

"Oh, God!" She shuddered. "I don't want to touch them."

"I remember where they are and I will keep you from them."

"There has to be a door. What do we do—wait for somebody to bring us food and tackle them?"

"No food. Tom has seen no one, except for the times when they brought us here."

"No food? Do they mean to starve us to death?"

"Tom has had nothing to eat since breakfast on Saturday. Water trickles from the top of the cliff to form a pool and thus prevents dehydration."

"Did you try to open the door?"

"Although made of iron it is not rusted. They drop into place to secure it on the outside."

"If we slid something between the door and frame . . ."

"I have no suitable implement. Do you have anything in your pockets?"

Beth checked the slicker and slid her hand into the pockets of her tight-fitting jeans. "I have nothing. What about the—them?"

"I searched them. The only thing I found was a cross and chain one of the men wore." He pressed something into her hand. "This belonged to one of them. It might give you some comfort."

Beth tucked the cross and chain into her jeans pocket. "You said there is water."

"I will take you to it. Are you able to stand?"

Beth struggled to her feet and Ishmael helped to steady her as she swayed, dizzy for a moment. She doubled over, vomited, and then wiped her mouth on the back of her hand. "I'm sorry."

"There is no need to apologise. I, too, was ill when I first regained consciousness."

"They must have caught us both at the same time."

"I had regained my faculties by the time they brought you here. Are you able to continue?"

"I think so." Beth took hold of Ishmael's jacket as he moved forward and the sound of water dripping grew louder.

"The pool of water is here."

Beth let go of his jacket and knelt to cup her hands in the water. It was icy and, as Ishmael said, it tasted earthy. She splashed her face and got to her feet.

"Are you able to continue?"

"Yes. I don't suppose there's a way out."

"There might be."

"Where is it? Show me."

"There is a fissure which I consider too narrow for a man to traverse."

"Did you try?"

"If it is a way out, it will lead down, almost vertical. Even if I could squeeze in, I would need two hands to descend, and my broken shoulder would not allow the use of one hand. Air comes from the fissure and I can hear the sea. Do you wish to attempt an escape?"

"Yes, we have no other choice."

"Very well, I will take you to the fissure. I cannot guarantee it will lead you out. It might become narrower as it goes down and trap you."

"I have to try. What else can we do?"

Ishmael shuffled forward again. "Our only hope of rescue lies with you." Ishmael stopped. "This is the fissure. I reached inside and discovered it would be too narrow for most men to navigate."

Beth let go of Ishmael's jacket, dropped to her knees and felt around for the opening. "If I get out, I'll go to Gwyn. What if I can't find him?"

"If you are unable to locate Gwyn, try to reach Chief Inspector Mathews at police headquarters in Carmarthen." He gave her shoulder a quick squeeze. "Be careful. I assume the fissure leads down to the cave. The roof is too high for you to fall from safely. You will have to wait for a high tide. Can you swim?"

"I've got medals."

"Excellent."

For a moment, she considered discarding the slicker, but the walls of the fissure were rough in places and the oiled canvas would give her some protection. She shuffled around and slid her legs into the opening.

Beth eased lower into the shaft until her waist was on level with the floor. "Before I go down, answer me one thing. Do you know who killed my aunt?"

"No. I do not."

CHAPTER TWENTY-FOUR

The oven had switched off an hour earlier. The casserole was barely warm but a zap in the microwave filled the kitchen with the rich aroma of the spices he'd used. Gwyn prepared the salad while Talia sat beside the door, a mournful look alternating with deep sniffs in the direction of the oven. A quick glance at his watch showed him Daniel-the-Shop would have closed so he couldn't buy dog food.

Glad of the dog's presence to take his mind from his worry about Bethan for a short while, he shared the casserole with Talia. "I suppose you're the only dog in Wales to dine on French cuisine tonight," he commented, putting down a bowl of water. "Not bad for a first effort, eh? Next time we'll try a bit more cumin and a lot less garlic."

Talia licked her plate clean and nosed it aside to check for food she might have missed. She lapped from her bowl then went to the door and gave a solitary bark.

"Was that your compliments to the chef, girl?" Gwyn let her out. He left the door open and returned to his dinner. He hadn't had a dog since he was a boy. If he had to have one, a full grown and trained dog would be his choice, but somewhere this dog's owners must be looking for her.

As the kettle boiled for coffee, Gwyn rang the number on the slip of paper Debbie had given him. A recorded voice announced the phone was out of service. He wasn't perturbed. The address was somewhere in Yorkshire. If Talia's owners didn't leave Derwen Bay until that morning, they wouldn't have reached home yet. People often asked the phone company to put the line out of action if they intended to be away. He'd try again in the morning. He was making coffee when Talia came back in and stretched out in a corner.

Gwyn felt sure the cave would provide a clue to whatever was going on in Derwen, and to Bethan's disappearance. The police-launch inboard would make too much noise for what he had in mind, but a number of people had rowboats he could borrow. Several would ask awkward questions while one or two would want to come with him. Emrys was the obvious choice, if Gwyn could catch him before he went to the Anchor. Gwyn rang the garage.

Julie answered, background shrieks almost drowning her out. "Hang on a minute, Gwyn. Emrys is bathing the twins."

Bathing the twins, an ordinary thing for an ordinary family to do with something going on right under their noses; something not ordinary and something not expected in a quiet place like Derwen.

Emrys laughed as he came to the phone. "Gwyn? What's up, mate? Bethan hasn't been in touch, if that's what you're calling about."

"No, but I intended asking. The car's still in the garage?"

"Locked up tight."

"Good. I need to borrow your rowboat if that's all right."

"Course it is; you know where I keep the oars. Are you going to do a spot of late night fishing?"

"Something like that."

"Any time, Gwyn. You help yourself."

"Thanks." Gwyn hung up and eyed the dog. "I can't take you with me tonight, girl, and I'm not sure how long I'll be so you'll have to be out in the garden."

Gwyn carried the dishes to the sink and Talia sat up with a growl. A few seconds later, someone rapped on the side door. Thinking it would be Bethan, he rushed across the kitchen to open it. "Linda?"

"Can I come in?"

"Of course." Gwyn stepped to one side to let her in and closed the door. "I didn't expect to see you." One part of his mind told him Linda was checking to see if Bethan was there.

"Ooh, a little doggie," Linda said in a baby voice. She held out her hand and Talia backed away with a low growl. "I don't think she likes me." Linda giggled.

"I expect she objects to being called *little doggie*." Gwyn hadn't quite got over their fight of Sunday night. "I'll let her out." After he closed the door on Talia, he turned to find Linda standing close. Her perfume wreathed itself about them. "Why are you here?"

"I came to say I'm sorry." Linda placed her hands on his chest, her face upturned. "Will you forgive me?"

Beautiful . . . Desirable . . .

The phone rang at the front desk. For a moment, Gwyn was tempted to ignore it, but it might be an emergency, it might be Bethan. He pushed through the doorway into the station and Linda followed. He picked up the receiver and she nibbled his free ear.

"Gwyn? It's Dilys. Is there any news of Bethan?"

Gwyn jerked his ear away from Linda's lips. "No news yet, but I'll stay in touch."

He hung up and pulled away from Linda. "I'm sorry. I have to be on duty."

She pouted, not an expression he often saw on her always-agreeable face. "Can't it wait?"

Gwyn shook his head.

Linda shrugged. "All right, but I left my earrings here. They must be in the bedroom."

"I don't think so. Let me check."

"I can do it," she offered.

"No, I will." He hurried into the bedroom, glanced around and even lifted the sheets and bedcover to check under them. He went back into the kitchen. "They're not in there."

The answer seemed to satisfy her. Linda brushed her lips to his cheek and left.

Gwyn went to let Talia in but the dog was nowhere in sight. First Bethan and then Ishmael, now the damned dog had gone missing, too!

Perhaps she'd found her way back to the campground. Gwyn checked his watch: ten o'clock. Catrin and Ifor would be watching telly.

Debbie answered the phone.

"Shouldn't you be in bed?" Gwyn asked.

"Yes." In the background, Ifor was shouting and Catrin shrieking.

"It's Gwyn Thomas. Is everything all right?"

"Yes." Debbie sniffed.

"Do you want me to come up?"

"No." Her voice had the nasal quality of someone who had been crying.

"Are you sure?"

"Yes."

"Talia ran away. I thought she might have come back up there. Will you watch out for her tomorrow?"

"Yes."

The line went dead.

Gwyn put the receiver to rest. Behind Debbie's voice, he'd heard a domestic dispute. He'd answered enough of them to know, but they hadn't called him to this one. Even so . . . Catrin was only a slip of a thing, and Ifor . . .

The house was in darkness when Gwyn got there. He left the Land Rover and stood for a moment in the shadows at the entrance to the campground. Stitch barked a warning and Gwyn returned to the police station.

The phone was ringing when he entered and he ran to answer it.

"Gwyn? It's Eleri. There's been no sign of Bethan and I'm just leaving Derwen House now. Snowy must be starving."

"Thanks, Eleri. You didn't need to stay there all evening."

"I'm aware of that, but Bethan is all I have left of Megan." Eleri's voice broke and then she took a deep breath that whistled over the line. "I'll take your key home with me, all right?"

"Thanks." If he needed to get into Derwen House, he had a duplicate of the key to the lock on the back door.

Gwyn went to the cupboard beside the bed to get the key but it wasn't there. He took the drawer out, tipped the contents onto the bed, found one of the police medals he'd forgotten about but not the key. He searched all his pockets, went into the living room and tore it apart, tumbling cushions from the sofa and feeling behind the seats of other chairs. Mystified, he gave up and went to the kitchen to clear the supper things.

Gwyn washed the dishes and wondered why Linda had tried to make up after their quarrel when she accused him of cheating on her with Bethan. What made her change her attitude? For the first time, Linda's behaviour confused him.

He changed into his uniform and checked the fax. There was still no message from Sergeant Jenkins, not about the deliberate tampering with Bethan's car or about the missing person's report. Disappointed and angry at the Sergeant's failure to respond, Gwyn returned to the kitchen and reached for his helmet where he always kept it hanging beside the door. The back door key to Derwen House hung from the next hook. Puzzled, he unhooked it and put it in his pocket. He set off convinced he was losing his mind. He was hearing voices and now he found the key in a place where he didn't remember putting it.

The tide was still running as Gwyn hurried along the Front. If he tried to row into the cave while the waves tumbled ashore, he risked damaging Emrys' boat. The Witch posed a danger, too. While the sea was active, she'd draw a rowboat to waltz around her skirts. It wasn't just the danger, such a thing would increase the chance of someone seeing him and wondering what he was doing. Until he learned who in the village was involved, Gwyn had to temper his impatience and wait until the sea went into its quiet hour. Now was not the time for rash behaviour.

Gwyn commended himself for keeping his emotions in check. The lack of response at Derwen House was no more than he'd expected but, when he found Ishmael's house empty, too, anger boiled. Damn the man! When he caught up with him, Gwyn had a good mind to box his ears.

Box his ears. *Duw mawr!* He sounded like his grandfather. That's what the old man always threatened. *I'll box your ears, Gwyn, if you don't smarten up!* Megan used the same phrase. She and his granddad would be about the same age but here Gwyn used the same expression and him just nudging thirty. The uniform did it; the damned uniform that made a man old before his time.

He strolled along the Front, keeping to the shadows that wrapped themselves around the dark of his clothing. He lingered in doorways, arms folded to hide the silver buttons marching down his front like twinkling lights. He could do nothing about the badge on his helmet, nothing about the length of chain attached to the whistle in his breast pocket. When he walked, the strong flashlight hanging from his belt tapped in a muffled way against the truncheon in the long pocket of his trousers.

He stood in the bus shelter, out of the wind, and listened for the waves to quiet, waited for the tide to lie still, and thought about Bethan—the way her eyes flashed when she was angry; the reddening of her cheeks when she realised she'd interrupted his private moment with Linda. The gentle, secret look she gave him when she picked the cobweb off his shoulder. She wouldn't have left without telling someone. She wouldn't have left without telling him.

"Gwyn?" A hand touched his arm.

He jumped and swung around, forearm raised in defence.

Eleri stepped back. "I didn't mean to startle you."

Gwyn lowered his arm. "I didn't hear you coming."

"You were deep in thought." She stepped into the shelter and out of the wind.

"What are you doing here?"

"I just remembered something Megan told me, but we'll have to go to Derwen House to check."

"What did she tell you?"

"When Bethan was little, she had a hiding place under the floorboards in their bedroom. Megan wasn't supposed to know about it."

Gwyn grinned. "It wasn't easy keeping anything from Megan. Do you think Bethan might have put something there that will tell us where she went?"

"It's possible."

Gwyn hesitated and eyed the sea. It would be a while before the tide reached its quiet hour. "I'll check it out." He stepped away from the shelter.

"I'm coming with you," Eleri said.

"There's no need."

"I'm coming."

If the prowler planned to visit the house tonight . . . "I don't want anyone to see us around the house at this time of night."

"Mrs Williams put her light out half an hour ago. She'll be asleep by now and giving her tongue the rest it needs."

"Eleri!" In the mellow light, he saw the smile on her face.

"Well, it's true, isn't it?"

He studied her. She was wearing dark clothes and had pulled a black knitted tam over her white hair. "You're dressed like a burglar."

She grinned and winked. "No point in letting everyone know this widow of the parish is out late at night chasing young bachelors, is there?"

Gwyn chuckled. "We'll have to go in via the back lane; less chance of anyone seeing us."

"Lead on."

CHAPTER TWENTY-FIVE

Slim as she was, Beth had trouble manoeuvring inside the fissure. Carved by eons of trickling water, even gravity didn't help her descent because the hole veered this way and that like a snake. This must have been how Jonah felt inside the whale. A vision of Powell-Pritchard came to mind. He frightened them with his tale of Jonah's trip and none of the children went near the beach for weeks.

Her toes ached as she fought for purchase, and her fingers were scraped raw, nails broken and ragged after only a few feet. For the most part, the damp walls of the shaft were uneven and rounded, but sharp edges caught her unawares. In one place, after the slicker ripped, Beth had no option but to graze her ribs on a jut of rock to squeeze lower. Ishmael must have heard her sharp intake of breath and he called down for reassurance.

"I'm all right," she shouted. But was she? If she couldn't get out at the bottom, she'd have to climb back. She'd never make it. Already exhausted, her hands were so tender she winced each time she reached for a handhold. It would be impossible to climb. If she didn't escape, she'd die in the shaft. She'd wither away until her bones fell into the cave for children to find when they played there. The only thing left apart from anonymous jeans and shirt would be the cross and chain that didn't belong to her. There was the slicker, of course, and Gwyn would recognise it but, by the time they discovered her bones, Gwyn would be long dead.

Beth cried, silent tears tickling a trail down to her chin but she dared not let go of the rock to wipe them away. If she died here, she'd never see Gwyn again. The last time they'd spoken, she'd called him all sorts of names. She'd been angry with him and said dreadful things, and now she was sorry.

But he's a policeman. He's a policeman! He's a bloody policeman! Beth chanted the words under her breath as she forced herself through the next tight spot.

Then she fell. She screamed and her voice echoed from the rocks above and below. A hundred screams, going on forever. A sharp jerk ended her fall and cut the cry short.

"Bethan! Bethan! Are you all right?"

Ishmael's voice reverberated around her, repeating the question a hundred times, but she had no breath to answer. The slicker had halted her fall, a part of it catching on the rock. She dangled from it by one arm hooked into a sleeve and it had a stranglehold on her throat. Gingerly, not knowing how long the slicker would hold, she probed about with her feet. She lost one boot in the effort but encountered nothing. She caught onto the slicker with her free hand and pulled herself up. The hold on her neck eased. "I'm all right" she gasped. "I'm all right."

"What happened?"

"What do you think happened!" she called up the shaft.

She jerked down a few inches and panic locked her windpipe. The slicker wouldn't hold for long. If she fell, she didn't know what she would land on. Although it was a safe guess it would be more rock, would it be smooth or jagged? Moreover, in this darkness, she couldn't tell how far she would fall. Then she found out.

Without warning, the slicker ripped free. Beth yelled once before she hit rock. She didn't hear the echo.

CHAPTER TWENTY-SIX

Eleri left the hall light on as a welcome to Bethan. It shone into the bedroom Beth had shared with Megan and moonlight added to the glow. Determined not to alert the prowler, Gwyn decided not to switch on more lights and explained why to Eleri. They went to different corners of the room and pulled back the carpet.

"There are loose floorboards here." Eleri pried them up and placed them to one side. "And there's something else." She took out a brown-paper package and handed it to Gwyn.

He opened the package and bundles of banknotes spilled out. Thousands of pounds; the money Bethan withdrew from her bank. He realised she would never leave Derwen without the money. Stunned with fear for her safety, he sat back on his heels.

"Gwyn?"

He dragged his attention back to Eleri. "What?"

"These were here, too," she said, handing him a bundle of notes, "brand new French francs."

He fingered the smooth surface of a franc. "Is Bethan planning to go to France?"

"I don't think so."

Something in her voice made him turn to her. "Why?"

"Because these are like the note Megan found, the one in the kitchen. Somehow she found more and put them in here."

"Where would she get . . . ?"

"It's a lot of money and Megan never mentioned anything to me about it. Why would she keep so much?"

"It isn't all Megan's; the pound notes are Bethan's," Gwyn said quietly.

"How can you be sure?"

"Before she left London, Bethan closed her bank account and withdrew the cash."

"Why didn't she just open an account here?"

"I don't know, Eleri, but it's the francs that interest me. Brand new uncirculated notes in this quantity . . ."

"Forgeries?"

He shrugged.

"But why? What good is forged French money here? Why not make pounds?"

"If . . ." Gwyn took off his helmet and scrubbed his fingers through his hair. "Forged French money won't be detected if it's used in Britain because we aren't familiar with the currency." He got to his feet, his mind racing. "Francs exchanged in small amounts at village banks would end up at the Bank of England for exchanging with France. The French bank would recognise a forged note . . ."

"And our bank would lose out."

"Yes."

"What that would do to our economy is . . . But there isn't enough money here to make much of a difference."

"I agree," Gwyn said, "but what if this is part of a larger operation? What if these notes are just a drop in the ocean? What if there are millions more? Other currencies?"

"How can we find out?"

"Me, Eleri. You have no part in this."

"You try stopping me! If it wasn't for me, you wouldn't know about this."

"I don't know anything now. It's all supposition."

"Then check with Carmarthen. Check with Metro."

He'd have to use the computer; get all his thumbs in order. Oh, hell! "Can you use a computer?"

"I've never tried. Too old to learn now, I suppose." Eleri put the floorboards back and spread the carpet over them.

"Oh, hell!"

"What's the matter?"

"I'm not good with computers."

"There's always the telephone."

* * *

"Oh, hell!" Gwyn saw the screen go blank, and clicking on different keys didn't alter a thing.

"What happened?"

"I hit something and everything went dead."

"Switch it on again."

"I'm no good at this, Eleri. I'm a pen and paper man." Gwyn bit his lip as the computer sprang to life.

"Isn't there someone in Carmarthen who can help?"

"At this time of night?"

"Try." Eleri prodded his shoulder.

Gwyn picked up the telephone and dialled. When someone answered at Carmarthen headquarters, he identified himself and asked to speak to anyone who could help with a computer problem.

"Are you aware of the time?" the voice asked.

"Yes, but I'm having trouble with my computer."

A sigh like a soughing wind came across the wire. "Hold on."

"It sounds as if someone who can help is on duty," Gwyn told Eleri.

"Let me listen." Eleri placed an ear next to the receiver.

A strident voice barked, "What have you done now, Thomas?"

Dorothy Driscoll! Gwyn cringed. "You're working late, Sarge."

"What do you want?" she snapped.

"I've forgotten how to access and search files. When I tried, the computer shut off."

"Idiot!" Although muttered under her breath, Gwyn heard. "What are you trying to research?"

"The Bank of England—"

"No, Gwyn, it's forgery cases you want." Eleri reminded him.

"Who's that? You got someone there with you, Thomas? It isn't the stick insect, is it?"

"No, it isn't," Eleri said. "I'll have you know I'm a respectable woman."

"Who are you? What's your name?"

"I'm Eleri Edwards, retired school mistress of this parish."

"What's the matter with you, Thomas? Are all your girlfriends old ladies or stick insects?"

"How dare you!" Eleri shrieked. "I earned my seniority and it's better than being a butch."

"Don't you mean bitch?" Dorothy retorted.

"No, I don't."

Gwyn cleared his throat, switched the receiver to his other ear and shook his head at Eleri. "Sergeant, do we have an active file on forgers in this area?"

"Forgers? Money forgers, you mean?"

"Yes."

"Hold on."

The sergeant's keyboard clattered away and Gwyn held his hand over the mouthpiece. "I don't need trouble with the sergeant, Eleri, especially not this one."

"Sorry, Gwyn, but she isn't a nice person."

"You'll get no argument from me, or anyone else who works with her."

"Thomas? What the hell are you into?"

Gwyn motioned to Eleri to be silent and she moved to where she could again hear both sides of the conversation. "What do you mean?"

"If I get another bollocking because of you . . ."

"Why? What did you find?"

"Something's going on, and I don't believe it's just in your patch. There is a file but they've locked it at London Metro. Hang on a minute . . ."

Eleri's eyes were like saucers. "What is happening?"

Gwyn shrugged. He'd wondered about smugglers, but what if they were smuggling forged notes? Either Megan or Bethan had a stash of them hidden away. How did they get them? Was that what the prowler was looking for? Did they bring in paper and ink by boat, or forged notes? Was it possible they hid notes under the rubble the lorries carried out of Plas Mawr? Plas Mawr! Reginald Plews! Was he involved?

"Thomas?" Sergeant Driscoll came back on the line. "I spoke to somebody and all he would tell me is that your patch is involved. He suggests you stay out of it."

Gwyn's hand tightened on the receiver until his knuckles turned white. Once again, they were keeping him out of the picture. "Tell me one thing, Sarge. Does this involve Reginald Plews in some way?"

The line was silent for so long that Gwyn wondered if she'd hung up, then:

"Yes, he's involved. Look, I can't say any more, not that I can tell you anything anyway, but my contact strongly suggests you leave it alone."

"I see. Thank you." Gwyn prepared to hang up and Eleri moved away.

"Wait! The desk will log your call to me. I need to give a reason if I'm to avoid another bollocking. You owe me, Thomas."

"What do you suggest?"

"I've got holidays due and Derwen Bay sounds like a nice place."

"I can book you into the Anchor."

"I can't afford a hotel. I'll stay with you."

Gwyn shuddered. "I don't have a spare bedroom."

"No, I don't suppose you do but I'm sure you have a double bed. I'll be in touch."

Gwyn hung up and buried his face in his hands. "Oh, hell!"

"What happened? What did she say?" Eleri asked.

"Give me a minute . . ." Gwyn walked into the kitchen and put on the kettle. "I need strong coffee. Would you like one?"

"Please." Eleri stood in the doorway and watched Gwyn bring sugar, milk and spoons to the table. "Why is the file locked? Why aren't they bringing you in on their investigation?"

"They must think I'm involved in whatever's going on." He'd asked about Plas Mawr planning permission days ago. In their minds, did that form a connection between him and Reginald Plews?

"Is this something you can't talk to me about?"

"Yes, but . . . look, you're the one who put me onto the forged money, if that's what it is, and . . ."

"And you're in a spot. You're not sure if you can trust me to keep my mouth shut, is that it?"

"No, that's not what I mean, but I don't know much more than you do." Gwyn spooned coffee and poured boiling water into the mugs before carrying them to the table. "All they'll tell me is that a locked file is being handled by London Metro that involves Derwen Bay."

"So we were right. They are forging French money here and Reginald Plews is involved?"

"Yes."

"A rich man like that?" Eleri dropped into a chair next to the table. "I suppose that's how he became rich."

"There's more. But I might be adding two and two and getting five." Gwyn spooned sugar into his mug.

"Tell me." Eleri took a sip of her black coffee.

He told her, trying to fit the pieces together as he spoke. "The lorries coming and going to Plas Mawr at all hours have been doing it for months. Plews is enlarging his cellar. How big does he intend it to be? The amount of rubble carried out seems excessive. A lot of new lumber is carried in, far more than needed in my opinion."

"He might be replacing wood in the rest of the house," Eleri ventured.

Gwyn shook his head in denial. "Then there are the boats coming in at night. Ricky's seen them go into the cave on the beach, and I don't believe the boy is lying. He and Bethan have seen a light flashing from the cave. He said Megan had seen it, too." He looked up at Eleri. He could almost hear her mind ticking. "I've heard a noise at night, like rock grating on rock, and when I was on the cliff with Talia earlier today I felt the ground vibrate."

Eleri's eyes widened with alarm. "An earthquake?"

Gwyn shook his head. "More like heavy machinery working somewhere underground, inside the cliff."

"The printing press?"

"It's possible. How big would one of those be?"

"Depends on how old it is, I suppose; unless Plews is extending his cellar close to the cliff."

"I doubt the Plas Mawr property line goes that far. There's something else—I examined the cave. High up, there's a shiny area on one of the rocks as if a boat has been tied up there."

"To what?"

"There is nothing to tie it to. I'm going in tonight when the tide is in to have a better look."

Eleri put her mug down with a clatter. "Be careful, Gwyn. What if the boat Ricky saw comes in after you?"

"I must take a chance. I must offer Metro something so they'll tell me what's going on and let me into the investigation. Right now all I have is suspicion and the word of a small boy."

Eleri was silent for a moment. When she spoke, it was with a quiver in her voice. "If Metro aren't letting you in on the investigation and you think they think you're involved . . . ."

"Yes," he answered bluntly. "They don't trust me. There was another matter I asked about a few days ago, and those files were locked too."

"How can they—They don't know you, Gwyn. If they did, they'd know you can be trusted. You're no law breaker."

"I must prove to them they can trust me; that I'm not involved with whatever is going on here. To do that, I have to take a boat into the cave tonight."

* * *

Aware Eleri huddled just inside the door to the public toilets; Gwyn perched on the steps at the side of the deckchair hut. Close into the shadows and with little moonlight, he had a clear view of the Front, the beach, and the path up the north cliff. Minutes earlier a courting couple came up from the beach, the girl giggling quietly at something the boy murmured. Now all was silent and dark outside the pools of light from the lamp standards along the Front.

A motorbike came down the hill fast, not the two-stroke job Sammy Williams rode but a more powerful machine. Gwyn stepped out of the shadows as the bike rounded the corner and made for Beach Road.

It stopped outside Derwen House; the rider got off and ran to the door. Gwyn recognised Doug Amundson. Emrys said Doug had been on his way home to London on Saturday, but here he was back again.

Gwyn fast-walked up Beach Road; he met Doug as he headed back to his bike. "Do you need help with anything?" Gwyn asked.

"Have you seen Tom? Tom Rowland?"

"Not since Saturday morning when he went up the north cliff with his painting gear. Mind you, I was away all day Sunday. Anyway, Bethan told Dilys he'd cleared out sometime on Saturday and taken all his stuff with him."

"Are you sure about that?" Doug's gaze swivelled from Gwyn to the bay.

"That's what she said. Goodnight." Gwyn continued up Beach Road. For whatever reason, knowing Tom had left made Doug jittery. Gwyn passed a few houses, crossed a property to the back lane, and returned to his post.

Doug had wheeled his bike to the car park and propped it against a wall. Now he ran along the beach towards the south cliff. Gwyn stayed in the shadows and watched.

Flat rocks at the foot of the south cliff jutted over the water. Splashing through the shallows, Doug climbed onto them and sat facing the north cliff. In his black-leather motorcycle outfit, it was difficult to see him but then a glint of something caught the moonlight. Doug had a pair of binoculars trained across the bay. As he swept them backwards and forwards across the cliff, Gwyn pressed deeper into the shadows.

Damn the man! Whatever Doug was up to, he hindered what Gwyn wanted to do. If it had been a local man, Gwyn would have sent him on his way. Doug wasn't breaking any laws but if he trained his binoculars on one of the houses, he'd have him for a peeping tom.

There! Doug pointed his binoculars at the top of the north cliff. Plas Mawr was the only building up there. Even if Doug couldn't see anything but the boundary wall around the house, Gwyn could still charge him. He was about to step into sight when Doug splashed back through the shallows and came racing across the sand.

Doug sprinted past, so close Gwyn heard his laboured breathing. Doug turned onto the cliff path and his pace slowed. Gwyn let him go as other footsteps scuffed towards him along the Front; Willy Ellis on his way home. At the Anchor, the last of the lights went out.

When he judged the tide had reached its high point and growing calm, Gwyn vaulted the sea wall and headed for Emrys' boat.

CHAPTER TWENTY-SEVEN

"Bethan?" The voice was far away, whispering from the walls.

She opened her eyes on a darkness that swirled around her. Years earlier, a so-called friend slipped something into her drink. When she went to bed and closed her eyes, she had the sensation of the room spinning. The feeling now was the same. She struggled to keep her eyes open and fought down the nausea.

"Bethan?" The voice came again.

"Who's there?" Her voice was weak, yet it deafened her and bile rose like a hot bubble. Beth rolled onto her side and retched.

"It is I, Ishmael. What happened?"

"Ishmael?" she whispered, then memory returned in a rush and she retched again. Her stomach was empty; nothing but a bitter liquid filled her mouth. She spat, laid her head on her arm and gasped for breath.

"Are you able to move?"

Beth touched the lump on the back of her head, bent her knees and winced. "I sprained my ankle." She fingered the swelling above the foot where she'd lost her boot.

"Oh."

Beth got to her knees, avoided the pool of bile, and gasped when her ankle protested the new position. "I'm all right."

"Where are you?"

"How in heck do I know! It's dark down here. I can't see a thing." Which direction was the shaft? Left or right? Straight ahead or back? "I don't know which way to go." She took a couple of calming breaths.

"If you follow the sound of my voice, you should be able to find the shaft. I think it will continue to go down to the cave."

Beth laughed, fighting hysteria. "The way your voice echoes I have no idea where it's coming from."

"Wait. I have an idea."

"It was your blasted idea that got me down here in the first place," Beth muttered, but Ishmael was right. This was their only chance of getting out. She didn't want to starve to death like the owner of the cross and chain and the others.

"Bethan?"

"What now!"

"I found a few stone chips. If I throw them down the shaft you can listen for where they land."

"They'll land right on top of me, or do you think I fell at an angle? Gravity still works down here, you know. Just shut up and let me find the shaft. I have enough to deal with so don't call me, I'll call you."

In an effort to ignore the pain in her ankle, she muttered curses under her breath as she crawled forward. Her head met rock. She manoeuvred around and moved in another direction. This time, nothing barred her way. A gentle breath of air bathed her face. Beth eased forward and her fingers found an opening leading down. "I've found the shaft," she called.

"Can you hear the sea?"

Beth dragged herself closer to the shaft and turned an ear to the opening. A seagull's cry reached her, then, as she strained to listen, the distant roll and crash of strong breakers that sounded as if the tide was racing in. She let Ishmael know and sat next to the opening. It might take a while before the tide was high enough to enter its quiet hour. She had no way of knowing if the shaft was steep or if it had toe or hand holds.

She dared not risk dropping into the water until the tide quieted because the waves would batter her against the cave walls. All she could do was wait and pray the shaft would be wide enough for her to get out at the other end.

Her head against the roughness of the wall, the torn slicker wrapped around her for whatever warmth it could offer, exhaustion and lack of food caught up with her. Beth dozed.

* * *

A loud clang jerked her awake. The nausea had left and a pang of hunger joined her thirst. She felt rested so she knew time had passed. As she came fully awake, she became aware of a whirring sound and air rose from the shaft with more force. Then a rumbling started somewhere in the cliff. The noise seemed to emanate from the rock and the echoes deafened her. Beth clamped hands to her ears and shouted: "Ishmael!"

When he didn't answer, Beth realised the racket drowned out her voice. She scooted away from the shaft, heading for the source of the sound. The whirring stopped as abruptly as it began and the air stilled.

"Bethan?"

"What was that noise?"

"I have heard it before. Do not be afraid. The cliff is not falling apart."

"The thought never crossed my mind. I'm going to check where it came from."

"No! Do not do that, Bethan."

"If you want to stop me, you come down here." Beth groped her way from the shaft. She ignored Ishmael's echoing protests and did her best to disregard the complaint from her ankle. It stiffened while she slept; now it throbbed in time with the dull thump-thump-thump in her head. The pain

231

made thinking clearly difficult, but the sound, accompanied by the stronger force of air, meant a fan. A fan was man-made. If she located it, she might be able to find another way out of here.

Beneath her hands, Beth discovered smoother planes of rock, machined rather than formed naturally. Someone had cut an airshaft, a sort of tunnel about three feet in diameter, large enough to suck in air from the cave below. Why? What for? And where did they place the debris? They couldn't put it on the beach, because people would notice the addition of a rock pile. Other caves might exist, like the one Ishmael was in, and they could put it there.

Strips of light suddenly fingered the rock, as if someone switched on a light beyond the fan. Then a rhythmic mechanical clanking reverberated, the volume increasing as Beth wormed her way forward until she was lying next to the metal blades. If the fan started up again it might be strong enough to draw her in. She struggled out of the slicker and weaved it around the hub, wrapping it as tightly as she could. The oiled cloth wouldn't hold forever but it might stop the blades long enough for her to squirm back along the tunnel. Safe from immediate danger, she inched closer and peered out.

The fan was set high up on the wall of a cavern. Below, two men worked at machinery Beth identified as printing presses, so old they looked to be falling apart. Several wooden crates sat on the floor. They held bundles of foreign banknotes, among them the same type of francs she found under the floorboards in Derwen House. By their red hair, Beth recognised the O'Malley brothers.

"Rory!" one of them called out. "I'm taking this load up." He pushed a handcart with rumbling iron wheels towards an incline and disappeared from view.

Rory stopped the press, took a grimy rag from his pocket and wiped his brow before going to a table. He picked up a flask and poured steaming liquid into a cup. Beth's stomach growled. The sight of Rory drinking drew attention to her own hunger and thirst. It would be worse for Ishmael because he'd been here longer. She had to get them both out, and Tom, too, but the fan didn't offer a way. Even if the cavern were empty, the only way down was to jump, and it was too high to do that without injury.

Another man came into sight, walking down the incline carrying an empty crate. Beth didn't remember seeing him before. She'd been away from the village but no one changed that much in ten years so he must be a newcomer. He was probably one of the men Emrys told her had come to work on Plas Mawr.

Plas Mawr. The piles of rocks in the garden . . . The tunnel was where they'd come from. They'd machined the airshaft and carried out the rock, but hadn't anyone heard? Had they attributed any noise to the renovations at Plas Mawr? The cavern must be beneath the house.

"At least now that halfwit isn't on the other side of the bay watching us." The new arrival set the empty crate next to the others.

"That's a good thing, eh, Andy?" Rory said. "He gave me the creeps, always sitting in the rocks. It was hard to see him because he kept so still."

"He was too daft to tell anybody about what he saw." Andy leaned against one of the presses.

"As daft as that old woman who pinched the money from our house."

"What the hell did she do with it?" Andy asked. "We've searched the damned place and turned it inside out."

Beth clamped a hand over her mouth. One of them was the intruder she heard the first night in the house.

"She must have given it to the bobby, but he hasn't done anything about it."

Andy laughed. "He probably took it for Monopoly money."

"That girl talked to him." Rory arched his back, hands to the base of his spine.

"It don't matter," Andy said. "She won't be talking to anyone else."

"I still say it was a mistake to bring the old woman's clothes here with the girl's things."

"We've been all through this. I just grabbed all the suitcases and filled them. I told you I didn't know which clothes belonged to the girl."

"You should have let me help you, Andy. I'd have known." A dark-haired woman stepped into view from where she must have been sitting close to the wall beneath the fan.

Bethan's training in fashion came to the fore and she studied the woman. Her tight black skirt, made from a cheap man-made weave, was beginning to stretch where she sat. The tight-fitting low-necked black sweater was a cotton-and-nylon mix that would pill up and turn grey after a wash or two. As for her shoes—they were scuffed imitation leather, with three-inch heels. She had a ladder in one of her black stockings.

Recognition dawned. Gwyn's girlfriend. Was Gwyn involved in this?

"Best if you stay clear of the house, Linda. Helping us borrow the key was enough." Andy found a cup and poured himself a drink.

"Yes. You can't be seen near the house," Rory echoed.

"At least that girl won't be spying on us over the wall." Andy gulped his drink and put the cup down.

"And she won't be walking around our cottage, neither," Rory added. "So there's nothing to stop you getting into that house and tearing it apart."

"Only Gwyn Thomas. He's been hanging around too much for my liking."

"We can't do much about him. If he disappears, too, we'll have the whole damned lot of them down here like that time the old woman was found."

Beth uttered a small cry. They killed Meg!

"What was that?" Rory asked.

"What? I didn't hear anything." Linda looked around.

"It came from the fan."

"Probably a bird; like the one that got sucked in last year. Earlier on tonight, I thought I heard one screaming up there. Just ignore it."

"Somebody's up there," Rory insisted.

"Don't talk daft. How can there be?"

"I'm getting the ladder and having a look." Rory walked from Bethan's sight.

"Jeez! Will you leave it be, man!"

Beth tugged the slicker free and the blade grated against the central cylinder. Wood knocked against the rock beneath the fan. As fast as she could, she squirmed away, balling the tell-tale yellow of the slicker because the colour reflected the light. She'd backed up several feet when a shadow cut across the pale glow on the other side of the fan. Would Rory take the fan out? Would he go as far as climbing into the tunnel?

A clanking sound came from the fan and Rory said. "This is bloody weird."

"What's that?" Andy asked.

"Come up here."

"How can I do that when you're standing on the only ladder? What did you find—a dead seagull?"

"It's a piece of yellow oilcloth, like our Mam has on the table back home."

"So?"

"It wasn't here last week when I had the fan out to oil it."

"It must've got sucked in when we put the fan on."

"And got caught in the workings? Get me my flashlight."

"Get it yourself."

Heedless of the pain in her ankle, Beth shuffled backwards while Rory took the fan out of its housing. A beam of light explored the tunnel. She kept still, shielding the white of her face in her arms, but he saw her and gave a shout.

Beth retreated as fast as she could. She passed the pool of bile, dropped the slicker into the shaft and wriggled after it.

Beth shimmied lower into the shaft, oblivious to the fresh scrapes and cuts of the rock, as Rory crawled closer.

"Ach! Shit! Will you look at that!"

He must have found the pool of bile.

How far down would she be able to go before Rory reached the top of the shaft? Would he be able to climb down after her? It was a tight squeeze, but Rory didn't look much bigger than she was, just taller.

She slid down. The sprained ankle protested as she searched for purchase with her toes. Raw fingers and shredded palms clutched at any protrusion that would allow a grip. Below, the waves dashed against the walls of the cave. How far down did she have to go? How far would she have to drop?

"Where are you, bitch?" Rory reached the top of the shaft and shone the light into it.

Beth smothered a scream as fingers brushed her hair. She jerked herself downward and the shaft turned at an angle. It was larger here, but jagged rock scored her back as she eased around so her body would conform to the bend. She ended up lying on a horizontal section, but she was on her back and the going was slow. Below her, the waves sounded wild, the last mad rush before the tide spent itself. She dared not fall into it yet; her weight would send her under the water. If there was any sort of undertow in the narrow confines of the cave, it would sweep her out towards the Witch.

Above her, Rory lowered himself into the shaft.

Beth waited. When the sea grew calmer, she'd move into what must be the last few feet of shaft. Meanwhile, she listened to the sounds Rory made. He descended slowly. Slim though he was, he had difficulty getting past the jagged outcrops. If he came too close, she'd make a last effort and take her chances with the sea.

An inch at a time, she manoeuvred until she was on her stomach. Different from the other hurts, something needle-sharp pricked and embedded itself in her shoulder. She reached to pluck it free, gasping at the quick pain. In the darkness, she traced the shape with raw fingers. Heart-shaped, a brooch like the one Meg always wore. Meg's brooch. With a sob, Beth held it to her lips. Aunty Meg had been in the fissure. It's why her fingers were raw, her nails chipped and broken.

P L Crompton

CHAPTER TWENTY-EIGHT

Gwyn judged the sea was in its quiet hour, a time when the tide was full blown. Some of the older wags said it came to hide in the bay and was lying still so the deep water wouldn't find it and lure it back. Even the gulls were silent. Full bellied after their feast at the fishing boats, they were no more than white blobs nestling in the dark cliffs.

Smooth as silver, undulating ripples caressed the surface as if wafted by a gentle breeze. The water welcomed the boat like a lover and Gwyn placed the oars into the locks. He pulled cautiously, anxious to make no sound to draw attention, and the boat skimmed across the water.

A few feet from the shore, a black and tan blur raced across the sand. It stood at the edge of the water and barked. Talia. If she kept it up, she'd draw attention and he'd have to explain what he was doing rowing a boat around at this time of night.

Eleri left her hiding spot and ran to the dog. She caught her by the collar and silenced her before waving to Gwyn. He waved back and bent to the oars as Eleri dragged Talia away.

Closer to the Witch, despite the calm appearance of the surface, he had to fight an undertow that tugged him towards her. He dared not take the boat close, because she would dash it to shreds against her skirts. He rowed harder and prayed. It took effort but he managed to pull free and guided the boat into the cave. He used the oars to keep clear of the rocks, and poled it deeper into the darkness.

After manoeuvring the flat stern against the back wall of the cave, he unhooked the flashlight from his belt and cast about. Above him, there was still six or seven feet of ceiling, but the place rubbed to smoothness by a rope was within reach. He stood up and grasped the rock, pulling the boat against the wall.

Above where he'd found threads of rope, rust stained the rock. Gwyn touched it and the colour came away on his fingers. Rust meant metal, but none of the rocks around showed evidence of iron ore in their makeup. He focused the light on the stain and saw a hairline crack. It travelled across the rock. A door conformed to the unevenness of the rock and no one would see it at a casual glance from the cave floor. As he reached up to try to pry it open, there was a scream and a splash in the water behind him.

Gwyn shone the light on the ball of yellow unfolding on the surface, and then a head bobbed out of the water. "Bethan?"

CHAPTER TWENTY-NINE

"Thank God!" Bethan swam for the boat and lost the second boot when Gwyn hauled her out of the water.

"Where have you been? I've been looking for you."

"Never mind that now. Get us out of here!" Beth reached for an oar. "Come on, Gwyn!"

A doorway opened in the rock above them and light flooded the cave. Gwyn raised a hand to shield his eyes. "Sean? Is that you?"

Beth moaned. "Oh, God, he's got a gun!"

"What the—!"

A roar echoed around the cave as Gwyn shoved her behind him. He jerked and fell against her. She tried to ease his fall into the bottom of the boat but his weight threw her off balance.

"Gwyn!" Bullets splintered the wood next to her head.

Beth tumbled the rest of the way into the water, the oar still clutched in her hand. She came up for air and bullets churned the surrounding water. Gwyn's helmet floated close by entwined in Meg's yellow slicker.

"Gwyn!" She hammered the side of the boat with her fist. "Gwyn!" She tried to pull herself up, to see if he was badly hurt, and tangled with the boat's towrope. She slid back into the water, grasped the rope and tugged. The boat drifted towards her. Beth dropped the oar, wrapped the rope around her hand and swam for the cave entrance using the light from the doorway in the roof as a guide. She knew the Witch

241

loomed in line with the cave but there was no other direction to take.

A splash sent ripples across the surface of the water, then a hand grabbed Beth's ankle and dragged her down. She let go of the towrope and lashed out with her elbows, knees and feet. For a second, the hold loosened. She sank until her feet touched bottom, and then she kicked for the surface.

As her head came clear of the water, hands wrapped around her throat. In the yellow light, she recognised Rory. Unable to break his grip, she curved her fingers into claws and tore at his face with jagged nails. He let go with one hand to protect his head. She curled her knees to her chest then aimed a foot at his crotch. She missed her target but it was enough for him to release her. Beth dived.

Like a bad dream, Rory came after her in the murky water. In a move he wouldn't expect, Beth swam under him, turned and grabbed his crotch. She squeezed with hands grown numb with cold and he jerked and stiffened. When she let go, Rory floated away.

Beth struck upwards and cleared the surface close to the boat. Rory was a few feet away, his face twisted in agony. A movement to her right drew her look in that direction. Sean was swimming to Rory. He must have run out of bullets, or maybe he noticed his brother was in trouble. In panic, Beth searched for the rope, grasped an end, tied it to her belt, and stroked for the entrance.

When she reached moonlight, Beth saw how badly splintered and bullet-riddled the prow was. She also saw the two men swimming in her direction. She increased her effort, trying to cut a path between the Witch and the cave, but Sean and Rory were closing fast.

A few feet beyond the cave mouth, an undercurrent tugged at her. For once, the Witch's help was welcome because it allowed her to increase the distance between herself and the two men. She gasped for breath, ached in every part of her body, so she let the rock draw them closer and called to Gwyn. She didn't know if he was alive or dead.

The tide began to turn. Around the Witch's skirts, waves flurried, battered, and sucked. Stronger now, the undertow pulled at Beth, and the Witch loomed dark as a nightmare. The rock dragged them to her seaward side, out of sight of any in the village who might have heard the shots. Sean was only a few yards away with Rory close behind him.

While the Witch sucked them towards her, Beth hauled herself onto the side of the boat with a grunt and reached for Gwyn. He didn't respond but his chest was rising and falling. He was still alive but unconscious.

A wave swamped the boat but Gwyn didn't move as salt water splashed his face.

"Gwyn! I need your help," she screamed. "The Witch, Gwyn! We're being pulled into the Witch!"

She had to do something to keep them from smashing against the rock. Beth hauled herself higher on the side of the boat, grabbed the second oar, and slid back into the water.

Beth wedged the oar between the boat and the rock. With her shoulders against the boat, she used the oar as a pole, digging it against the Witch as she tried to force them out of the current. She looked for Sean and Rory and saw they were dog paddling out of danger at the edge of the undertow. The brothers had only to wait until the current carried her back within reach.

The boat rode like a bloodstain on the lace of foam around the Witch's skirts and Megan's yellow slicker joined the dance. Beth thrust with the oar again, jousting with the Witch as she tried to keep them clear. At one point, as she shouldered the prow, the boat swung around and dashed against the rock. Wood splintered and the boat settled deeper in the water.

The current carried them to the narrower end of the rock and the current lessened. The undertow was deeper here, farther from the surface. Beth gathered what she was certain was the last of her strength, kicked at the rock and gave a final thrust with the oar. They broke free of the undertow for a moment as they came into sight of the village, and then the Witch drew them back into her caress.

Above the crash of water, an engine rumbled and then something hit her shoulder and fell into the water. Instinctively, she grabbed it. A lifesaver with a rope attached. Not caring who'd come to help, she hooked an arm through the device.

The rescuer fought the Witch for possession, almost tearing Beth in two. The lifesaver she'd hooked her arm through threatened to rip it out of its socket and the towrope pulled at her belt until she could hardly breathe. She had to let go of the lifesaver.

The police launch hovered in the safety of calm water but she didn't know who was driving it. Beyond the launch, she saw Sean and Rory swimming towards the beach. Beyond them where water met sand, a black-and-tan dog barked and ran backwards and forwards in a frenzy. Several houses were lit up and a dark mass of people had gathered on the beach. Friend or foe? Was there anyone she could count on; anyone who wasn't part of the conspiracy? "Gwyn!"

The boat settled deeper, the water inside almost level with the sea. It was sinking and the tug at her waist threatened to drag her under the surface. If she untied the rope, the boat would drag her away from Gwyn, leaving him at the mercy of the Witch, but Gwyn was going down with the boat. When the bulk of wood sank level with the water, Gwyn floated free. For an instant, he lay on the surface. Beth lunged for him and hooked her fingers into the uniform epaulet on one shoulder as the boat disappeared beneath the waves.

Though lighter now, the boat still weighed her down and Beth had difficulty keeping her head above water. Only a silver button fastened the epaulet to the uniform shoulder and it couldn't hold for long. Beth dragged Gwyn closer and let go of the epaulet in favour of a handful of jacket.

The undertow took possession of the boat. It was dragging her closer to the Witch. Waves washed over her face as she struggled to untie the rope from her belt while she fought to keep Gwyn's head above water.

"Bethan!"

Beth glanced towards the police launch. "Doug?" Tom's contact, Ishmael said.

A second lifesaver snaked towards her but landed too far away for her to reach. Doug drew it back for another throw and the current whirled Beth around to face the open sea. Above a swirl of phosphorus, something sped towards them, a dark splodge on the moonlit water. No lights showed on board and the engine gave a low purr as the shallow keel skimmed over the water. She'd seen it before in Doug's painting.

The yacht was close but it wasn't slowing. Beth realised it was going to run them down.

"Gwyn!" Beth shouted at him. "Dear God, Gwyn!" The yacht was almost on top of them.

She had to dive and drag Gwyn with her. Even as she decided on the course of action, the police launch motor growled when Doug shifted gears. The launch swung to intercept the yacht, but the yacht was almost upon them.

Beth prayed she didn't drown Gwyn, and dived. They sank quickly and the black keel and churning prop passed overhead close enough to touch her hair.

Their dive took them onto the edge of the boat weakened by the spray of bullets, and their combined weight split it apart. Only a section of the prow stayed attached to Beth's belt. She kicked for the surface, hauling Gwyn with her. Gulping air, she heard Gwyn cough and splutter. "Gwyn! Can you hear me?"

"Bethan?" He groaned.

Even as Beth sobbed her relief, the yacht turned and hurtled towards them. The police launch cut at an angle in the direction of the black danger but the yacht was too close to them for it to intercept in safety.

"Take a deep breath, Gwyn! We have to go down again."

They sank as the dark shadow passed overhead. She rose fast, one hand caught under Gwyn's arm.

Several boats were heading out from the beach and Davy's speedboat took up a stance opposite the police launch. Like sheepdogs, they herded the yacht away.

Gwyn passed out again. She held his head above water even as she sank beneath the waves. She fought for the surface and a rowboat came alongside. One of the men threw her a lifeline.

"You!" She gasped. She might hate the man, but he was a welcome sight now.

"This is what comes of not going to chapel on Sunday, Bethan Davies." Reverend Powell-Pritchard reached out to help her into the boat, "But God was on your side when you jousted with the Witch."

Beth pushed his hand away. "Help Gwyn; he's been shot."

"*Arswyd*!" Powell-Pritchard shouted to the second boat as it drew alongside. "We need help here. Gwyn Thomas has been shot."

"*Duw Mawr*!" Emrys leapt into the water and swam to them. "You grab his shoulders, Reverend, and you, too, Sammy," he said to the boy in the boat with Powell-Pritchard, "and I'll try to lift him from here."

"Very well, Emrys," Powell-Pritchard agreed. "But you didn't need to blaspheme, did you?" he asked as he and Sammy lifted Gwyn, almost upsetting the boat. "Will you bloody mind what you're bloody doing!" Powell-Pritchard shouted. "You'll have us all in the bloody drink."

For a moment silence reigned as three pairs of eyes focused on Powell-Pritchard, then Emrys let out a roar of laughter. "He's bloody human, after all."

As they hauled Gwyn into the boat, Emrys turned to face her. "I had to borrow Dat's boat. But what did you two do to my boat, *cariad*?"

"Probably the same as the Witch is doing to that one over there," Powell-Pritchard said. "Sammy—you take Gwyn and Bethan back. Emrys—we'd better see what we can do to help Mr Plews. That's his yacht over there." The minister clambered onto the other boat and helped Emrys out of the water.

Beth climbed into the boat with Sammy's help. She sat and took Gwyn's head in her lap. He didn't respond. Eyes closed, his breathing was shallow.

While Sammy rowed for the beach, she looked across the bay. The Witch had the yacht in a dizzying spin. A powerboat, there were no oars to pole it away and it was being repeatedly smashed against the rock as the man on board screamed for help. The lifesavers thrown to him either missed or fell short. Beth watched in horror as the prop tore free and the yacht fell apart. The masts with the black, furled sails floated on the water for a moment before the Witch dragged them under her skirts. Meg's slicker marked the spot, a yellow arm raised on the rock as if it waved farewell.

The police launch and Davy's speedboat took a safe position opposite the narrow end of the rock with the other craft behind them; they could do nothing but wait at the edge of the current. If they went closer, the Witch would get them, too.

As Sammy beached the boat, Beth saw the men in the flotilla stand with their heads bowed.

The dog stopped barking, leapt into the boat, and began licking Gwyn's face.

"Bethan?"

She gave a sob of relief. Gwyn was conscious. "We're safe."

Despite the blood soaking into his uniform and the lines of pain on his face, he grinned. "I could do with more of those kisses, *cariad*."

Beth thought about telling him what he felt was the dog's tongue then she smiled and said, "Only one, because you're a bloody policeman." She bent to touch her lips to his.

THE END

Other books by P. L. Crompton:

The Last Druid

In Roman-occupied Cambria, a powerful druid does all he can to undermine Roman authority and influence the future.

He claims a young girl as novice because she has the Sight, but her sight opens into the past and she wonders how she can be of help to him. When the answer comes, it is not what she expected.

A well-researched preface to P.L. Crompton's The Last Druid promises a realistic tale of Rome's retreat from the British Isles.

The book was just as challenging as Tolstoy's "War and Peace" and Kay's "The Far Pavilion".

The imagination and description of each situation were so real to me I could see what was going on as if it were a movie.

It seemed well researched which lent it authenticity and the style was very readable.

The Agency

In 2033, governments worldwide are bankrupt. There is no unemployment insurance, no social services or welfare, no pensions, and no health care subsidy. Unemployment sits at close to 60 percent, and those with jobs are the new elite.

Sheila Davenport owns a successful employment agency. When other agencies begin to go out of business, she attributes it to their inability to compete. Then she hears a hellish rumour: Sign with Davenport: they'll find you a job even if they have to kill someone.

Other agency owners are murdered and the Davenport Agency comes under police scrutiny. Sheila investigates and uncovers a sinister plot.

This one is a keeper and I look forward to reading her next release.

WOW! is the only single word I can use to describe this book while Holy! Good Gosh! Jumpin' Geehosafats! comes closer to describing how blown away I was reading The Agency.

The Agency is a gripping, well-paced story that paints a disturbing picture of the future. As thrillers go, this is at the top of my list.

The Agency has a great premise, cast of characters, and most importantly a main character that holds it all together.

Land of My Fathers

A collection of interrelated stories set in a Welsh valley during the 1930s and 40s.
Sometimes funny, sometimes sad, a glimpse of life as it may have been then.
Some stories based on true events.

Such interesting stories involving a village in Wales, it's people's traditions, superstitions, ghost stories, prejudices, romances, enjoyments, and tragedies held my interest throughout the book.

A well-written book with vivid descriptions of the countryside, the people, and the events.

Strongly recommend it to anyone who is Welsh.

All books are available worldwide as paperbacks or e-books at outlets like Amazon, Kindle, Barnes & Noble, Smashwords and many others.

P L Crompton

www.ingramcontent.com/pod-product-compliance
Lightning Source LLC
Chambersburg PA
CBHW060312260626
47160CB00007B/2576